To Catch a Traitor

BOOKS BY D. B. SHUSTER

SINS OF A SPY SERIES

To Catch a Traitor — August 2018

To Hunt a Spy — January 2019

KINGS OF BRIGHTON BEACH SERIES

Mafia Rules (prequel) — January 2019

Kings of Brighton Beach — June 2015

NEUROTICA SERIES

A Bundle of Neurotica: Eight Neurotica Short Stories — June 2015

Please visit my website http://dbshuster.com for FREE reads and
special offers.

To Catch a Traitor

Sins of a Spy Series Book One

D. B. SHUSTER

CRIME BYTES MEDIA
NEW YORK

For Gene, my favorite Ruski
and
For Kristine and the Deer Park Moms Book Club

AUTHOR'S NOTE

THANK YOU FOR choosing this book. Like all juicy sagas, this one has a large cast of characters. You'll find a character list included at the end for your reference as well as a glossary of foreign terms. You're also welcome to download the family tree from my website.

This is a work of historical fiction. The characters and the family saga told in this series are purely fictional, but aspects of the story come straight from historical accounts of the Cold War. I have drawn deeply on the history of Soviet Jews, particularly of the Refusenik community. Their daily trials—the surveillance, the menial jobs, the anti-Semitism, and the harassment by the KGB—are all well documented, although I have taken liberties here. I have also drawn on autobiographies and journalistic accounts of American and Russian spies to give richness and realism to this part of the tale. In particular, Sofia's use of the Tropel cameras and her methods of signaling the CIA were drawn from the exploits of Adolf Tolkachev, powerfully told in David Hoffman's *Billion Dollar Spy*.

In conducting research for this book, I was struck by how often the men dominated the story, with the women relegated to the roles of wives and daughters, supporters in a public struggle, but seldom the main actors. I was similarly struck by how seldom women took central roles in the accounts of spies on both sides of the struggle. Indeed, in the Soviet Union, it seems few women served as agents, and many of those that did were relegated to the role of "dangle," luring in the prize but not managing it once caught. This exclusion seemed to reflect a far-reaching prejudice, especially since the Refusenik and dissident narratives almost never included details of women being regularly followed and harassed by KGB tails, and since women also seemed to receive lighter sentences at trial.

As a sociologist, I do not doubt that few women rose high in the spy ranks. This dearth from the 1980s is still evident today when we look at the numbers of women in top leadership positions in the intelligence community. But as a researcher myself, I do seriously question the second-fiddle role women ostensibly played among dissidents and Refuseniks. I suspect that the published histories also reflect the subconscious biases of their authors in terms of the questions asked, the people interviewed, the weight given to particular activities, and the attribution of credit. I couldn't resist exploiting these seeming blind spots to create this thrilling saga.

Finally, I have an odd personal connection to this material. I grew up in America, a child of the Cold War. I remember learning in school about the evils of Communism and the nuclear threat. I remember when Sting's "Russians" came out in 1985 and the radical notion that our "enemy" might be just like us. In middle school, I heard the famous dissident and Refusenik, Natan Sharansky, speak at my synagogue, and my family was moved to participate in the March for Soviet Jewry in Washington, D.C. in 1987. But this history became even more personal for me when I met Gene in the 1990s. At our wedding, he thanked President Gorbachev for letting his family emigrate from the Soviet Union so that he could come to America and meet me.

TABLE OF CONTENTS

Chapter ONE 1

Chapter TWO 7

Chapter THREE 16

Chapter FOUR 23

Chapter FIVE 28

Chapter SIX 34

Chapter SEVEN 39

Chapter EIGHT 45

Chapter NINE 50

Chapter TEN 53

Chapter ELEVEN 57

Chapter TWELVE 61

Chapter THIRTEEN 65

Chapter FOURTEEN 71

Chapter FIFTEEN 76

Chapter SIXTEEN 85

Chapter SEVENTEEN 94

Chapter EIGHTEEN 98

Chapter NINETEEN 102

Chapter TWENTY 108

Chapter TWENTY-ONE 112

Chapter TWENTY-TWO 118

Chapter TWENTY-THREE 122

Chapter TWENTY-FOUR 126

Chapter TWENTY-FIVE 132

Chapter TWENTY-SIX 140

Chapter TWENTY-SEVEN 147

Chapter TWENTY-EIGHT 154
Chapter TWENTY-NINE 160
Chapter THIRTY 165
Chapter THIRTY-ONE 171
Chapter THIRTY-TWO 176
Chapter THIRTY-THREE 180
Chapter THIRTY-FOUR 185
Chapter THIRTY-FIVE 193
Chapter THIRTY-SIX. 199
Chapter THIRTY-SEVEN 208
Chapter THIRTY-EIGHT 216
Chapter THIRTY-NINE 223
Chapter FORTY 230
Chapter FORTY-ONE 234
Chapter FORTY-TWO 241
Chapter FORTY-THREE 251
Chapter FORTY-FOUR. 257
Chapter FORTY-FIVE 263
Chapter FORTY-SIX 270
Chapter FORTY-SEVEN 274
Chapter FORTY-EIGHT 278
KINGS OF BRIGHTON BEACH EXCERPT . 282
ACKNOWLEDGMENTS 289
ABOUT THE AUTHOR 291
CHARACTER LIST 292
GLOSSARY 294

CHAPTER ONE
SOFIA

Sofia hurried past the KGB agents who constantly tailed her father. They stomped their feet and rubbed their gloved hands together to fight off the lingering winter chill and kept their eyes trained on his cement-block apartment building. They acted as if they hadn't noticed her, but she was no fool.

Head ducked against the March wind and the cold drizzle in the air, she headed in the direction of the subway station, the way she always did a few evenings a week, carrying the same tote bag she always did, full of the same items she always carried.

Nothing about her errand should pique their attention.

When she reached the corner at the end of the block, she regarded them out of the corner of her eye. Aside from a small difference in height, they seemed nearly identical in their wool coats and fur hats. One of the agents turned his head in her direction. She couldn't see his eyes behind his dark sunglasses, but she felt the heavy weight of his gaze.

Should the agents stop her, as they sometimes did, they would find nothing of interest. At least not at first glance.

It was the chance of the second glance that made her nervous.

She waited impatiently for the light to change. The longer she lingered at the corner, the greater the risk they would approach, especially with this raw weather that surely exacerbated the miserable monotony of surveillance.

Her father, their focus, was cozy upstairs in his apartment and would be all evening, waiting for her son to come home from school and then helping him with his homework and enjoying the hot borscht and potatoes her mother would prepare for them.

The second agent checked his watch and nodded. He remarked to the first. She couldn't hear or read lips, but his companion's face cracked into a creepy smile. She knew she was right on schedule, and they knew it, too. Likely they joked that they could set their watches by her.

She smiled to herself. Predictability was one of her best tricks. The KGB imagined she was setting off to clean toilets at Moscow State University, when in reality she was off to change the world.

The light changed. She scurried across the street. Several blocks and a subway ride later, she arrived right on time for her shift. The professors and students were heading home for the day, leaving a warren of mostly empty offices, hallways, and classrooms.

She stopped at the security desk in her building to retrieve her name badge. The new guard, Grisha, hadn't given her any real trouble yet, but he seemed to enjoy ogling her. He made a cursory inspection of her tote.

His fat hands lingered on the slacks folded on top, but he didn't dig around, didn't notice the heavy key fob tucked in the pocket.

She went to the supply closet to change into her work clothes. She fastened the slacks and checked the pocket, making sure the precious key fob was securely in place. Then she gathered her mop, rags, rubber gloves, and bleach and hauled them up the stairs to the third floor.

Grisha followed her up the stairs. There were three bathrooms up here for her to clean, one on each end of the hall and a third, more private, within the suite of offices that included Max's old laboratory.

Taking a chain of keys from his pocket, Grisha searched for the one that opened the door to the suite.

She waited impatiently and shifted the bucket and bleach from one hand to the other to relieve the growing ache in her muscles. Finally, he unlocked the door and ushered her inside. Together, they crossed a small reception area to another wooden door, and Grisha again began the process of searching through the keys for the right one.

She could have told him it was the one with the green plastic holder over its end and sped up the process, but she didn't want him to think her overly interested in the security measures.

When he finally finished fumbling with the keys and the lock, Grisha held the door open for her. Her hands were full of cleaning supplies, but he didn't ease her burden. Instead, he pinched her bottom as she passed defenselessly by him.

Her shoulders tightened. They were alone up here.

She clutched the mop handle and worried what she would do if he made a more aggressive advance—how she would fend him off, how she might disarm him and still manage to keep this job.

Too much depended on her ongoing access to Max's office and the valuable secrets inside.

The hallway was dark. Instead of turning on the lights, Grisha held the door open and let the light from the outer office guide her. Sofia counted the doors as she hefted her supplies down the corridor. The third on the right had been Max's. The sixth was the bathroom.

She unlocked the door to the bathroom with the key she had been given. Once inside, she pressed her ear to the door. When she heard the sound of the hall door closing, she crept back into the hallway and tiptoed to Max's office.

No one had thought to revoke her brother-in-law's access to the research laboratory that used to be his. If they ever thought about him, it wouldn't be as a risk to the security of their information. No one had heard from him in the seven years since his trial. He was either in the gulag or dead.

Just like her husband.

She slipped the chain from under her shirt. The keys hanging from it were warm from her skin. She kissed them once for luck and tried the lock, first to the office door and then to the file cabinet. *Success!*

It amazed her every time that with all of the other security measures, the university never bothered to change the locks.

She only hoped her luck would hold.

The office's new occupant had a meticulous filing system. Sofia easily found the report she wanted. She stuffed the file under her shirt, closed the cabinet, and eased open the door. Still no sign of Grisha.

She raced back to the bathroom and closed herself in the big stall at the end near the window. The radiator connected to the wall, and a wooden box covered the metal pipes. Heart pounding, she opened the file over the fat shelf of wood atop the radiator. The report was nearly 100 pages long. She had been working on this one slowly, five to ten pages at a time.

She retrieved the key fob from her pocket. She unscrewed the top to open the lens of the tiny Tropel camera hidden inside.

Working with the Tropel was a slow and painstaking process. Picking up where she left off, she slid page 30 into the brightest spot in the middle of the ledge. Holding the tiny camera with both hands, she propped her elbows around the first page and held the camera above it. She lined her hands up with the notch she'd made in the window frame, the requisite 28 centimeters from the shelf.

She took a steadying breath and clicked the shutter.

The bathroom stall was hot. She would have cracked the window, but she didn't want to risk a breeze ruffling her papers.

Sofia wiped her damp hands on her thighs before picking up the paper and flipping to the next page of the report. She couldn't risk leaving sweat on the pages. If and when the laboratory researchers pulled the file to review, they would surely be suspicious if they found stray wet marks on their report.

She set up the next page. She worked methodically and with a sense of quiet power.

These photographs wouldn't change history. They wouldn't save her husband or Max and his family from trial and imprisonment.

They wouldn't restore the years that had been robbed from them all.

But they could change the future.

They could be used to weaken the Soviet military and pressure the Kremlin to let her people leave a country that hated them.

She glanced at her watch. Eighteen minutes had passed since she'd stolen the file. She still had more than half of the file left to photograph, but she returned the report to its folder and sneaked back to Max's office.

She exercised strict discipline, never stealing more than twenty minutes at a time. It was too hard to conceal her activities if she took longer. The slow pace frustrated her, but over the course of six years, twenty minutes of photographs several times a week had nonetheless yielded an impressive flow of information.

The cabinet drawer was full, and the file was a tight fit. She took pains to push it down into its spot and straighten the edges to hide the evidence that it had been removed.

In the process, she noticed the corner of another file sticking up above the others. She glanced around, satisfied herself no one was coming, and pulled the file. She flipped through the first few pages of what seemed to be a report on a recent long-range missile test, discussing the impressive capabilities of a new prototype.

Reluctantly, she put the file back in its place. "I'll be back for you," she whispered.

She locked up the cabinet and the office and then returned to clean the mirrors. She wiped the pipes so that they appeared clean and shiny. No one would give her high marks for diligent cleaning, but the bathroom would have the appearance and smell of having been washed and tidied. Good enough that her job would be secure.

She finished quickly and moved to the other bathrooms in the building.

Grisha never came to check on her. She changed out of her clothes and checked compulsively—as she changed, as she folded the slacks, as she placed them in her bag—that the mini camera remained tucked in the pocket, hidden in her bag.

She kept her bag tucked close against her side as she left the university campus. The wet wind clawed at her with cold fingers. She was dressed for the cold in her coat and knit woolen hat, but she was shivering when she arrived a few minutes later at the subway station.

The station was warm inside, but as she descended the stairs, she immediately spotted two KGB agents on the platform. They stared openly at her, and the cold chill inside her didn't abate.

They made no attempt to hide or to fit in with the handful of people waiting for the next train. Stiffly formal, they had the same bland look edged with irritation, the same leather loafers, the same heavy wool coats and fur hats with ear flaps.

She clutched her bag closer to her side and turned deliberately away from them as if she hadn't seen them, as if they couldn't possibly be here for her, as if the threat of their presence made no difference.

She gazed sideways at them and saw them moving toward her. Although she stood stalk still, her heart started to pound as if she were running hard.

Maybe someone did suspect after all.

Would the agents search her bag? If they discovered the tiny Tropel inside the key fob, they would know what it was and guess where it had come from.

They would execute her.

She glanced around, wondering if there was somewhere she could stash the camera or some way to buy time and get away. She was so consumed by her fear of discovery and her frantic search for an escape that she didn't notice the third man coming toward her.

She turned away from the tracks, ready to head back up the stairs, when she barreled into him. He rocked back with the force of the impact and clutched her shoulders.

"Easy," he said hoarsely. "Easy."

She started to dodge out of his grasp, and his fingers tightened on her.

"Don't." He hissed a warning under his breath. "Don't run. You'll only make things worse."

CHAPTER TWO
ARTUR

NERVOUS WITH ANTICIPATION, Artur sat in a booth at the back corner of the restaurant. He had an unimpeded line of sight to the Jew, his target, Edouard Soifer, aka "Edik," who slouched at the bar and waited for the bartender to refill his shot glass with vodka.

Jewish traitors were passing dangerous propaganda and information to their compatriots abroad and endangering the whole country's prospects for peace. Edik and his father were known to host foreigners in their home, making Edik a potentially valuable informant and perhaps even a prospect for passing on misinformation.

If tonight went well, Artur would prove to Victor his skill as a spy handler, capable of turning civilians and even hostiles into valuable assets.

He had butterflies in his stomach and the delectable thrill of the chase. Spy work was perhaps more heady even than falling in love.

The bartender delivered Edik his next shot, his fourth by Artur's count. Drinking alone, Edik looked lonely. Almost handsome but for his perpetual frown and penchant to overindulge in liquor, he seemed to Artur the kind of man who would easily be dazzled if a beautiful woman showed him some interest. A woman like Lilya.

Artur fondled the miniature listening device, no bigger than a kopek, in his jacket pocket and nodded to Lilya, the dangle he'd requested for this evening.

Lilya sashayed up to the bar. Her innocent, wide-eyed expression made her seem younger than she was and camouflaged her jaded cynicism and years of expertise. She was his ace in the hole on this one.

Artur wagered that with inhibitions already weakened by drink, Edik wouldn't stand a chance against Lilya's charms. The only question was how long it would take her to lure him to her hotel room.

Lilya seated herself on the stool beside Edik and brushed her hand along his arm, a subtle move to get his attention. Edik swiveled to face her. She leaned forward and put her plump cleavage on full display, a less subtle effort, but undoubtedly effective. Edik's pasty face flushed a bright pink.

Artur rubbed his hands together. This was going to be easy. By midnight, the lonely man would be proclaiming his undying love. They wouldn't even need to plant the listening device in his shoe to get all of the information they wanted from him.

Lilya murmured something to Edik, and he fumbled his drink. He dropped the full shot glass on her. The bartender rushed over with a stack of cloth napkins, and Edik awkwardly mopped at Lilya's lap.

Apologizing profusely, he became more flustered and awkward with each passing moment.

Lilya reassured him and tilted her head. Edik should have leaned in at Lilya's coy invitation, but he abruptly grabbed up his coat and hat, turned, and walked away from her.

Artur swore viciously under his breath. He couldn't let Edik walk away before the approach had even happened.

He didn't know when he would get another chance like this one. He couldn't fail.

He threw a few rubles on the table and got up from his booth. He moved nonchalantly to the door, readying himself to intercept Edik, though unsure what he would do to detain him.

"Wait!" Lilya cried. She cut in front of Artur and chased after Edik. "What about these?"

She held up a pack of cigarettes with English script on them. Marlboro.

Edik patted the breast pocket of his suit and frowned. "Those are mine."

Lilya smiled triumphantly. In a husky voice, she said, "Maybe they're mine now."

"Give them back," Edik insisted, sounding much like Artur's four-year-old son.

"Come back. Sit with me," she invited.

Shoulders hunched, Edik skulked after her. He tossed his hat onto the bar and reclaimed the seat he'd prematurely vacated, draping his heavy coat over the back.

"They're not yours." He sulked over the cigarettes.

"You can get more. Can't you?"

"A whole carton," he confirmed.

Artur had made an excellent choice in Lilya. She was as good at this work as everyone had said. Already, she'd tricked Edik into admitting he was involved in black market trade. With his revelation that he had access to American cigarettes, Edik had just unwittingly handed them something to use against him if they needed to coerce rather than seduce him to their side.

"Are you interested?" Edik asked.

"Oh, I'm very interested," Lilya said, voice low and full of innuendo. She shimmied for him. As Artur's own attention diverted to her round, jiggling breasts, he thought no coercion would be necessary.

But Edik kept his attention riveted to the pack of Marlboros.

With a sigh, Lilya laid the cigarettes on the bar. Edik seemed immediately to relax once she abandoned her claim to the pack.

Lilya fluttered her lashes and flashed him her most flirtatious smile. This time when she leaned toward him, she managed to draw his gaze to her lovely body.

She touched his arm, leaned closer, and lowered her voice so that

Artur had to strain to hear. "We could bargain. Couldn't we?"

"Sure. We can bargain." Edik sat up straighter and finally, finally exuded the confidence of a man who understood a woman was interested in him. He took command of their interchange for the first time and asked, "How much?"

"I'm not a prostitute," she said as if affronted. Artur snorted softly under his breath. Lilya might have an agent's title, but in reality, she was little better than a whore—a useful whore who used her services toward a worthy cause, but still a whore.

"I didn't say you were." Edik scratched his nose with his finger. "What would you say to forty rubles?"

"Forty? That's offensive!" She drew away, but Artur knew that no matter how offensive Edik might become, Lilya wouldn't walk away. "I could get at least a hundred."

"A hundred? Are you out of your mind?" Edik protested her price. "That's almost as much as my father gets every month in his pension. Even Sofia can't get a hundred."

Sofia? Who was Sofia? Did Edik have another prostitute that he visited?

"One hundred," Lilya insisted. She stuck out her chin in a display of stubborn pride.

"If you say so, then one hundred it is," Edik agreed, a little too quickly after his previous outrage. Artur caught himself leaning toward the couple and pulled himself back, but he suffered a strong misgiving that something had just gone wrong. Edik had seemed eager to haggle before, confident even, and outraged at Lilya's stated price. So why had he suddenly caved in to her demand with no additional fuss?

"I'm glad you're so agreeable," Lilya purred. "I can be agreeable, too."

She put her hand on his knee and slid it up his thigh. "Maybe we'll have to rethink that hundred rubles."

Edik jerked away and nearly fell off of his stool. He pushed her hand off of him.

"Hey! That won't work on me."

"Why not? You feel like a strong, healthy fellow to me," Lilya simpered.

Edik frowned at her. "I won't renegotiate with you now that we've got an agreement. Sofia says that's not good business. One hundred rubles. Or no deal."

Again Edik mentioned Sofia. Who was she? Artur didn't recall her name from the file, and Edik's briefing hadn't mentioned a wife or girlfriend.

Edik eyed Lilya suspiciously. "Do you have the money or not? I don't do this on credit."

"What?" she sputtered. "You want me to pay you?"

"Why would I pay you?" Edik asked, confused or else doing a good job of pretending to be. "You said you're not a prostitute. And you offered me a hundred rubles for a carton of cigarettes."

A misunderstanding! Artur held in a frustrated sigh as he realized what had happened, why Edik had agreed to Lilya's price without further haggling. Edik had been asking how much she would pay for the cigarettes, not how much she charged for her services.

Either their target was a social idiot, or he was brilliantly adroit at dodging snares, the admission of selling items notwithstanding.

"You're an idiot!" Lilya shrilled and marched on her tall stilettos to the exit. She wasn't supposed to leave. Artur wanted to shout at her that she couldn't give up. She had to try again. But he couldn't give himself away.

He also couldn't give up. He would lose any respect his fellow agents had for him if he did. And Victor would never view him as an equal.

Artur slid onto the stool beside Edik. "What happened with the woman?"

"A misunderstanding." Edik sounded depressed.

"I could help clear it up. Get her to come back if you want," Artur offered, trying to get the plan back on track and put Lilya back in position.

"No," Edik said adamantly.

"Why not? She's very pretty," Artur wheedled.

"She's a prostitute."

"Are you sure? What if she isn't a prostitute? Would you be interested?"

"No," Edik said.

Maybe they needed a different dangle, someone more Edik's type. Artur fished for information. "What's the matter? She not your type?"

"She's not as pretty as Sofia," Edik grumbled under his breath.

"Who's Sofia?" Artur asked.

"You ask a lot of questions," Edik observed and shut down the conversation.

"What'll you have?" the bartender asked.

"Same as him," Artur said. The drink was almost instantly placed before him. "*Zdarovya.*"

He raised his glass to Edik, who grunted to acknowledge the toast and then looked away. Artur swallowed the shot of vodka in one burning gulp.

He contemplated his empty shot glass. He still couldn't get a read on Edik. Had the man evaded their trap or been too awkward to get himself ensnared?

Artur thumbed the listening device in his pocket and considered his options. He usually excelled in social situations, but with Edik, his natural charm seemed to be failing him. He had done covert operations, but he had never done undercover work, never been face to face with his target. And he doubted Edik was typical, or else Lilya would already have him upstairs in her hotel room.

He groped for a way to kindle conversation between them. He couldn't come up with anything better than a bad pickup line. Finally, he was reduced to asking, "Do you come here often?"

"Every Wednesday," Edik said.

"What's special about Wednesdays?"

"Nothing," Edik said. "That's just when I come here." The bartender poured Edik another drink, and Artur lost Edik's attention to the clear liquid in the man's glass.

Edik didn't seem drunk, but Artur had watched him toss back quite a large quantity of alcohol. Maybe he merely needed to wait for the man to become inebriated, and then he could question him.

It wasn't the worst strategy as a last resort, but it was hardly the shining success he needed.

Once the bartender moved off, Artur asked, "Then why here? There are other bars in Moscow."

"Like I said, you ask a lot of questions."

Blyad! He couldn't afford to alienate Edik. If only he weren't so green.

"Sorry, sorry." Artur dropped his voice as if imparting a confession. "It's just that I'm new in town, and I haven't had anyone to talk to." He matched Edik's sullen tone and slouched posture. Sympathy flickered in Edik's eyes, and Artur sensed he had found a promising avenue. "I moved here for my girlfriend," he improvised. He mimicked the high voice of his pretend woman. "'I'm so in love with you,' she said. 'Come with me to Moscow,' she said. 'Move in with me,' she said. 'We'll be so happy.' And then as soon as I show up—pow!—she takes up with some other guy."

"She cheated on you? But you're so, so…" Edik waved his hand as if he couldn't find the right words. He leaned against the bar and propped his head in his hand, as if having trouble holding it upright.

"So Jewish?" Artur supplied, suddenly inspired.

"You're Jewish?" Edik blinked at him several times, openly trying to study his face. For what, Artur couldn't say. He expected the inspection would find him lacking.

He wasn't Jewish. He didn't even know anyone Jewish.

His closest Jewish connection was that his father once-upon-a-time had a Jewish friend in the army.

"Says so on my passport," he lied. "That's why she broke up with me."

"That's awful," Edik said and waved to the bartender. "Another drink for the new guy," he called out. "Whaz your name?"

Artur was gratified to hear the growing slur in Edik's consonants. He'd get him drunk, wring whatever information he could from him, and then drag him up to the hotel room and doctor his shoes while he was passed out. *Not long now.*

"Koslovsky." Artur reached for the first and only Jewish name to pop into his head, the name of his father's friend from his Army days. "Yosef Koslovsky. And you?"

"Edouard Soifer. They call me Edik."

"Nice to meet you, Edik."

The bartender delivered them both fresh drinks. They clinked their glasses together. "To new friends," Artur said, and Edik echoed him.

Edik drank his shot in one swallow and wiped the back of his hand across his mouth.

"Okay, pal. You've had enough for tonight." The bartender handed Edik a tab.

Edik bobbed his head in agreement. "Six shots. 170.48 milliliters."

What an odd statement, Artur thought.

"Whatever you say," the bartender said with patronizing tolerance. Artur wasn't sure what to make of his target, except that Edik was a little strange.

"You're leaving already?" Artur asked, his newest plans crashing to a halt.

"Reached my limit," Edik said.

Edik flipped the bill over and squinted at some handwriting on the back. It looked like a shopping list, cigarettes being one of the items. Edik stuffed the note in his pocket before Artur could glean more.

"All set?" the bartender asked.

"All set," Edik confirmed, and Artur intuited that they weren't talking about the bar tab.

Edik pulled out his wallet, revealing a fat stack of rubles. For someone with no job, he was flush with money.

Artur made note of the money. Finding out where it came from, how the Jewish community continued to be so well funded despite chronic underemployment and the crackdown on Customs, was part of the mystery he'd been charged with solving. He expected to uncover a lot more than a carton or two of black market cigarettes.

As Edik counted out the bills, Artur palmed the listening device in his pocket. Adept at sleight of hand, he slipped the bug into the cuff of Edik's fur-lined cap.

Although better than a coat pocket, the hat cuff wasn't an ideal hiding place, not nearly as good as the shoe that had been their original plan. In the hat, the device could easily fall out and be discovered.

"I'll be back next Wednesday," Edik called to the bartender as he buttoned up his coat.

"*Molodetz*," the bartender said.

"Good night." Edik started to walk away, leaving his hat on the bar counter, once again sidestepping Artur's snare. Had he seen Artur plant the bug?

"Hey, wait!" Artur called. "You forgot your hat." Artur carefully handed the hat to Edik and held his breath, hoping the listening device wouldn't fall out.

"Thanks, friend. Sofia would've been angry with me if I lost another one."

Sofia again. Who was she?

Edik pulled the hat down low over his fat head. When Artur saw that the device remained safely hidden, he slowly exhaled.

Artur wasn't close to getting what he needed out of Edik. He consoled himself that all wasn't lost. The listening device was planted, if precariously, and he'd gained some new leads.

Even though he hadn't been able to wring Edik for information tonight, he could easily find him next week without any trouble and try again, perhaps with another dangle.

"You want me to show you around Moscow? Introduce you to people?" Edik offered.

"You mean that?" Artur asked, surprised by his own sudden success. Obviously there was more than one way to seduce a target.

CHAPTER THREE
SOFIA

DESPITE THE PADDING from her bulky winter coat, Sofia could feel the stranger's fingers dig into her shoulders. He asked, "Sofia, don't you recognize me?"

Painfully thin, shrouded in a tattered coat, his face hidden beneath an unkempt gray beard that hung past his chin, this man was no one she knew. But he also didn't look like the KGB agents behind her. His bony fingers dug painfully into her shoulders.

The wind picked up in the station as a subway train approached, offering a new set of avenues for escape and evasion. She wouldn't get far if she lost herself to panic. She calmed her mind and began to assess her options.

She studied him, noticing details she had initially missed. He wore no hat, only a slim black skullcap. She'd seen such things before on some of her uncle's American visitors, the ones whose wives wore long skirts and wigs that reminded her of fake straw. The ones who were religious Jews. But he didn't have the smugly secure, assured air of the Americans or their butchered, toothy accents. His Russian was perfect.

"I'm sorry," she said.

He cleared his throat as if embarrassed, and his voice had a different quality when he next spoke. "Kolya didn't recognize me, either."

Kolya. Her son. And that voice saying his name. She had waited long years to hear that voice again. "Mendel?"

It couldn't be. Her husband was a young man, and there were six months still left in his prison sentence.

"I've come home," he said loudly, over the sound of the approaching train.

She gave a cry and threw her arms around him. He was alive—for almost five years she hadn't been sure of even that much—and home. At last!

"How is this possible? We weren't expecting you. Why didn't anyone tell us?"

Mendel awkwardly folded his long scarecrow arms around her, as if he didn't really want to touch her. His mouth pressed close to her ear as the train screeched to a noisy halt. "We'll talk at home," he whispered. "It isn't safe here."

She nodded once to show she understood, and he immediately released her.

He took her by the arm, and they walked together through the train doors. The KGB agents followed.

Mendel nudged her into an empty seat. Although there was another beside her, he didn't sit. Instead, he stood in front of her, as if to shield her. He cut his gaze to the KGB agents, and she immediately understood they were there for him.

For him. Not for her.

He'd had a contingent of watchers before he'd been arrested, too.

Like her father's detail, they added a layer of complication and danger, but she had experience evading them.

Surreptitiously, she checked the tote bag tucked firmly against her side, assuring herself that the work pants were still there, undisturbed, neatly folded. She would have liked to pat the pocket to make sure the Tropel was still hidden there, but she couldn't risk inadvertently drawing the agents' attention where she least wanted it.

She wasn't in the clear yet. She still needed to hide the Tropel until she could get it to her contact, but she breathed a little easier.

Her worst fear hadn't come to pass. They hadn't somehow learned of her espionage and set a trap for her. They hadn't suddenly turned their sights to her. She hadn't attracted any new attention or suspicion.

And now Mendel was home.

She stared up at him in wonder, scarcely believing he was here. How many nights had she prayed for his safe return?

She cataloged the changes in him, trying to reconcile his appearance with that of the dashingly handsome man who'd swept her off her feet.

She could still see the hints of him, but she had to look hard. There were deep crags around his eyes, a sallow tinge to his now baggy skin, and a stoop to a frame that used to stand almost arrogantly straight and tall. But his eyes still shone with the same bright intelligence, and his lips still held the same darkly sensuous curve. He still had a head full of hair, although it was thinner now and streaked through with gray.

The physical changes didn't matter, not really. They made her wonder what he had suffered, but they didn't trouble her overmuch. They didn't change the intensity of her love for him, a love that had burned brightly through the long years of their separation.

The important thing was that he was home now. At last. Maybe different. But alive and safe!

She was impatient to hold him, to talk to him, to restart the life they'd both had to put on hold when he was taken.

She stood at the next stop, but he signaled for her to sit back down. "Kolya's spending the night with your parents. They thought we could use the privacy."

"Did you get to talk with him?" she asked, but he gave a swift shake of his head and mouthed, "Not now."

She pressed her lips together to hold back the torrent of words, the outpouring of years' worth of stockpiled and bottled up love, the hundreds of questions.

He'd said he'd seen Kolya, and she couldn't even ask him about that. Their son had been a chubby toddler when Mendel had been taken from them, and now he was seven, reading his own books and going to school. She wanted to tell Mendel how much of him she saw in their studious boy, how very proud she was, how she'd tried to keep Mendel's memory alive for him, about the hopes she had for them both now that they were all back together. About her overwhelming desire for another baby before she was too old.

She tried to communicate all of this with her eyes, but Mendel's own expression remained shuttered and severe.

She wondered what he might be thinking. Maybe he resented the agents for dampening the joy of their reunion with their ever present menace, for making them wait this little bit longer when they had already been waiting for what seemed a lifetime.

She cut her glance sideways to the agents and realized suddenly that they weren't actively interfering. They stood a respectful distance away, as if giving them space for their reunion. Several seats away from her and Mendel, they were even out of range for eavesdropping if she and Mendel kept their voices low.

That fact in itself ratcheted up her constant current of anxiety. When had the KGB ever been respectful or made anything easy?

Her father liked to say that the agents on the street were meant to lull you into a false sense of security, thinking that only two such men spied on you.

People accused him of being paranoid, but she knew better. Someone was always watching, always listening, always waiting to catch you.

The KGB had a vast army of people, agents and informants, who observed and recorded. Anyone—even her newly returned husband—could be a spy or turned into an informant, even unwittingly.

Mendel had mentioned danger, she realized, but he hadn't signaled what kind. What if the agents weren't the biggest threat?

At the subway stop near their apartment, Mendel motioned for her to stand. She reached for his hand.

His skin was dry but warm, but he pulled away with an odd little shiver, denying her even that small touch.

She didn't understand. What could it hurt? Wouldn't the agents think it strange if they didn't touch?

Or had his feelings for her changed during their forced separation?

She turned up the collar of her coat and stuck her hands deep into her pockets, walking with her stranger of a husband through the quiet Moscow streets, the KGB agents trailing silently after them. Mendel moved slowly, stiffly, as if his whole body ached, as if he were an old man.

She had a deeply uneasy feeling. Something wasn't right.

When they reached their apartment building, the agents didn't follow them in. They remained outside, standing watch a little distance from the door, the way her father's agents did whenever he came to visit her.

They rode the elevator up to the seventh floor in silence, she following his lead. Soon, she thought, they would go into the apartment where they could be alone and everything would be as it should, the way she had imagined it night after lonely night—passionate kisses, tender words, embraces that chased away the gnawing loneliness.

He didn't look like the man she'd imagined would return to her, but her love had always been about more than that. Pent up desire gave way to a hot, steady flow, expectant and searingly sweet.

As soon as they were alone in the apartment, she locked the door behind them and secured the chain. She was eager to connect, to reclaim him, to find in him the man she'd loved.

She threw herself into his arms and wrapped her arms around his neck. He tilted his head away, and her kiss glanced his chin. Then he cradled her head against his shoulder, against the rough wool of his coat.

His fingers lingered for the briefest moment in her hair, and then he released her, long before she was ready.

It felt like a rejection. And she couldn't begin to guess why or to stop the tears that spilled from her eyes. The old Mendel had never been able to get enough of her. They had always been touching, kissing.

"What's wrong?"

"I don't like to be touched anymore," he said. Again, he wouldn't look at her.

"What did they do to you?" she blurted.

"I can't—won't—talk about it," he said. "I'm home now. And it's done."

She turned away from him to shield him from her potent disappointment and unbuttoned her coat. He was the one who had endured the harsh treatment. Her suffering was nothing in comparison to his. Just look at him!

She wouldn't press him, she decided. It was his pain, and he could tell her when he was good and ready, but she did have other questions.

What was the danger he'd mentioned earlier? Had it only been the presence of the agents, or was it something more?

She hung their coats in the coat closet and stuffed her tote bag deep into the back, some innate caution driving her to keep the camera safely hidden, even from him.

She went into the kitchen and filled the tea kettle, needing to keep her hands busy. She left the water running, a trick she'd learned to muffle what surveillance might pick up.

"Why were you released? You still had several months left to go," she said. "And how come no one told us?"

"Still seeking plots everywhere," he said. "I guess some things haven't changed." He sounded as if he were scolding her.

"Nor should they," she said a little tartly. He used to cheer her efforts and share her caution. "You didn't answer my question."

"Who knows why they do the things they do?" he said evasively. "I just thank God I'm not there anymore." He shut off the running tap, effectively ending their conversation.

He knew more than he was letting on. He had returned a full six months before his sentence was up, something nearly unheard of.

Her thoughts alighted on a minefield of devastating possibilities. Had he made a deal with the KGB? Could he be trusted? Was he their spy?

"I want to go to bed," he said. "I'm exhausted."

There was no invitation in his words. Likely he was exhausted, but he was also avoiding further conversation.

He still hadn't talked to her about the danger he'd mentioned in the subway station, but she had a heightened sense of it now, crowding into the room, filling all of the space between them.

He compounded her sense of separation from him, saying, "I'll take the couch tonight. I'm not ready to share the bed."

Not ready. Maybe she only needed to be patient. Maybe there was hope. She would wait as long as he needed if there was a chance he'd truly return to her.

But what if he were already gone?

CHAPTER FOUR

ARTUR

RTUR SAT AT his cubicle typing up his report on his first encounter with Edouard "Edik" Soifer. The sounds of hushed, angry conversation from his supervisor's office carried to him.

"How can you saddle me with him? He's never even handled an informant," Artur's new partner, Victor, complained.

Victor hadn't stopped at his cubicle next to Artur's. He'd arrived and marched straight to their supervisor's office, likely not expecting Artur to be in earlier than he was, especially after the late night out.

"He's an excellent agent," their supervisor defended. But Kasparov didn't sound fully convinced himself, adding, "So I've been told."

"So you've been told," Victor grumbled. "By whom? By Semyon? This is a simple case of nepotism. And there's too much at stake. How can you expect me to produce results on the Reitman case when I have to babysit the Spymaster's son-in-law?"

Artur blew out an exasperated breath. He wished he weren't privy to the argument, one that repeated with troubling frequency. He was a victim of his own success.

"You're letting your ego get in the way. You need to give him a chance," Kasparov said.

"A chance to what? Tank my career? Just because he's greener than grass doesn't mean I'm willing to get mowed down with him," Victor said. "I already talked to Lilya. She said last night was a total bust. They got nothing."

"She got nothing," Kasparov clarified. "Artur's working on his own report."

"*Blyad!* He's here?" Victor asked.

"See what he has to say. You might find a benefit sticking to the side where the grass is greener," Kasparov said.

Victor emerged from Kasparov's office a moment later. Although he likely realized Artur had heard the whole conversation, he made no apology. He didn't even have the good grace to look slightly sheepish, at the very least for not having noticed Artur's presence.

Instead, he swooped down on Artur's cubicle like the fat hawk the other agents agreed he resembled. "I heard last night was a bust."

"Not exactly." Artur tried to sound upbeat. The truth was he was disappointed himself. He typed the last sentence of his report and pulled the paper from the typewriter, handing it to Victor with feigned bravado.

When he'd set out with Lilya last night, he'd expected to have a book's worth of secrets in his hands by morning. In reality, he hadn't gathered enough information to fill a complete page.

Victor skimmed the paper. "So you know Soifer's involved in black market trade. He carries around gads of cash. And he comes to the same bar every Wednesday night to take orders for merchandise."

"And he has an associate named Sofia with a talent for price gouging for cigarettes," Artur added.

"That's it? That's all you got out of him?" Victor asked, incredulous.

"It's a start," Artur said.

Victor snorted dismissively. "It'll take a lot more than this to demonstrate you have what it takes to be a spy handler. This isn't enough to take to the Spymaster without embarrassing yourself."

Artur couldn't help but agree with him. He had hoped to do far better.

"Although, to be fair, this was your first experience with an informant," Victor added with unexpected sympathy. "Sometimes these things take time."

Before Artur could wonder at the change in Victor's tone, he heard the telltale slap of leather-soled shoes on linoleum, the confident stride of the Spymaster, the Chief of the Second Directorate, Foreign Intelligence. Victor must have seen Semyon coming down the hall and was now trying to put on a good show.

Semyon paused at Artur's desk. Even before Artur had married Maya, Semyon had taken an interest in him, but the new proximity since his assignment as Victor's partner increased the number of visits.

Judging by the presence of his gold cuff links, the medals from his military service, and his "lucky" red tie with the gold star at the bottom, Semyon had just met with the heads of state. He carried a notepad and a leather folio.

He scrubbed a hand over his face, and Artur noticed the dark circles under his eyes and the deepening lines. His father-in-law seemed to have been involved in an endless string of meetings lately. Yet he never failed to grace Artur with some small, fatherly acknowledgment,—a smile or wink or pat on the shoulder.

"Hard at work, I see," Semyon said.

"Yes, sir."

Artur hoped he wouldn't have to report to the Spymaster on the poor results from his first spy handling assignment. He didn't want to disappoint the man.

"Good. Good," Semyon said distractedly. "I'm counting on you both. I just came from the latest briefing. President Reagan is using the Jewish question to stall negotiations for nuclear disarmament. They're standing on the Helsinki Accords and accusing us of human rights violations."

Semyon huffed derisively. "The hypocrites accuse us of racism and discrimination. They should take a good hard look in the mirror."

"This isn't about what's true," Artur said. "The Main Enemy has always wanted to interfere in our internal affairs. It's what the Americans do all over the world. They pretend they're interested in peace, while they occupy countries and build up their arsenals. We all know this is just an excuse to continue Reagan's Star Wars program."

Semyon clapped him on the shoulder. "You get it."

He turned to Victor. "You'll be interested to know the American ambassadors are naming Jews by name—Sharanksy, Nudel, Reitman, Abramovich. By name!" Semyon exclaimed and then gave a weary, disgusted shake of his head.

"Reitman?" Victor asked, looking pale.

"Yes, Reitman," Semyon confirmed. "I want a full status report." Although a KGB Chief, Semyon wasn't technically their supervisor. Victor and Artur worked for the First Directorate, domestic intelligence, and reported to Igor Kasparov. But investigating the Jews, who were communicating with foreign governments, crossed into areas of foreign intelligence, too.

"Everything's in place," Victor said. "Mendel was welcomed home yesterday, no questions asked. And so far, he's been very cooperative."

"Glad to hear it," Semyon said, as if surprised and pleased Victor could impart any good news.

"And how are you faring?" Semyon asked Artur.

"I went after a potential informant last night," Artur said.

"I heard you ran into some unexpected trouble," Semyon said.

"The target didn't take to Lilya," Artur said.

"She mentioned that," Semyon said, leaving Artur to wonder whether Semyon was secretly keeping tabs on Artur's performance. "Will you try again with another dangle?"

"Actually, I'd like to see if I can get anywhere with him myself," Artur said.

"Why? Is he *goluboy*?" Semyon asked with surprise.

"No, I don't think he's gay," Artur said. "I think he's just really awkward with women and happened to take a liking to me. I told him I was new in town, and he offered to show me around."

"Interesting. So you're going undercover," Semyon said, gracing him with unexpected approval. "Seeing if you can befriend him and pump him for intel yourself."

"It's going to take a lot of time," Victor complained. "Sex or blackmail would be so much faster."

"Yes," Semyon agreed. "But those are blunt instruments. Sometimes it's better to be more subtle and use a needle, so sharp they don't even feel the pinch until it's too late."

"He's never been undercover before," Victor said.

Semyon shrugged. "We all have to start somewhere. And obviously he has a natural talent if the target invited him on his own."

He gave Artur a wink, patted him on the shoulder, and, in much higher spirits than when he arrived, Semyon started to whistle as he headed down the hall.

"He has big plans for you," Victor observed. "Wants to see you cut your teeth on the kinds of assignments needed to advance."

"Yes. But he'll also understand if there's something more pressing," Artur said. "Like the Reitman case."

"You stick to your thing, and I'll stick to mine," Victor said. "This is a good opportunity for you. If you succeed, it will show that you're ready for big assignments. You know, deep cover or Embassy work."

"But the Reitman case?" Artur asked, knowing that this was Victor's major focus, the assignment on which he thought his own career rose or fell.

"Is well in hand," Victor said. "And it's in everyone's best interest if we all keep the Spymaster happy."

CHAPTER FIVE
SOFIA

W HEN SOFIA AWAKENED the next morning, Mendel was gone. If not for the blanket and pillow crumpled on her living room sofa, she might have convinced herself his return was a troubling dream.

Her little sister stopped by before school, bringing Kolya so that he could change into clean clothes.

Despite a ten-year age gap between Vera and Kolya, they both went to the same school. Vera rode the city bus with him every morning.

"Is Papa here?" Kolya asked. His slim shoulders were tight and high, and his face pinched. Rather than being overjoyed to have his father back, Sofia's little boy seemed anxious.

When she told him Mendel had left for the morning, Kolya's shoulders relaxed, but his face stayed pinched as if he were concentrating hard. "He looks weird, and he smells funny."

"He's had a hard time," Sofia said. "But we'll take care of him, and things will get better." She tousled his hair, dark and curly like hers, and spoke with a confidence she wished she felt.

"He had a funny hat," Kolya said, reminding Sofia about the *yarmulka* she'd noticed last night. She hadn't asked Mendel about its significance, but she wondered now. Her husband used to teach Hebrew, but he had never been a religious man. Other than the rabbi and her uncle's foreign visitors, they had never encountered anyone religious, anyone who wore a Jewish skullcap. But now Mendel was wearing one. What did it mean?

There was so much about him that was different on the surface. She couldn't begin to guess what might have changed inside.

Kolya retreated to his nook, a semi-private corner of the living room partitioned by two large bookcases to form a bedroom. She heard him open and close his dresser drawers, taking out his clothes.

She knew better than to ask if he needed her help. Only seven, he refused to be coddled or treated like a child. Mama called him her "little man." Sofia hoped that with Mendel's return, Kolya might allow himself to be a little boy again.

"Mama wanted me to tell you to bring Mendel by later," Vera said. "She said she's looking forward to baking for him again."

"She said she's going to fatten him up," Kolya said, his voice slightly muffled by the bookcases. "And that she can make him handsome."

Vera rolled her eyes. "She also said to ask you to bring some sugar. She's running low."

Sofia was surprised her mother had asked Vera to pass the message. The request had precious little to do with needing actual sugar, but she doubted either Kolya or Vera suspected. They had both been carefully insulated from what Sofia thought of as the family business.

Neither could be trusted yet. Vera too easily telegraphed her thoughts and feelings, and no one could predict what a young boy might tell his friends or teachers.

She wondered why her mother hadn't phoned. They had long suspected a wiretap, but it had never stopped them. The KGB wouldn't know they were up to anything out of the ordinary, especially if Sofia actually delivered a container of sugar along with what was really wanted.

She and her mother had become adept at using routine to hide their other activities.

Unlike the men in her family, save for Edik, Sofia and her mother didn't have regular KGB escorts. Sofia stuck religiously to the humdrum routines of visiting family, going to work, and shopping for groceries. Occasionally, an agent would follow, but the KGB seemed to think that watching a housewife stand in line for bread and sugar or catch the metro home after work hardly rated their close attention.

The Soviets didn't seem to imagine a mere woman could cause them any real trouble. Sofia exploited this blind spot as often as possible.

Mendel returned before they left. He had a brown paper bag in his hand and a hammer. He gave a terse greeting to her and to Vera and asked after Kolya.

Kolya emerged, his white shirt buttoned and tucked neatly into his dark trousers. Kolya's gaze slid away from his father, but Mendel stared at him as if soaking in and memorizing every detail.

"All set?" Kolya asked Vera, as if he were eager to leave.

"You should wear this," Mendel said, and he pulled a black skullcap from the bag in his hand. He pushed the round piece of cloth at Kolya. Kolya took it and inspected it warily.

"Are you crazy?" Vera balked. "You can't make him wear that thing."

"It will draw unnecessary attention," Sofia agreed.

She didn't like the idea of little Kolya wearing a *yarmulka*. In school would be bad enough, but he also had to ride the city bus. Muscovites could be very anti-Semitic. They might not care that he was just a child. She didn't want any trouble for him. Or for Vera.

"It will protect him. God will protect him," Mendel said.

God? They had never before talked of God.

"Protect him?" Vera objected. "You might as well paint a target on his back."

"Don't tell me how to raise my son."

"Mendel, she's right," Sofia said.

"She's a child," he said, dismissing them both.

"I'm like a mother to him. I spend almost every day with him," Vera said with bristled dignity. "You've been home one night."

"I'm his father!" Mendel roared.

Kolya moved close to Vera in solidarity. He handed the skullcap back to Mendel. "I won't wear it."

"You'll do what I say. This is for your own good."

"No," Sofia said firmly. Mendel looked at her with surprise, as if he'd forgotten she was there or hadn't expected any argument from her. "Vera's right. It's not safe for him to wear the skullcap outside."

Mendel opened his mouth to argue, and she held up her hand. "No."

He regarded her silently for a moment. The man she remembered could be bullheaded, but maybe he remembered that she had never let him trample her.

"Inside then," Mendel said staunchly. "When you get home from school."

"I'm going with Vera after school. Like always." Kolya stared mutinously at his father, and Sofia expected this was the beginning of a drawn out battle.

"We don't need Vera," Mendel said, and Vera drew back as if he'd slapped her. "You'll come straight home now that I'm here."

Sofia reached out and squeezed her sister's shoulder. She tried to soften Mendel's ungracious treatment. "You're always wanted," she said. "But these two do need a little time to get used to each other again."

Vera pressed her lips together and gave a tight nod, bottling up her obvious hurt. Sofia had always thought Mendel's homecoming would be a cause for celebration and joy. She hadn't expected it to be so painful an adjustment for all of them.

After Vera and Kolya left to catch the bus, Mendel went to the kitchen with his paper bag and hammer clutched tightly in his hands.

"What do you have there?" Sofia asked as he opened the bag and gingerly placed the contents on the kitchen table.

He held up a small rectangular object with a Hebrew letter on the front. "It's a *mezuzah*," he said and took two more from the bag.

"A what?"

"Inside this case is a scroll with a prayer on it. Words of God," he explained. "We are commanded to teach them to our children, to recite them when we wake up and go to sleep, and to put them on our doorposts," he said. "I'll put them up for protection. On the door to every room, except the bathroom. The scroll helps safeguard the home."

"How? And from what?" The little boxes certainly wouldn't offer any protection should the KGB decide to bang down her door, not unless they contained explosives. And even then.

In fact, to her eye, the rectangular cases looked like the ideal vehicle for spy gear. She couldn't help but wonder if, like her key fob, they contained tiny cameras or other surveillance equipment. They were certainly the right size and shape.

Mendel changed the subject, not bothering to explain what kind of protection he thought the objects offered. "The rabbi gave them to me and also the *yarmulka* for Kolya. To welcome me home."

"When did you see the rabbi?"

"Yesterday. And then this morning again. At the synagogue. I went to pray." His answer surprised her. The Jewish community gathered at the Moscow Choral Synagogue every Saturday, but most people stayed *outside*, flocking to the synagogue as a cultural center, not a religious one. Almost no one in the Soviet Union was religious. Good Soviet citizens reserved their fervent beliefs for the State.

While Mendel had never been a model citizen, in all of the years she had known him before his arrest, he had never ventured inside the synagogue building. Now he had been there twice in less than twenty-four hours. And he had spoken to the rabbi.

She reached behind her and turned on the faucet to drown out the sound of what she wanted to say. Even if the objects had surveillance in them, she could make it hard for their audience to decipher her words.

"I don't understand. You used to say the rabbi was our enemy. A puppet for the Kremlin." Behind her, the faucet noisily sprayed water into the metal sink.

Mendel had strongly argued that Moscow's rabbi didn't represent Jewish interests in the USSR, but rather undermined efforts to highlight their plight.

"I was idealistic and foolish back then," he said. "I thought anyone who disagreed with me was an enemy." The rabbi had not supported their desire to leave the Soviet Union for Israel or their social activism for human rights.

"I know better now," he said. "I've seen the true face of evil."

"In the gulag?" she asked.

His whole body tightened as if she'd hit him with a live wire, and she was sorry she'd asked.

"Yes," was all he said.

He turned abruptly and picked up a *mezuzah* and his hammer. He stalked from the kitchen to the front door, and she couldn't tell if he was angry at her for poking at a topic he'd made clear he didn't want to discuss or haunted by what had happened to him.

She heard him near the front door, intoning what she recognized as a Hebrew blessing. She inspected the two cases he'd left on the table. They had removable backs. She slid the back off of one and peeked inside. As he'd said, there was a parchment scroll inside the box's compartment.

Mendel banged the hammer, ostensibly to affix the *mezuzah* to the front doorpost, but she didn't go to see. Instead, she carefully picked up the thin parchment and inspected it. It was wound around a black object the size of a thick kopek. A listening device?

She nearly dropped the scroll in her surprise. She had never actually seen one of the KGB's bugs before.

Did Mendel know the bug was in there? Did the rabbi?

The hammering stopped. She hastily popped the scroll and listening device back into the compartment.

Maybe Mendel knew. Maybe he'd made a deal with the KGB. Or maybe he'd been duped and was installing the bugs without knowing they were there.

Either way, he was helping the KGB spy on her and her associates. She had to be careful. More careful than usual.

She always assumed someone was listening in. Now she knew for sure.

What she didn't know was whether her husband, the man who used to be her comrade in arms, was willfully complicit.

CHAPTER SIX
VERA

"**Y**OU'RE COMING TO my party, aren't you, Masha?" Larissa asked loudly with a sly glance at Vera.

Vera wasn't invited to the party, and Larissa wanted her to know it. The other girls in the classroom quickly got on board with the new scheme, and they chatted excitedly about the party, casting haughty looks in Vera's direction.

Vera sank lower in her seat and doodled in the margin of her notebook. She pretended she wasn't listening to them, that being excluded didn't bother her.

But she stank at pretending. She could feel the heat in her face and knew her red cheeks easily broadcast her distress to everyone. She could feel her teacher's gaze raking over her, and she didn't dare look up to meet the woman's eye.

Larissa, the other students, even their teacher all seemed to enjoy being cruel to her. They just didn't know that they didn't have to aim all that precisely today to pierce Vera's heart.

Mendel had already done that.

We don't need you, Mendel's words echoed in her head, breaking her heart all over again. She'd spent every afternoon with Kolya and sometimes Sofia for years. Other than her parents, she had no one else. No school friends. No boyfriend.

Now she had nothing to fill her time after school, other than her own studies.

She focused on her notebook. She had written Gennady's name there again, not that he ever noticed her, and circled it with hearts and flowers. She retraced the design now, digging into the paper with her pen until the paper ripped.

She crumpled the page into a ball and got up from her desk to throw it out, grateful to have something to do, some reason to move away from Larissa and the taunting conversation about her upcoming party.

"Tovarish Soifer," her teacher called in a deceptively sweet voice. "Come here."

Vera dropped her paper in the trash and shuffled to the teacher's desk. She knew that tone, and it didn't bode well for her.

"Did you see the paper this morning?" Her teacher waved a copy of *Pravda* in her face.

"Yes, ma'am."

"And I suppose you read the article about Israel?" She blinked at Vera from behind lenses that made her eyes appear huge.

Vera swallowed hard. She hadn't read the article, but her father had railed about it. "Lies, all lies," he had cursed and thrown the paper in the trash in a fit of disgust.

"No, ma'am."

"I'm surprised. Given that you want to trade in your citizenship to move there."

That wasn't what Vera wanted. It was what her parents wanted. What Mendel had convinced them to want.

She had only been a young girl when her sister married Mendel, but she well remembered the way he had relentlessly argued with and cajoled her father, the way he had painted a vision of leaving for the Jewish homeland.

He had convinced the entire family to embrace their Jewish identity and request to emigrate to Israel. And Vera, only a child then, had had no say, just like Kolya had no say.

The family hadn't been allowed to leave, and now they were no longer Soviet citizens either.

And it was all Mendel's fault.

"Why would anyone want to give up Moscow for a third world desert?" Larissa piped in. "Israel's a horrible place. Full of savages. Always ready to wage war on their peaceful Arab neighbors."

Larissa was the teacher's obnoxious little pet and gleefully regurgitated the slurs she'd made on other occasions.

"Here, Vera. Enlighten all of us about Israel. Read the article to us." Her teacher forced her to read aloud to the class.

"Israelis taught Nazis genocide," the headline read. The article went on to detail how top-ranking Israeli officials had been involved in teaching the Nazis how to slaughter millions of people with smooth efficiency.

Vera choked on the words. That her father insisted they weren't true was no consolation right now. Her classmates looked on her with horror, and she burned with embarrassment and shame as she stumbled through reading the many horrific atrocities detailed in the article.

"Take a close look, class," the teacher said, standing. "See Vera here? She's a traitor. A Zionist. A Jew."

"A Nazi sympathizer," one of her classmates added.

There was nothing she could say. She couldn't fight back, or they might kick her out of the school, just months shy of graduation. She knew she had been privileged even to be allowed to stay in the prestigious math and science school. Her teachers and the other students regularly reminded her that her slot should have been given to someone more deserving.

The students booed and shouted insults, and Vera was crying by the time her teacher finally let her go back to her seat at the back of the room.

She wished she could be anywhere but here, but not Israel. The place sounded like a nightmare. So uncivilized and foreign, a land of tyrannical zealots like her brother-in-law.

She still couldn't believe Mendel had tried to force poor Kolya to wear a skullcap. To school. Kolya would have been lucky to survive the day without a black eye and a broken nose. He wasn't a girl, and so he wouldn't be spared the physical violence the way she was.

And she hated to imagine him being shunned and shamed as she was. She cried a little harder, for herself and for him.

She knew Sofia wouldn't have cried. Her sister would have lifted her chin in proud defiance.

But Vera wasn't tough like her sister.

She hunched in her seat, shoulders stooped under the weight of her misery. If only she could fit in here. If only she could be like her classmates. She loved Moscow. It was one of the best cities in the world. She wanted friends and a future here, not this terrible limbo of waiting for permission to go to a country she'd never seen, a country she'd only ever heard terrible things about.

She wrapped her arms around herself and stared at her desk. She couldn't bear to look into the malicious faces of her classmates. The teacher instructed them to take out their notebooks and present their homework. She walked up and down the rows, inspecting each student's work and doling out praise.

When she stopped in front of her desk, her teacher didn't say a word. She merely dropped a folded piece of paper on Vera's desk. A note.

The teacher walked back down the aisle to her desk and sat down. Vera felt the eyes of the other students on her as she unfolded the note.

It was from Petya, another one of their classmates. "Dear Vera," it began, "You are one of the best student in our class, and I need your help." His solicitous flattery put her on guard. No one gave her compliments.

She was tempted to stop reading and crumple up the note. But curiosity made her continue. It seemed he needed a tutor, and he wanted her.

She was leery of this request for help. Maybe it was another prank, timed perfectly to kick her when she was down, right after her teacher's harangue.

Maybe the plea was real. Everyone knew Petya had been ill. He'd already missed weeks of school, and he was absent again today.

Or maybe this was a nasty trick. Like the time she'd been invited to a picnic in the park and showed up at the appointed time to find everyone leaving for home, the picnic over.

In her mind, she could hear the echo of her classmates' laughter over her disappointment at being excluded yet again, of having her nose rubbed in how much they hated her.

She folded Petya's letter back into a neat rectangle. Maybe she should refuse the invitation and rob them of their amusement.

But what if Petya really needed her? She would like the opportunity to be helpful, to spend time with someone her own age for once, to maybe make a friend.

She would brave the risk, she decided. What was a little more laughter at her expense?

CHAPTER SEVEN
SOFIA

LATER THAT MORNING, Mendel went out onto the balcony to smoke. Knowing Mendel would be occupied for at least a little while, Sofia took the opportunity to sneak into the crawl space unobserved.

The crawl space looked like a wide, wooden cabinet set into the upper third of an otherwise empty stretch of wall in the kitchen.

She climbed onto a kitchen chair, opened the hatch, and levered herself up into the storage area. Only a few feet high, there was no way to stand. Boxes full of an interrupted life cluttered the space. They belonged to Max, Irena, and Nadia, Mendel's sister's family, who had all been shipped off to the gulag. Sofia crawled to the back corner, behind the boxes, where she hid her own secret things, including her mini cameras.

She easily found the twine and paper package where she kept a stack of rubles, once as thick as a hardcover book. Her store had been depleted over the last several months, but she trusted it would be replenished after her next drop.

Moving quickly, she took a pile about a centimeter thick, stacked with bills worth a few hundred rubles, and replaced the rest in the package.

When she finally shimmied out of the crawl space, less than a minute had passed. Following a familiar pattern, she took the opaque canister she used for sugar from the cabinet. She poured most of the sugar into an empty bowl, placed the money in the cannister, and then poured the sugar back inside to cover the rubles.

Eying the *mezuzah* Mendel had placed on the kitchen doorway, she called her mother on the telephone. "Vera said you wanted us to come over today."

"Yes, how are things with Mendel?" Renata asked.

"Some things haven't changed," Sofia said. "He's outside smoking." It was a habit she had never liked. She hadn't missed the stale smell of cigarettes in her apartment.

She felt petty for even thinking of it now, though. She should just be happy he was home.

"But other things have changed?" Mama asked meaningfully.

"You've seen him." She couldn't voice her suspicions over the phone. Even in person, she would have to be very circumspect. Most of all, she couldn't let Mendel know she suspected him.

"Do you still need sugar?" she asked.

"Yes. Can you spare a cup?" Her mother asked, playing along, acknowledging the coded request.

"*Konechno*," Sofia said as Mendel poked his head into the kitchen. She told him, "I'm on the phone with my mother."

"Ask him what kind of cookies he likes now," Renata said, and Sofia relayed the question.

"Oatmeal raisin," he said. Renata heard him. "Ah, that hasn't changed either," she said. "I'll start on them now. Don't forget to bring me more sugar."

"No problem," Sofia said, but she had a niggle of worry. In the years she had been delivering these weekly installments of cash to her parents, she had never been stopped. Not once.

But she had always run the errand alone. Now she would have Mendel and his KGB entourage in tow.

"Your *yarmulka* might attract attention," she said as they put on their coats to leave.

The last thing she needed was for them to call attention to themselves. Carrying that much money around wasn't as dangerous as toting the Tropels, but it could still land her in hot water.

"You might want to take it off for when we walk through the neighborhood."

"No," he said.

"Cover it with a hat then? It's cold out, and that won't keep you warm," she suggested, pulling on her own knit cap.

"No," he said firmly. "And that's final."

She didn't argue with him, and a few minutes later they exited their apartment building together.

Two agents sat on the bench by the door, waiting for them. One had a paper folded in his lap, the other a cup of coffee, but their casual air didn't fool her. Like snakes lazing in the sun, they could strike in an instant once stirred.

She glanced nervously over her shoulder at her husband. He glared with undisguised hatred at the KGB men on the bench. Maybe he wasn't working with them after all, she hoped. Or maybe he was being coerced into cooperating.

Maybe she hadn't lost him. Maybe there was hope he was still on her side.

The new addition to his wardrobe set him apart, and the people they passed on the street ogled him and muttered. Mendel held his head high, in proud defiance of the interest he drew.

His arrogant display of Jewishness offered sufficient provocation for the agents to harass him, if their anti-Semitic neighbors didn't lash out first.

Did he imagine this flimsy piece of cloth, like the scroll on the doorpost, would protect him from harm?

She was glad Kolya wasn't wearing one.

The two agents fell into line behind them, silent and keeping an almost respectful distance, just as they had last night.

Knowing Mendel had, wittingly or unwittingly, recently installed bugs in their apartment, she had to wonder whether the tail was just for show and their non-interference stemmed from knowing he was their creature.

When she and Mendel reached her parents' apartment, Mendel's KGB agents joined up with her father's. No one interfered with them or even made a rude remark.

Something was off.

Renata greeted them at the door and fussed over Mendel. "You poor thing! You're so thin. They didn't feed you at all. Well, don't worry, I'm going to make all of your favorites. I just put the oatmeal cookies in the oven." Her mother turned to her next, kissing her on both cheeks. Renata smelled of cinnamon and vanilla. She asked Sofia, "Did you bring the sugar?"

Sofia extracted the canister from her handbag.

"Let me go put this away," Renata said. "Ilya, Sofia and Mendel are here," she called over her shoulder and bustled to the kitchen.

"*Molodetz.*" Her father, Ilya, rose slowly, heavily from his easy chair, pretending it was an effort to come greet them, when in reality he was giving Renata cover to hide the canister.

Like her, her parents were always acting for an audience, aware the KGB or their army of informants were watching and listening.

They always had to be careful. The information they shared or concealed had implications for so many other people. Like other Soviet Jews, her parents had both lost their jobs when they declared their intention to emigrate. Her mother, once a respected surgeon, now worked as a lowly dishwasher and her father an elevator operator on the late shift in a hotel. Unlike others, though, they were at the heart of Jewish resistance.

Renata tended to the members of the community and judiciously doled out the money, medications, and medical supplies the community received from their friends abroad, while Ilya's *samizdat* published and disseminated reports on the persecution of Jews, especially the mistreatment related to the seemingly regular arrests, trials, and imprisonments.

For her part in the family plot, Sofia, along with her cousin, Edik, fenced black market goods provided by their western contacts. She led her parents to believe the money she delivered every week came entirely from these sales.

"Come, Mendel, maybe you want some tea? And some cookies, too, of course. We need to put a little weight back on you." Renata had always loved to dote on Mendel.

"I'll have some tea," Mendel said, gracing Renata with a shy smile he had yet to bestow on Sofia.

As Mendel followed her mother to the kitchen, Ilya pulled her aside. He led her into the living room, where the TV played at full volume on a station full of static, her father's favored technique for foiling the KGB's attempts to eavesdrop.

"Did the agents give you any trouble?" he whispered directly in her ear.

"No."

"Surprising," he said. "I wonder why."

"Maybe they think prison scared him out of causing more trouble?" she suggested, even though she had other, stronger suspicions.

Ilya scowled at her. "He was an activist, a known troublemaker. Do you really think they're that stupid and lazy that they wouldn't do their best to intimidate him, at least for the first few months after his release?"

"No," she admitted.

"We have to be extremely careful around him," Ilya said. "He can't be trusted."

"I know," she said. For a brief moment, she squeezed her eyes shut, her heart rebelling. She envied her parents their partnership. They shared their secrets, while she hoarded all of hers. For five years, she had told herself everything would be different when Mendel came home.

She had imagined she wouldn't be alone anymore.

Spying was a lonely business. She felt the pressure of all of those secrets building inside her. Sometimes she wondered how long she could remain self-contained without bursting apart.

She hadn't survived this long by blinding herself with denial and hopeless wishes. Her life depended on being clear-eyed about the dangers and risks she faced. She took a deep breath and opened her eyes.

The time for wishing was over, and she splashed back into her frigid reality.

"He seems to have allied himself with the rabbi," she said.

Ilya raised a bushy eyebrow as he contemplated this news. "Does he know about the money? Or the lists?"

"No, I haven't told him anything." And she hadn't told her parents the whole truth either.

"Keep it that way," Ilya advised.

CHAPTER EIGHT
VERA

VERA CLUTCHED HER schoolbooks nervously and waited for Petya to answer the bell.

She waited a long time at the door. She rang the buzzer a second time. Anxiously, she moved from foot to foot.

Finally, the door opened. She was greeted, not by the skinny boy she knew or a laughing gaggle of classmates, but by her own fantasy man.

He was real enough, flesh and blood, not a daydream. Petya's older brother had been the heart throb of the school until he graduated two years ago. Vera vividly recalled the girls' fighting over whether Gennady had glanced at one or another of them, posturing over who could and should win his favor. Since he was the best at everything in school,—math, science, language, sports—the girls had decided that whichever of them he chose must also be the best.

The interest had continued even after he had left them for university. His commuting schedule still put him on the city bus with a large group of them, and Vera had gathered he sometimes hung out with Petya and his friends.

Of course, she had never been invited to join the fun.

Her cheeks flushed at the sight of him. She was embarrassed by the juvenile fantasies she herself harbored, of the way she sighed over his yearbook picture and drew foolish hearts around his portrait, of the way her breath caught when he got on the bus in the morning a few stops after hers. Her infatuation was so obvious that even her seven-year-old nephew had caught on, and yet she doubted Gennady even knew her name. He had never spoken to her.

She hovered in the doorway and looked down at her feet. Maybe Petya's invitation was a cruel joke after all. Maybe someone had glimpsed the hearts and flowers in her notebook and dreamed up a new way to torture her. If the invitation were a prank, it would be ten times worse now, the humiliation so much more poignant if it happened in front of Gennady.

She summoned enough courage to mumble, "I'm here to see Petya. He said he needed help with his schoolwork."

"He doesn't really," Gennady said.

"Oh." She bristled inside. She had made a mistake coming here. She fell for the same tricks again and again, always hoping this time would be different.

She was about to turn away, bolt back down the stairs, and pretend the whole thing had never happened, pretend she had never received Petya's prank of an invitation.

Gennady opened the door wider. "I'm sure he just used that as an excuse to spend some time with a pretty girl."

Wait! He thought she was pretty? No one had ever told her she was pretty before. No one really ever paid her much mind, not even her parents.

"If I were in his place, I would have sent a note to lure you here, too," he said. "Are you going to come in or what?"

"I—" She found herself tongue-tied and deeply flattered. He seemed to shine so brightly before her. She couldn't look directly at him.

He took her by the arm and relieved her of her textbooks. "Come inside, Vera," he said gently. "I had no idea you were as shy as you are pretty."

He knew her name!

And he thought she was pretty.

She felt as if she were floating in a dream as she followed him into the apartment. She hung her jacket on the stand beside a glossy hall table. There weren't many decorations in the apartment, but she noticed that everything was of the highest quality.

A gilt-framed photograph in the hall showed a man who looked like Gennady, probably his father, in military regalia, decorated with all manner of insignias and medals, standing beside General Secretary Andropov.

She quickly looked away, pretending to herself that she hadn't seen it. She had forgotten that Petya and Gennady's father was a high-ranking general in the army. Her father, with his longstanding hatred of the Soviet government, would never have approved this visit. He would say she had let some petty flattery go to her head and lure her right into the enemy's domain.

But there couldn't be any real danger to her here, even if Petya did plan to embarrass her. She had never run afoul of the authorities, and she never would.

"Vera!" Petya called. "I'd come greet you, but I don't want to get you sick." He sat at the dining room table with his books spread out before him and a pile of crumpled tissue and sheets of paper at his side. "I'm so glad you're here. I've been struggling over these math problems for the last hour." He sounded nasal, and his face was pale. Dark circles ringed his eyes, and his cheekbones were more pronounced than usual.

She supposed that on a better day Petya might be as handsome as his older brother. The other girls had shifted much of their attention his way once Gennady had graduated. But to her, there was no comparison. She had an incurable crush.

"Why didn't you ask your brother to help you?" she asked.

"What makes you think he didn't?" Gennady placed her books on the table across from Petya. "The truth is, I'm a terrible teacher," he said. "I know things, but I can't explain how I know them."

"But *you* can. Right, Vera?" Petya encouraged. "I've seen you with your nephew. You're a natural teacher." The little bit of praise suffused her system like a drug, making her feel warm and loose.

"I can try," she said, and the nervous tension, the awful suspicions, eased out of her. Petya really did need her and want her here. "What are you working on?"

She sat down at the table beside him, and they started to discuss the math problem that had been eluding him. Gennady left them alone to work, and she relaxed even more. Slowly, her self-consciousness fled.

She enjoyed the role of teacher and, more than that, the company of someone her own age. Petya was a quick study. His issues stemmed from missing the material the teacher presented in class rather than from any lack of understanding.

She didn't know how much time had passed before he started to yawn. She had so enjoyed this stretch of time with Petya, even though all they had talked about was math problems and the quirks of their teacher. She glanced up at the window and noticed it had grown dark outside.

"I'm sorry," Petya said. "I'm so tired all of a sudden. Can you come back tomorrow?"

Her paranoid father would undoubtedly disapprove of her being in General Morozov's home to help a boy who was an erstwhile friend at best. But she pushed the niggling feeling of wrongness aside.

"I guess," she said, pretending nonchalance, even though this new invitation made her giddy. Tomorrow was a school day. In the past, she would have had to babysit Kolya, but Mendel didn't want her hanging around.

She was free. But the luxury of having no responsibility didn't give her any satisfaction. She was eager to accept his invitation to fill the time. To avoid being home all alone for hours with no one to talk to while both of her own parents worked, when other families, normal families, might be having dinner together.

At least for this little while she had mattered to someone and wasn't all alone or invisible. She wondered, when Petya finally returned to school, would he acknowledge her the way the others wouldn't?

She collected up her books. He rose from the table, and she saw that he had lost a significant amount of weight. His slacks hung loosely from his frame. He had always been slim, but now he looked as Mendel did, as if he'd been starved.

"Sit. Sit." She waved him back into his seat. "You look exhausted. I can see myself out."

He sank back into his seat, seemingly grateful that he needn't exert himself. "Thanks," he said. "I really mean it. It was good of you to give up your afternoon for me. And I know it's selfish of me to ask you to come back again. You're a true friend."

"It's fine," she said because she couldn't tell him how grateful she felt for this reprieve from solitude. "Try to get some rest."

She hugged her books to her and headed for the door, happy for the first time in as long as she could remember.

Gennady had called her pretty, and Petya had called her a friend. Deep down, she knew it wasn't much, but she savored those little crumbs as if they meant everything.

CHAPTER NINE
SOFIA

I N THE MORNING, Sofia climbed up on a chair and threw open the *fortoshka*, the small ventilation window in her bedroom.

The open window was a signal to her contacts that she wanted to meet. She needed to leave the window open for an hour, from nine to ten in the morning.

Mendel came into the room. "It's chilly. Why's the window open?"

"I like the air," she said. "Especially when I'm folding laundry." She gestured to the basket of clean laundry she'd just brought up from the machines in the basement.

The prospect of folding laundry was enough to send him fleeing to the other room. "Should I shut the door?" she called. "So you don't feel the air?"

"No," he said, and she couldn't help feeling he wanted her to leave the bedroom door open so that he could keep an eye on her activities.

She folded the laundry and put everything neatly away and still had time to spare. She made the bed and folded the blankets Mendel had left in a nest on the floor. He had vacated the living room for the bedroom at night at Kolya's request, but he slept on the floor.

He had yet to join her in the bed. He had yet to touch her. And she couldn't help but wonder why.

Had he turned against her? Or was he just so damaged from his ordeal? And could time and patience heal either problem?

When the hour was up, she closed the window, hoping her contacts had seen it. Now she needed to wait an hour. At eleven, they would call with information about when and where to meet.

"Are you going to the store?" Mendel asked. "We're out of kasha and milk."

She wished he would go out job hunting. She hadn't pushed. He hadn't even been home a week, and he was entitled to some peace and quiet. Perhaps he even wanted her out of the apartment to enjoy a little solitude, the same as she wanted him out.

But he was going to need to find a job and soon. Not so much because they needed the money, but because otherwise the government would have a ready excuse to round him up and pack him off to the gulag again, this time on charges of parasitism.

"I'll go later," she said. "I have some things I want to do first."

"What things?" he asked, and he sounded suspicious.

"Cleaning," she said. She needed to keep busy, if only to satisfy his curiosity. She changed the sheets on Kolya's bed and spent extra time tucking the corners tight. Then she hauled the ancient vacuum out of the closet and pushed it slowly through their three rooms, doubling the time it took to accomplish these simple chores.

A few minutes before the hour, she positioned herself in the kitchen near the wall-mounted phone. It rang at eleven on the dot. She snatched the receiver from the cradle before Mendel could lever himself off the sofa, where he was reading a book on Jewish history.

"Hello?"

"Hello. Is Marat home?" The name signaled the time and place to meet her contact, later this evening in a quiet residential neighborhood near the university. An easy stop for her to make on her way home without rousing suspicion due to lost time.

"I'm sorry. There's no one here with that name," she said, agreeing to the proposed time and place.

When she hung up, Mendel leaned in the doorway, his hand braced under the *mezuzah*. "Who was it?"

"No one. Wrong number," she said. She spared a moment to think about the hours of nothing that would be recorded from her apartment, the monotony of laundry, vacuuming, a seemingly random wrong number.

Inside she burbled with mirth. It overflowed into a smile she couldn't supress.

"What? What is it?" Mendel asked, searching her face with what seemed a frisson of alarm.

"Nothing," she said. "I just look at you, and I think how happy I am that you're home at last."

What she really felt was optimism. That things could change. That there was a chance for a better life. That she could best the Soviets, stealing secrets out from under them without their ever suspecting, even when they violated the sanctity of her very own home. Possibly of her marriage.

Mendel blinked at her, obviously caught off guard, and he didn't return her smile. She still wasn't sure what to blame for the distance between them, but she knew better than to follow her instinct and reach for him.

He would only pull away.

He retreated anyway, seemingly chased off by her pleased smile and pretty words about his homecoming. He ducked his head as if he felt guilty and returned to the corner of the sofa and the book he'd been reading, making her wonder why he'd even bothered to get up and come over to her in the first place.

The rest of the day passed quickly. She didn't have to work tonight. She stayed home to give Kolya his dinner. They did a puzzle together, while Mendel watched them, his expression unreadable.

In the evening, she claimed she was headed to the library for her book club. She did indeed have a book club meeting, and she did indeed go.

But afterward, she took a small detour on her way home.

CHAPTER TEN
VERA

AS SOON AS Vera got outside, it started to rain, but even the big fat water droplets couldn't dampen her mood.

"Hey!" someone called after her, and she turned around to see Gennady jogging toward her. He carried a large black umbrella. When he caught up to her, he pulled her close to him to share the umbrella and shield her from the rain. "You left without saying good-bye," he scolded.

She had no words. She could only look up into his eyes and wonder that they were standing so close together and that he'd cared enough to chase her down to say good-bye.

"Let me walk you home," he said. "I don't like the idea of your being out here all alone."

"All right," she agreed. He put his arm around her shoulder to keep her under the umbrella with him. She knew the touch meant nothing, but she liked the feel of him next to her all the same. She had never stood so close to him, close enough to feel his heat and to smell the good, clean scent of him.

"How do you like university?" she ventured.

"It's good," he said. "I'll be finished with my courses next year and heading off to my officer's training," he said. "Following in my old man's footsteps."

She was sorry she had asked. Her emotions rolled and knocked around, like a bag of marbles spilled to the ground.

He was so confident and self-assured, easy in the knowledge of what his future held. She was graduating this year and had no plans for the future, no prospects.

No university would take a *Refusenik* like her.

Their paths couldn't be more divergent. He would go on to become the kind of man her father hated, following in the footsteps of one he would never respect. Why did her father have to be such a rebel? And why did Gennady have to be seeking a military career?

Meanwhile, she would languish in Moscow, maybe cleaning toilets for a living like her sister, letting life pass her by while she waited for permission to leave that was never, never, never going to come.

They walked along in an easy silence. What did it matter what his future held or how far it would take him from her, she thought. Realistically, there could never be anything between them. Just her silly crush and a rainy night when they shared an umbrella.

He had never even spoken to her before. Likely he wouldn't again.

But could he maybe hold her a little tighter? The scent of him tickled her nose and her tongue, a familiar flavor she couldn't quite place, and she wanted a deep inhale, a taste.

"You're awfully quiet," Gennady observed as they approached her building.

Her father's KGB escort sat on the bench across the street under big umbrellas of their own. She glanced up at the window to her family's apartment. The lights shone brightly, and she guessed they had guests. Her parents always seemed to be entertaining friends.

They would still be sitting on the sofa next to the partition where she made her bed, and she would have to wait for who knew how long before she could lie alone in the dark and imprint all of the sweet details of the evening into her memory.

"What's the matter? Don't you like me?" Gennady prodded.

She couldn't tell him that she had too many words to share a single one. She couldn't tell him that she was halfway in love with him and that only the sheer impossibility of it all held her back.

"Everyone likes you," she deflected.

"But, Vera, I didn't ask about everyone." He stopped walking and turned to her. "I asked about you. Do you like me?"

Desperately.

Her heart began to pound so hard she could barely catch her breath. She couldn't look him in the eye. She managed a quick nod in answer to his question.

"So shy," he whispered and kissed her on the cheek. She raised her hand to the spot, as if she could hold the kiss there. He cupped the back of her neck gently and pressed his mouth softly to hers. "So sweet," he murmured against her mouth.

Someone whistled at them, one of the KGB agents, she realized, mortified.

Gennady pulled away and laughed.

Laughed at her.

The kiss, her first kiss, wasn't real.

Only this time, the KGB rather than her classmates, bore witness to her humiliation.

She turned on her heel and dashed into the building.

Behind her, she thought she heard the laughter growing louder. She couldn't bear to look back and see Gennady mocking her.

She had misjudged him. Wasted sentiment on him.

She rushed up the stairs to her own apartment. The familiar buzz of the television coupled with snatches of conversation grated on her already jangled nerves. She retreated to the kitchen, where she wouldn't be expected to smile and perform for the latest in a constant stream of intruders, who dominated her parents' focus and attention.

She put on water to make tea and busied herself tidying the kitchen, forcing herself to keep moving, to focus on her tasks so that she didn't replay the kiss and the laughter over and over again.

The sugar bowl on the table was empty, and she searched in the cabinet for one of the large canisters where her mother stored the rest. She spied it on the top shelf and reached up on tiptoe to retrieve it.

The container was heavy. She screwed off the top and then carefully poured the granules into the bowl. There was a sudden large avalanche of sugar, and a large chunk of something fell onto the bowl and toppled it. Sugar spilled onto the counter.

When she put down the cannister and inspected, she found a large wad of rubles wrapped in plastic. She didn't know how much was there, but she immediately recognized it was a significant amount.

What was it for? Where had it come from? Why didn't she know about it?

She tossed it back into the cannister and hastily put the container back where she'd found it, recognizing that she'd discovered a secret she wasn't supposed to know. As she cleaned up the mess from the sugar, the tears flowed freely.

Her parents had their own life, their own secrets. She was the outsider, even in her own home. They had each other, but she had no one.

CHAPTER ELEVEN
GENNADY

GENNADY HAD NEVER kissed a girl, only to have her turn and run. Vera's mewl of distress haunted him as he walked home. The rain tapped on his umbrella, like restless fingers drumming on a table.

He had noticed Vera before tonight. She had a distinct look, large dark eyes, sun-kissed skin, and a bounty of wavy dark hair. Up until this year, she'd had a girl's figure, but her curves had filled out, and now with her dark beauty, she stood out from the other women he knew, earthy and exotic among a sea of pasty faces.

He had tried to catch her attention on the bus, but she never sustained eye contact with him, always looking immediately away, and she always had her nephew in tow. He'd told himself she was shy. But now he was humbled to think maybe she'd never had any interest in him at all.

His long legs carried him quickly back home, making the trek in half the time he'd taken up escorting Vera. His thoughts were consumed with memories of the warmth of her skin and lips on this cold rainy night, with the feeling of exhilaration he'd had when she'd admitted to liking him, with his sense, before everything had gone wrong, that this was meant to be, that somehow they'd been waiting for one another.

None of it was real. He'd merely been chasing down a little comfort to ease the stress of all of his responsibilities, and he'd followed the wrong scent.

When he arrived, he caught Petya asleep at the table, his face buried in his recently finished homework. The past month with Petya repeatedly falling ill had been hell on both of them. Their father was off on assignment, and no one would say where or for how long.

Their mother had long ago abandoned them. She hadn't loved them enough—not his father, not his brother, not him—to weather any adversity. She had left the men in his family to fend for themselves.

So maybe he'd scared Vera off. Better to have that happen now rather than later when she was truly under his skin. He shouldn't be interested in such a skittish girl, likely to bolt at any moment. He didn't need a woman like his mother, who would abandon him when life got hard, as inevitably it would.

"Petya, wake up and take yourself to bed," he said more harshly than he intended. He had grown tired of playing nursemaid. Over the past month, his brother hadn't been well for more than a few days at a time.

This last bout of flu had so weakened Petya that he couldn't cook his own kasha or keep up with his studies. That left Gennady to fill the roll of mother, father, and teacher, while he faced his own pressures and deadlines. His future rested heavily on his performance this year. He needed to score highly enough on his exams if he hoped to follow in his father's footsteps and have an officer's career in military intelligence.

He pushed open the window behind Petya's chair. The room smelled of stale sweat and sickness.

Surely Vera had noticed the unpleasant odors. She must have longed for fresh air during the hours she'd coddled his brother through his homework. Yet she had sat here for hours and endured the unpleasantness without complaint.

But she had darted away faster than a frightened rabbit when Gennady had tried to kiss her.

Petya startled when the window groaned. Upon waking, he peppered Gennady with uncomfortable questions. "Did you get her to promise? Will she come back tomorrow?"

"What difference does it make?" Gennady asked grumpily.

"I need her!" Petya complained.

"You don't need her." Such weakness simply didn't happen to Morozov men. Petya merely needed to rest up and refocus. "Admit that you just wanted to spend time with a pretty girl."

When Gennady had caught his first glimpse of Vera through the spyhole, he had been certain the tutor request had been a flimsy pretense to garner sympathy and attention from a very pretty girl.

A girl his brother fancied.

A girl Gennady had tried to kiss.

A girl who maybe hadn't welcomed his kiss, despite the hunger he thought he'd glimpsed in her exotic, tilted eyes.

"She's not pretty," Petya protested.

Gennady raised his brow at the bald-faced lie.

"Fine, she's pretty," Petya conceded. "More than pretty." Petya rubbed his hands over his face and released a long, exhausted sigh.

An uncomfortable, cold feeling chased over Gennady's skin. Guilt settled like ice in his gut. How sick was Petya? And how much did he like Vera?

His brother had failed tonight to break out the flirtation and compliments. Petya hadn't shown Vera the small courtesy of walking her to the door, let alone home. At the time, Gennady had thought Petya had blown his chance or wasn't interested, leaving the field open to him. In retrospect, he wondered if his brother had been too sick to exert himself.

Had Gennady tried to steal Vera from his sick brother?

"That's not why I asked her to come. I need her. She's the only one with the smarts and the patience to explain this stuff to me," Petya complained. "And she was my last resort. Everyone else was too busy. Including you."

"You asked other people?" The revelation gave him a frisson of alarm. His brother really did need help, more than Gennady was able to give him. Petya needed Vera, much to Gennady's chagrin.

"I asked all the top people in the class. They're all tied up with university interviews. No one else was willing to risk catching my plague."

"If no one else was willing, then how did you get her to agree?" Gennady asked.

"I honestly don't know," Petya said. "I'm guessing she has a crush on me." Did Petya like her, too?

Petya had offered Vera nothing in return for her help, and she hadn't seemed to mind. Perhaps Vera had feelings for her classmate. Would she have preferred Petya's interest, Petya's kiss?

"I'll fix this," Gennady said.

"Fix what? What did you do?"

"Nothing," Gennady lied. "But I'll make sure she comes back."

CHAPTER TWELVE
SOFIA

S OFIA CIRCLED THE tree-lined block in the residential Moscow neighborhood a second time. The faces had all changed in the few minutes since she'd circled the block and come back, but the KGB had networks of spies working together.

Someone could be watching her even now, no matter how much she planned or checked. Her heart beat as if she were running hard, and her body yearned to take flight, but she maintained a sedate pace.

Even if she could run far and fast enough to save herself from danger, the Soviet system held everyone she loved captive.

The only choice was to fight, secret and dirty, for as long as she could.

As she rounded the corner, she spotted her contact standing near a parked car on the quiet, residential street. He dressed in the ubiquitous wool coat and fur hat that Muscovites favored in this cold weather, but his gleaming smile betrayed him as an American.

His big, white teeth glinted in the moonlight, inviting her to smile back.

Ever aware they might have an audience, she made eye contact but showed no other sign of greeting, not even a sly smile or tilt of her head. She kept walking, and Paul fell into step beside her.

They walked side by side on the empty sidewalk for a minute or so without speaking. It was late in the evening, after the book club had ended and the library closed, after she had gone out with the friends she'd met there for tea and pastry, after they'd parted ways and she'd headed in the direction of the subway station.

Theoretically, this was a perfect time to meet. Very few people were out on the street, just the drunks and people walking their dogs. But it wasn't so late that someone would think it odd to see people out like herself, heading home after a late evening.

She kept her eyes moving, surveying their surroundings, but she couldn't help but be aware of the man beside her. Tall and broad, he moved with graceful athleticism and exuded robust good health. She couldn't help but be struck by how different he was from the husk of a man her husband had become.

"It's clear. So far," Paul assured her finally. She repeated his English words in her head, making sure she understood. Sometimes his accent was difficult for her to unravel. Her own teachers had used the British pronunciations, and Paul had the added curse of what he claimed was a "Brooklyn accent."

Sofia wouldn't know. She had never been outside of Russia.

"We're not picking up any activity on their radios," he said. Out of the corner of her eye, she glimpsed the tiny earpiece and the flesh-colored wire that disappeared into his collar. The Americans sure loved their fancy gadgets. Obviously, judging by the bug she found in the *mezuzah*, the Soviets did, too.

She imagined the war of spy versus spy, with each side trying to outdo the other in surveillance and counter-surveillance. Aside from the Tropel, of which she wasn't all that fond, Sofia didn't rely on any hi-tech gadgetry.

"There's a new guard at the laboratory," Sofia said in her best English, skipping the social niceties. At best she could have only five minutes with Paul, the time it took to walk four blocks together and then part ways. They couldn't afford to be seen together for too long, and she had a lot to tell him.

"He's taken an interest in me. He notices if I'm in the bathroom too long," she said.

"I don't like the sound of that."

Neither did she. "I'm hopeful it's merely an attraction and not based on suspicion," she said. "But it's limiting my time to make the photographs. And the Tropel needs a lot of set up. It's—how do you say it—fidgety."

"Finicky," Paul corrected.

"*Tak*. Finicky," she said. The little cameras were attractively discreet, but they were hard to operate.

"I managed to fill up the last camera, but it took longer than I had hoped." She slipped a glove from her pocket. The little fob-shaped Tropel fit neatly inside the thumb.

Paul accepted the glove and stuffed it in his own coat pocket.

"Military intelligence said your last few rolls of film were invaluable. They've sent a wishlist of requests. It's all in my note." He seemed almost abashed when he told her, "There are five cameras in the package this time."

"I don't know what I can do about the requests, but I definitely have enough material for all of those cameras," she said, thinking of the report on the prototype that she was itching to get her hands on.

He surreptitiously handed her a heavy pack wrapped in brown paper and twine. Five cameras. This was a sign of the true value of the information she provided. Each camera alone was worth more than the average Soviet citizen earned in a year.

"I had them disguised as lipstick tubes for you this time," he said. "I thought it would be easier to explain their presence if someone found them."

Someone like her husband, she thought, and only if he didn't inspect them. Although the cameras were petite and easily concealed as everyday objects,—key fobs, lipstick tubes, lighters—anyone discovering the camera lens would have no doubt what they were used for or that they were spy gear.

Two militia men appeared at the end of the next block. An ambush?

Sofia fought the impulse to turn and walk the other way. "Look," she alerted Paul.

"I see them."

She forced long, slow breaths into her lungs as she walked slowly in their direction, expecting at any moment that they would grab her and make her disappear into the night.

CHAPTER THIRTEEN
ARTUR

A RTUR AND EDIK sat alone in a booth in one of the few pizza places in the city, a landmark Edik had been eager to share in his self-imposed role of tour guide. Edik had delivered on his offer to take Artur around the city, but he had yet to introduce Artur to his inner circle.

"Her husband is home," Edik whined.

They were on their second bottle of wine, or rather Edik was. Artur had been careful to nurse his glass while making it look like he kept filling up, all the while topping off Edik's glass again and again.

"Whose husband?" Artur asked.

"Sofia's," Edik hiccuped. Sofia again! Edik was incredibly discreet, or else he had few connections. He hadn't mentioned any names, except Sofia. The woman who doled out all manner of useful advice and could get more than forty rubles per carton of Marlboros, but not quite one hundred.

"Who's Sofia?" Artur asked.

"She's the best person in the world," Edik said, sloshing the wine in his glass.

Ah, finally! It had taken five days and the better part of the second bottle before Edik seemed to feel loose enough to discuss the mysterious Sofia instead of merely citing some nugget of wisdom she'd imparted to him.

"And she's married," Artur clarified.

"She hasn't been married. Well, no. I mean she was always married. To Mendel. But Mendel, he was in prison." Edik rambled, his words running together.

"Mendel Reitman?" Artur asked. He knew Victor was investigating Reitman, but he hadn't connected Victor's high-profile assignment directly with his own before now.

"On the nose," Edik said. He lifted his finger to touch Artur's nose, but missed. If not for Artur's quick reflexes, he might have been poked in the eye.

"So, you're in love with Sofia, but now her husband is back from prison."

"I'm not in love with her," Edik protested feebly. "She's my cousin."

His cousin? Edik obviously was connected directly to Reitman, an important fact that bore directly on the information Artur should be trying to cull from Edik. A fact that Victor surely knew and had deliberately neglected to share.

Edik's family connection to Reitman and his regular contact with foreigners placed him at or near the very center of a plot the Spymaster himself had taken a special interest in foiling.

Holding back critical information about the connection between Edik and the Reitmans, Victor had sent Artur unprepared into the field. Artur could easily guess a myriad of reasons why, and all of them rankled.

"If you're not in love with her, then what difference is it to you if her husband's back?" Did he suspect what Mendel's return represented, the noose tightening around them?

Edik stared morosely at his glass and didn't answer right away, as if thinking over his words carefully.

He seemed far too sober to interrogate. But much more alcohol, and he wouldn't be coherent, Artur thought ruefully.

Finally Edik said, "I'll tell you a bad secret."

Artur leaned in, ready to snap up a juicy tidbit of information, hoping that maybe he had Edik where he wanted him.

"I was hoping he wouldn't come home," Edik said.

"So you could be together?" Artur guessed. Edik's confession provided no new leads.

"She's better off without him," Edik said. "He's not a nice person. Not like she is."

"Why was he in prison?" Artur asked, already knowing the truth.

"For teaching Hebrew," Edik said.

The lie surprised Artur. Teaching Hebrew? No; Mendel had been arrested for drug dealing and sentenced to five years in a Siberian gulag.

"She thinks he's a hero," Edik said.

"She must be happy to have him home after so much time," Artur said.

"She doesn't seem happy," Edik said.

"When did you see her?" Artur asked.

"This morning," Edik said. He seemed to be telling the truth, but the KGB's surveillance hadn't picked up a conversation between Edik and his cousin. In fact, the listening device hadn't picked up much at all, aside from the muffled sounds of Edik and his father moving around their apartment. Edik constantly forgot to bring his hat with him, and the listening device picked up precious little from its perch on a shelf in the front hall closet.

Had Edik met Sofia in the brief few moments when he went out to get the paper and forgot his hat? Edik still seemed far too sober for Artur to interrogate outright.

"Well, you know what they say," Artur said. "Absence makes the heart grow fonder."

"What does that have to do with anything?" Edik asked. "Mendel isn't absent now."

Artur cocked his head and regarded Edik. Was his target putting him on, or was he genuinely confused? "Maybe she forgot what he was really like when he was away, and now that he's back, she's remembering all the problems they used to have," Artur explained. "Living with him again, she's bound to see all of his flaws. All of the things that annoy her. That's what happened with my girlfriend. She loved me when we were long distance."

"And now she doesn't love you," Edik said with a bluntness that might have stung had the girlfriend been real. He stared morosely at his glass of wine and then said, "I thought you said she dumped you for being Jewish."

"She did," Artur said quickly. The Jew handled his liquor entirely too well. His speech might be muddled, but he retained an irritating lucidity. "It was one of the many flaws she found in me when she looked close."

Artur turned the conversation back to Edik and Sofia. "Are you in love with her?"

"I'm not in love with Sofia," Edik said again.

"If you're not in love with her, then what's the problem? Why is it so bad that her husband's back?" Artur asked, willing Edik to start talking about what Mendel's return actually threatened.

Edik changed the subject. "I have to go to the OVIR tomorrow to renew my emigration request."

"You want to leave?" He tried to connect the dots of Edik's drunken logic and failed. He wasn't sure there was a connection at all. Perhaps Edik was adroitly redirecting their conversation, but Artur doubted it. Edik raised his finger again to tap Artur on the nose, but Artur ducked out of Edik's way and poured more wine.

"Do you think they'll grant you the visa?" he asked. Unless Edik had a whopper of a bribe and possibly even then, he knew for certain Edik's request wouldn't be granted.

"No," Edik said. "They've hardly let anyone go the last few years. Even with family in Israel."

"You have family in Israel?"

"Sure; don't you?" When Artur shook his head, Edik said, "Don't worry. I know someone who can arrange it."

Artur wasn't surprised. The Kremlin had long suspected the Jews' plaintive requests for family reunification were based almost entirely on manufactured family trees. Lies, lies, and more lies.

"Who?" Artur asked, fishing for the name of the contact, but Edik switched subjects. Again.

"Anyway," Edik said, "I'd prefer to go to America."

Straight into the arms of the Main Enemy, Artur thought. It figured. What else did he expect? The Jews talked about oppression and human rights, but all of that rhetoric hid the reality. Some of them might have Zionist dreams of the Jewish state, but the majority had capitalist dreams, fueled by American propaganda.

"America?" Artur asked with disdain. "You know America's full of homeless people," he said, noting one of the more visible failings of the capitalist system. There were no homeless people in the Soviet Union. "And race riots."

Edik only shrugged. "It hardly matters," he said dismissively, clearly not willing to confront the issues and have his eyes opened. "My visa request has already been rejected a bunch of times. I'll probably never get to go."

"Did they tell you why?"

"Different reasons. First, because I served in the Army. I had to wait five years so they couldn't say I had access to sensitive military secrets. Then, because I didn't have family in Israel."

"But you took care of that," Artur said. Edik probably had no legitimate blood ties at all to anyone in Israel. Or America.

"Right. But they said the family relation wasn't close enough. Not a parent or sibling." He drained the remainder of his glass of wine. Artur poured what was left in the bottle, but only a few drops were left. They coated the bottom of Edik's wine glass. "Last time, no reason. They threw me out of the office and told me not to come back."

"Then why go back now?" The last visit should have provided enough disincentive to return.

"Sofia says we should go every six months to keep our requests active. What other choice is there?"

"Indeed," Artur said, but he could easily supply other options, beginning with keeping quiet and accepting fate.

The Jews' vocal desire to emigrate was causing considerable political trouble. His country's future rested on shutting down the dissension. The Jews were never going to be allowed to leave.

"Will you come with me?" Edik asked.

"To OVIR?"

"I get nervous when I have to deal with those offices. I'm not good with people. Not like you," Edik said.

"I'm good with people?" Artur asked.

"Yes," Edik said. "So will you come with me?"

"I'd be happy to." Artur readily accepted the excuse to continue their acquaintance.

"You're a true friend," Edik said. He put down his empty glass and wiped his mouth with a napkin. "If they approve me, then my father will need to rent out my room to someone. Maybe you?"

Artur nearly choked on his surprise at the invitation. "Maybe," he said, not wanting to sound too eager, as a plan unfolded neatly in his mind for going deep undercover and infiltrating the Jewish conspiracy.

CHAPTER FOURTEEN
SOFIA

EVEN IF THE militia hadn't come for Sofia and Paul, the two men in uniform would surely take an interest if they heard them speaking English or caught a fragment of Paul's lousy and heavily accented Russian.

Sofia began to rant at Paul in Russian. "There's so much to do. You have to do your part," she said, and listed a range of household tasks from watering the plants to taking out the garbage.

"Do you have a light?" one of the militia men interrupted, directing his question to Paul.

"No. Sorry," she said, preempting Paul's answer. She caught him by the sleeve and pulled him forward with her, her voice rising in pretended anger. "And last week I asked you to fix the oven. But did you do it? No, of course not. You had to go out with your friends."

Whether or not Paul caught the full gist of her tirade, he glanced sheepishly at the militia men, who watched them pass with sympathetic nods, likely thinking him a hen-pecked husband.

"And don't think I didn't hear about how you looked down Olga's shirt. I can't believe you!" She batted at him.

They rounded the corner, out of range of the policemen. Paul was unusually quiet, even after the danger had passed.

Finally, he said, "There have been too many close calls lately. I can't even tell you the lengths I had to go to in order to get out of the Embassy undetected." The Embassy was guarded by Russian militia men and closely monitored by the KGB. "The team had to smuggle me out in the back of a van."

He cleared his throat. "You're a mother, Sofia. I appreciate what you're doing. But what if you're caught?"

"We both know what will happen if I'm caught," she said soberly. "And we both know your government would agree it's worth the risk."

"The government would also agree you've done enough if you feel ready to stop," he said. "Now that your husband's home—"

She cut him off. "How do you know he's home?"

"I can't tell you how we know it, only that we do." He grinned, his wide American grin, and she supposed he was smug that the CIA had filched intelligence from the KGB.

She was about to ask whether they had heard anything else about Mendel when he said, "You should give some thought to exfiltration."

"That would mean telling Mendel about all of this," she said.

She didn't know what terrible things had been done to Mendel in the gulag or what deal he might have made out of desperation. The KGB had had five years to warp him and wear him down.

Even if he had heroically resisted them, one thing was achingly clear. The man who had returned to her wasn't the same one who'd left.

"Yes, you'd have to tell him," Paul confirmed, and she gathered from his answer that the CIA hadn't picked up any intelligence that Mendel might be an informant for the KGB.

"I'm not ready to do that yet," she admitted, but she didn't tell him more, didn't share her doubts.

She wasn't sure she could trust Mendel, not the way she once had. Not the way she trusted Paul.

Not yet, anyway.

She shifted topics. "I'll contact you when I'm ready with a drop."

"Godspeed," he said. They had worked together long enough that he likely realized further argument would be a waste of his breath.

"Please be careful," he said.

"Always."

They parted ways, and she didn't dare look back at him.

When she arrived home, her apartment was dark. She didn't turn on the lights. She hung her coat in the closet by the door.

With Paul's package in hand, she then crept quietly toward the main room, which served as a living room by day and as Kolya's bedroom by night.

She listened for Kolya's deep, rhythmic breaths behind the bookcases in his sleeping nook. He didn't stir, even though a floorboard squeaked as she tiptoed toward the bedroom.

She couldn't see any light under her bedroom door. She pressed her ear to the door, but she didn't hear Mendel moving around.

She padded softly to the kitchen. She scrambled up onto one of the chairs and pried open the hatch leading to their crawl space. She lay the package by the opening and then levered herself up inside.

The space was small and dark, but dry. Crammed with boxes from Mendel's sister's family, there was just enough room for her to sit cross-legged on the wooden planks. She pulled the string to turn on the lightbulb.

She untied the twine and opened the paper around the package Paul had given her. As he'd said, there were five tiny cameras, all of them disguised as lipstick tubes. The tubes were different colors: cherry red, mint green, shiny metallic blue, gold, and silver. He'd also included a new book to use for decryption, a thick roll of rubles, and a lengthy note.

She unfolded the pages of the note and began decoding the tightly scrawled numbers into English text. She matched the numbers to the book pages, taking the third letter on each page. As she worked, she listened for any sounds of stirring in her apartment.

She couldn't afford for Kolya or Mendel to find her up here with so much incriminating evidence in her lap, but she didn't have a better alternative.

This little hideaway was the best place available to decipher the notes without detection. Sofia's father was convinced that the KGB had broken into their homes and set up cameras to spy on them.

Any camera would have a hard time seeing what she was doing in the thick shadows. But also, Max's things were here, and she could almost feel her brother-in-law's presence.

She couldn't confide in anyone about her work for the CIA. But her connection to Max had made her espionage possible, and she liked to imagine him supporting her in her efforts and approving of her choices.

Choices that might free him, his wife, and their daughter.

Once she finished the work of matching numbers to letters, she began to translate in her head. Paul's note included the usual flowery language, the gratitude for her information, the praise of her efforts and savvy. She skimmed the flattery and the information about the bank account they claimed to have set up for her and went straight to the requests.

She found them on the bottom of the second page, a list of two pages of typed questions about radar and nuclear capabilities.

She discerned that the file on the new missile test might not answer their questions directly but would go a long way toward addressing their areas of greatest interests.

She would make that document her priority.

She jumped when she caught the sound of a creaking floorboard. Quickly, she wrapped the paper around the cameras and other contents and stuffed them into a corner behind the storage boxes. Then she shimmied out of the crawl space.

She had just managed to shut the door when Mendel entered the kitchen. He flipped on the light and rubbed wearily at his eyes. He wore a pair of pajamas she had given him years ago as a birthday present. They'd been the perfect size back then, but now they draped loosely around his body.

"What are you doing in here in the dark?"

"I didn't want to disturb you or Kolya with the light. I thought

I'd have some tea before bed," she lied.

"You didn't turn the stove on for the kettle," he observed.

"Not yet," she said. "I was just taking a moment to enjoy the quiet."

He didn't respond. She sensed he didn't quite believe her.

CHAPTER FIFTEEN
ARTUR

AFTER PARTING WAYS with Edik for the night, Artur headed to KGB headquarters. The large yellow and gray brick building was impressive and imposing, perhaps more so in the middle of the night, presiding over the empty square.

Artur had not yet become immune to the effect of the tall doors and endless corridors, designed to humble the building's occupants. Entering the building, he still had the awed sense of his own lowly significance, his small role in something so much greater.

But if Victor's behavior was any indication, he expected that many of his fellow agents had become immune to the building's powers, entering with their great arrogance unchecked.

He rode the usually crowded elevator alone and exited on his floor. The lights were off. He was the only one here tonight. No need for stealth as he headed for the cubicles where his desk adjoined Victor's.

He sat down at Victor's desk, not his own. He flicked on the small lamp and rifled through the files and papers heaped on top. No surprise, the fattest file belonged to Mendel Reitman.

It was time to play catch-up.

He settled into Victor's chair and began reading the files on Mendel and everyone associated with him, paying special attention to his wife, Edik's beloved Sofia.

As he studied Sofia Reitman's photograph, Artur couldn't understand Edik's unrelenting fascination with his cousin. Her hair was inky, nearly black, and bushy with curls. Thick eyebrows slashed over her slightly slanted almond-shaped eyes. She was homely, unless you preferred dark, Mediterranean-looking women.

Artur most certainly did not. His own wife was a pure Russian, a paragon of beauty, long-limbed and fine-boned, with milky white skin and platinum hair.

Sofia's file was thin on details. She had once been a doctoral student and then a lecturer at Moscow State University, until she had been kicked out after applying to emigrate. Like Edik, she had applied multiple times for an exit visa. She had been repeatedly denied on the grounds that her work in Max Abromovich's laboratory had provided her with access to sensitive information.

Max Abromovich. Artur recognized that name, too. Abromovich was an infamous dissident. The physicist's name got trotted out every time foreign diplomats wanted to scold the Soviet regime about supposed human rights violations.

Max had been Sofia's thesis advisor. Just prior to his arrest, she had married his brother-in-law, Mendel Reitman, whose name was also frequently thrown in their faces like an insult. And who was the target of Victor's current assignment.

If Sofia wasn't their traitor, then she was highly likely to know who was, more likely than the hapless Edik.

Indeed, Sofia had a highly intriguing set of family ties. Edik was the least of them, it seemed. Her father and uncle, Edik's father, had both been assigned KGB tails, with surveillance on them going back years, information that had been omitted from the case file Victor had given Artur on Edik.

Artur spent several hours alone in Victor's cubicle, piecing together the information that had been denied him. The more he read, the more he suspected Victor had been deliberately hoarding information.

He closed the last of the files, put everything back into the haphazardly organized disarray in which he'd found it, and went home.

He found his wife and son asleep, cuddled together in the armchair in the living room. In sleep, they both looked so sweetly innocent— white-blond angels, a dangerous illusion.

At four, Aleksei was prone to kicking, screaming tantrums that could last hours. Maya, Artur had learned, bottled the same brand of rage when thwarted, but she had perfected the art of distilling hers, and serving her potent poison chilled.

He leaned down to plant a kiss on her cheek, and her blue eyes fluttered open. "You're home," she murmured with a flush of sleepy pleasure. "Tell me everything."

He couldn't ever tell her everything. She didn't have security clearance, even if her father was a Spymaster, seated high in the KGB organization. And even if she had, there were some concerns better kept to himself.

"Let's put Aleksei to bed first," he stalled. He needed the scant extra minutes to sort his thoughts and figure out what he could and couldn't share.

He lifted their little boy out of her lap and carried him to his bedroom. He hadn't seen Aleksei all day, but he was glad the child didn't awaken. Despite his undisputed handsomeness, the high cheekbones from his father and the coloring and refined features from his mother, the boy was prickly and difficult.

Artur found fatherhood far easier when he didn't actually have to interact with his son, a fact he would never share with the boy's mother, who thought the sun rose and set only for him.

He tucked the covers around Aleksei's small frame, gently tousled his spiky hair, and utilized his considerable training to slip swiftly and soundlessly from the room before Aleksei could rouse.

Maya waited for him in the study with a glass of cognac. "You're so late," she scolded. Irritation seemed to have replaced her earlier pleasure at his arrival now that she'd consulted the clock. "It's almost morning."

Despite her ambitions for him, she jealously guarded their time together. She seemed to need constant proof that she was first in his esteem and affection, even above her father, his boss.

She would have wanted him to come home first with his suspicions about Victor and the case, would have preferred for him to lay them at her feet before heading to the office to gather the facts.

"I was out late with the target."

Maya perched on the corner of his carved mahogany desk, crossed her long legs, and asked, "Is she beautiful?"

"No. No one would say *he* is beautiful," Artur said, killing her jealousy at the root. "But the man does drink like a fish."

He swirled the cognac in his snifter, Waterford crystal. The brandy set was a lavish gift from his father-in-law in recognition of his latest promotion. Artur regarded his wife over the rim. The window behind her looked out on a nighttime view of Moscow, dark and quiet. With her moonlight-pale hair and her luminous skin, she looked almost ethereal, a fairy queen reigning over the slumbering city.

His work had long been a dangerous point of contention in their marriage, even if it was the precise reason she'd been attracted to him in the first place. She didn't like his long hours or his keeping secrets from her or his membership in a club from which she would forever be excluded.

A club to which, Artur knew, she dreamed of belonging. But the KGB wasn't the place for a woman like Maya. Her skills and intellect could be put to far better use.

"It took a long time to get him drunk enough that he would tell me what I wanted to know," Artur said.

"Maybe a truth serum next time to speed things along?" she suggested. She liked to try to participate in his cases to the extent he could let her, which was usually not at all.

"I know you have great faith in chemistry," he said. She worked as a chemist. "But truth serums work better in theory than practice. Interviews with truth serums take forever. The subject spills his guts about anything and everything in his mind, and the whole thing sounds like crazy ramblings. It's hard even to know what's real and what's just stuck there in his head."

"Alcohol is also a chemical," she said a little sharply, and Artur held back a sigh.

It might always be a sore point in their relationship that he could tread where she could not. At least he knew how to placate her, a skill he hadn't yet mastered with their child.

"I know it's late," Artur said with honest regret. He would have liked nothing better than to crawl into bed with her and try again for the second child she wanted so very badly. "I'm sorry for waking you, but I wanted to get your advice before I have to head back out again."

"My advice?" she preened. She took the cognac snifter from his hand and sipped from the glass she'd poured for him. "Tell me everything," she said huskily, putting him in mind of Lilya.

Before Aleksei's birth, she had campaigned hard with her father to be an agent. Artur expected she would have made an even more alluring dangle than Lilya, but Semyon thought such a role unseemly for his only child, besides which Maya's constitution was far too delicate for such sordid assignments.

"The interview went very well tonight," he said, without giving her any particulars.

"How well?" she asked. She caressed the polished wood of his desk with her fingertip.

"Well enough that I can establish myself as an effective spy handler," Artur said.

"Effective enough for a station position?" she asked with a wide dreamy smile. She hoped to accompany Artur on an international assignment. Posing as a diplomat's wife, a real-life role that would suit her well, given her intelligence and cool demeanor, was the closest she could hope to come to any real espionage.

He wanted to give that to her. He wanted to give her everything.

"Possibly," Artur said. "But there's a wrinkle."

The instant crinkle of worry in her smooth brow made him flinch inwardly. She could have had any man in the KGB, and she had hitched her lot to him, choosing him above all of the others, handing him the proverbial brass ring.

He never wanted her to think she'd chosen wrong or to admit to himself that perhaps he had.

She took a long sip of cognac and said, "Tell me."

"During the interview, I realized that my informant was linked to a high profile investigation and that, for whatever reason, Victor had withheld that information from me."

Her expression remained neutral as he spoke, but her foot kicked back and forth, like a pendulum marking time.

"And that's why you want my advice?" Maya asked.

"Yes. What's he up to?" Artur had his own ideas, but he wanted her perspective.

Daughter to a career politician, Maya had often accompanied Semyon to events and had cultivated an uncanny knack for reading people and situations, establishing herself as an asset to her father and now her husband. She paid special attention to the members of the First Directorate, Artur's department, and of the Second Directorate, Semyon's. It was common for agents to move between the two, and she and Artur hoped he would establish his credentials in the First Directorate and then move onto foreign intelligence assignments abroad, working as an intelligence officer for the Second Directorate under Semyon.

"Victor, Victor, Victor." She tapped her finger thoughtfully against her rosy lips. "Victor Zhirov, right? No one likes him," she said finally, "but no one talks against him, either. He's been steadily promoted, but very slowly. He's—what?—a good ten years older than you?"

"Yes," Artur confirmed. He'd been married to Maya for five years, only slightly less time than he'd been with the KBG. Their marriage had catapulted him through the ranks. He'd been handed coveted assignments and leapfrogged the line for promotions and recognition. But his charmed life, the speed with which he met his ambitions, came with an unseen burden.

He constantly had to prove to everyone—especially to Maya and her father—that he was worthy of the favor they bestowed on him.

Victor had made it clear he doubted Artur's true value as an agent.

"I'm sure Victor resented it when he got stuck with me as a partner." Artur had deferred to the more seasoned agent, trying to smooth Victor's ruffled feathers at being assigned such a novice as partner. He had thought to use his own charisma to circumvent the KGB's internal politics and the agents' professional jealousies. A mistake.

"Only because he doesn't recognize your talent yet," Maya said loyally. She had grand ambitions for him, for them. Of course, he wanted the same things she did. But he suspected that if he couldn't climb to the heights they both imagined in whatever time frame she'd secretly allotted, he would lose her love.

"Victor played me," Artur confessed, despite his reluctance to admit any shortcomings to her. "He wanted me to believe this spy handling assignment was a chance to prove my skill to him."

"He fooled both of us," she said. "You talked about spy handling, and I immediately started imagining the possibilities. A posting at station Budapest. Or even Paris."

"Or New York," Artur said ruefully. "I let him distract me with visions of opportunity, when he was only sending me after a marginal suspect. The guy's little better than a dead end as an informant."

"He handed you the barest crumb," she agreed. "Something that wouldn't hurt his case if you failed but also wouldn't steal his thunder if you succeeded."

"Maybe he wanted to keep me out of his way, but I suspect he also wanted me to fail. He sent me in blind."

He leaned on the desk beside Maya, his hip touching her thigh. She didn't censure him and pull away.

"He sabotaged me. At best, I'd report to Kasparov looking overly pleased with myself for an insignificant contribution to the case." Kasparov, his supervisor, would not have been at all impressed.

"And at worst?"

"Grossly incompetent. Having no clue what the case was about and gleaning nothing useful." He took the glass from her and took his own sip. The hot burn of the alcohol didn't ease the pain of his own gullibility.

She touched her palm to his cheek, and he turned his face into her caress, grateful, so grateful, that she was sympathetic.

She didn't begrudge him for his foolishness and inexperience. Not this time, anyway.

"It was only luck that I stumbled onto the right trail," he admitted.

"It was more than luck, darling," she said, but he knew better.

For now, he was simply content that Victor hadn't succeeded. He had a lot more to lose than his standing in the KGB.

He nuzzled Maya's long, elegant neck and breathed in her subtle French perfume, a signature combination of lavender and lilacs.

She pushed at his shoulder. "Later," she said. "Let's figure this out first. What options are you considering?"

Artur stood, clearing his head. He moved to the window and stared out at the darkened cityscape, a habit that helped him think. The lights were off in the apartments he could see from his window, a large swath of Moscow. He imagined the residents sleeping peacefully in their beds, untroubled by the kinds of worries that plagued him.

"I can't take the problem to your father," Artur said finally. "It would seem disloyal. No one likes a tattletale. But sabotage is also out of the question. This case is too important."

"That didn't stop Victor."

"No, it didn't," Artur agreed, and that disturbed him as much, if not more, than the threat to his own reputation.

"Which means you have the key to him," she said.

"He cares more about his own selfish ambitions than about our country?"

"Typical, I'd say. Not everyone is as patriotic as you are." She came up next to him and took his hand, interlacing their fingers. "Which makes this easy to work to our advantage."

"How?"

"I'm sure Papa wants you on this case, or else why saddle you with Victor, who's going nowhere fast? We all know that if anyone can solve it, you can," she said. "So all you have to do is make it clear to Victor that you don't need him and that he can either get behind you or get gone."

"All I need to do," he echoed, not hiding his bitterness. "And for my next trick, I'll turn straw into gold."

Maya laughed and kissed him on the cheek. "Of course you will, my love. I bet you already know exactly what you have to do," she said.

CHAPTER SIXTEEN
GENNADY

INSTEAD OF HEADING home after his last class at the university, Gennady got off at the stop near Petya's school. He waited there for school to let out, expecting Vera to appear any moment.

Her classmates appeared, but she didn't. The bus came and went, and still he waited.

Finally, he spotted her. His breath caught, and the memories that had haunted him all day—of that sweet kiss, the flash of desire in her dark eyes, and of her running away—hit him with their full force.

He replayed the scene over and over, tortured himself with it.

Do you like me? Her face had been so open, all of her emotions there for him to read.

Or so he had imagined.

He had been satisfyingly confident until that last moment. Why had she run?

"Stop pulling me," her nephew, Kolya, complained as she dragged him toward the bus stop. "I don't want to go home."

"Your Papa's waiting for you," she scolded.

"He's not my Papa. He's mean. And I hate him."

"You just need a little time to get used to each other," she said, bending her head toward him. Her voice was soft and soothing.

"I want to go home with you. Please let me come home with you," the boy begged.

His words had an uncomfortable resonance. *Please, Mama. Please don't leave. Take me with you.* Gennady rubbed at his own chest.

Vera didn't notice Gennady. Or at least she pretended she didn't.

"You don't have a choice today. I have to be somewhere," she said.

"I hope that somewhere's with me." Gennady's voice came out hoarse, rather than confident. He cleared his throat and cursed the small show of weakness.

She glanced up at him, startled. Her large, luminous eyes widened. Her cheeks flushed a charming rose. She looked away quickly, and he wanted to crow in triumph.

Maybe she was embarrassed. Or nervous. Or shy. But she was definitely not indifferent to him, not unaffected by their kiss the other night.

He hadn't imagined her responses to him. Some of it, at least, had been real.

So what had gone wrong? Was she in love with Petya?

Kolya planted his hands on his hips and squared his shoulders. "Who are you?"

"I'm Vera's friend," Gennady said. Vera made an inelegant snort.

"You mean her boyfriend," Kolya scoffed, as though Gennady had tried to conceal a bigger truth.

"He's not my boyfriend," Vera said, dismissing Gennady all too quickly.

Because she preferred Petya?

"But I'd like to be," Gennady admitted. A dark possessiveness swelled in him. He wanted to kiss her again, deeper this time, so thoroughly that she would lose all thought of his little brother, so well that she wouldn't ever think about running away from him.

"Your auntie's a very pretty girl," he told Kolya.

Vera's lips pressed together in a tight, thin line, as though he'd deliberately insulted her instead of paying her a compliment.

"Very pretty," Kolya agreed. "And nice." Kolya narrowed his eyes at him and with fierce protectiveness asked, "Are you nice?"

"If I'm not, I bet you'll have something to say about it." Kolya gave a fierce nod of his head, and Gennady couldn't hold back his chuckle. "I like you, kid."

"I don't know if I like you yet," Kolya said.

"Fair enough," Gennady said.

For her part, Vera remained sulkily silent. Gennady suspected he'd somehow offended her, but he couldn't figure out what had set her off.

He wanted to make amends, if only he knew how.

The bus pulled up to the stop. Vera slid into a seat beside Kolya. Gennady stood next to them, rather than take one of the empty seats, but she refused to look in his direction, as if she couldn't stand the sight of him.

His stop came first. He intended to ride with her to hers and then escort her back to his apartment, but she pressed the bell for the bus to stop.

"This is your stop," she said with great dignity.

He had grown up with the general. He knew an order when he heard one, no matter how softly spoken.

He hesitated to leave her. He had promised Petya he'd make sure she returned, and he had somehow made another critical misstep.

"What about Petya?" he asked.

She leaned in close to him, speaking so only he would hear, but her tone cut like acid. "I'll help him. But you stay away. I'm not a toy for you to play with."

A toy? Where did she get such an idea? The bus lurched to a stop, and she nudged him ungently toward the door.

He took her cue and headed home alone. He puzzled over her words, over the seeming depth of her anger. He didn't understand her rejection.

At home, Petya lay asleep on the sofa, a book folded over his chest. His color had worsened since yesterday. Despite the doctor's pronouncement that he was on his way to recovery, his pallor had taken on a gray tinge.

"He looks worse than the last time I was here," a familiar voice said from behind him.

Gennady was usually aware of his surroundings, but he hadn't noticed the other person in the room.

Maybe he had been too tangled up in his thoughts of Vera. Or, more likely, his uncle had simply perfected the art of stealth, moving like a ghost or hiding in stillness.

Gennady would expect no less from a KGB Spymaster.

He turned slowly and pretended he had known his uncle had been sitting there all along.

His uncle lounged in the armchair behind him, an unlit cigar in his hand, his face shrouded in shadow.

"You want a light for that?" Gennady asked, pointing to the cigar, and his uncle huffed softly, a small chuckle of amusement and what seemed to Gennady like a hint of pride in him.

He felt himself puff up under the man's warm appraisal. He wasn't close to his uncle. He couldn't even say he liked the man. There was something coldly calculating about Semyon that reminded Gennady of his mother, of the way she had weighed, measured, and then discarded people who didn't suit her ambitions.

But Gennady did admire him.

He suspected Semyon's civilian post outranked even his father's prestigious military title, not that they ever discussed such things.

"I was afraid it would give Petya a coughing fit," Semyon said. "I decided to wait and let him rest."

"I'm awake," Petya said weakly.

"How are you feeling?" Gennady asked.

"Better," Petya said. Petya closed his book, sat up, and turned so that his feet touched the floor. "Is Vera coming?"

"Vera Soifer?" Semyon asked. "So you finally followed my advice and asked for her help?"

"Yes," Petya said impatiently. "Genna, don't keep me in suspense.

Is she coming back to help me?"

"Soon," Gennady told him. The plaintiveness in his brother's voice made him feel guilty. He shouldn't have flirted with Vera the way he had, shouldn't have told her that he wanted to be her boyfriend. Even if it was the truth.

"You really like her. Don't you?" he asked Petya.

"Nobody likes her," Petya said, catching Gennady by surprise.

The knot in Gennady's chest loosened. He might have bungled things with Vera, but at least he hadn't encroached on a budding romance.

"I told you she was my last resort. My friends will tease me no end when they find out I begged her to help me study."

"Why? What's wrong with her?" Gennady hadn't seen any signs of defect or bad character.

"It's not her. It's her family." Petya ticked off the demerits on his fingers. "Jews. Criminals. Traitors."

Gennady knew he should have been impressed by the recital, but he couldn't make himself care. Even with this information—even knowing his father might not approve, even knowing that a relationship with Vera might prove a liability to the military career he planned to have— he wanted to kiss her again, to hear her whisper that she liked him.

He wondered whether his fascination with her was a mere act of teenage rebellion—one Vera had easily observed. *I'm not a toy for you to play with.*

Petya looked to their uncle for support, but Semyon sat back in their father's favorite armchair, an inscrutable expression on his face.

Gennady could feel the weight of his uncle's judgment boring down on them both. He straightened his own spine. He wasn't a child, ruled by petty impulses and immaturity. He was a man.

"I would hate to be judged by our family," Gennady said sternly.

"Our father's a general," Petya objected, drawing himself up.

Only a few years divided them, but Petya seemed impossibly childish in that moment. A man's worth was measured in his actions, not his accolades or accidents of his birth.

"And Semyon could very well be the next Chief of the KGB or

even the General Secretary," Petya added with a nod to their uncle.

"Yes, and our mother?" Gennady reminded him. "Would you want to be judged for her actions?"

Momentarily shamed, Petya hung his head and sighed.

Gennady spared a glance for his uncle. Semyon's only outward reaction was the agitated drumming of his fingers against the arm of his chair, as if he were growing impatient.

"Vera's never done anything to anyone, not that I've seen. But we treat her like an untouchable." Petya scratched at his limp hair. "She's never invited around, unless as a joke. Frankly, I was surprised she actually showed up to help me."

"Maybe that shows you her measure." Brave and caring, willing to take a risk to help a person in need, the direct opposite of his worthless mother, who'd turned her back on her own sons.

"Pathetic and lonely?" Petya offered, slipping from shame back to antipathy.

Gennady didn't often see this side of his brother, and he couldn't say he liked it. He could too easily imagine the way Petya and his classmates must have tormented and picked on Vera. *I'm not a toy for you to play with.*

Gennady scowled at him.

"Don't give me that look," Petya snapped. "You have no right to lecture me. Just because you're two years older doesn't mean you get to stand in for Papa."

"Does your father still have that excellent French brandy?" Semyon asked. He rose from the armchair and headed to their father's study. Gennady took his departure as silent approval. He hadn't intervened.

"I didn't lecture you," Gennady told Petya. "But it's telling that you think I did."

With that parting shot, he followed his uncle to the general's study. Semyon helped himself to a glass of brandy and poured one for Gennady too.

Rather than sit behind the desk in the general's chair, Semyon came around to sit in one of the club chairs and invited Gennady to take the other, treating him as an equal.

"From what I hear, you're doing very well in your classes," Semyon said.

"You're keeping tabs on me."

Uncle Semyon undoubtedly had very detailed information. Like Gennady's father, his uncle had access to a vast network of informants and contacts. Gennady just hadn't expected Semyon to deploy them over something as trivial as his performance in his courses.

"Genna," Semyon said, "you're like a son to me. Of course I'm keeping tabs on you." He smiled self-deprecatingly and admitted, "I'm hoping I can steal you away from the military and sign you for the KGB. Hand down my legacy."

His father wouldn't have liked to hear that. There was a longstanding rivalry between the military and civilian intelligence agencies.

"You have your son-in-law," Gennady said.

"Artur, yes," Semyon agreed. "But *you* I've been helping to groom since before your birth. And you're blood."

His uncle's ambitions for him made him a little uncomfortable. He craved the approval more than he knew he should, especially in his father's absence.

Semyon cleared his throat, perhaps also uncomfortable with the show of emotion. Gennady changed the subject.

"You pushed Petya to have Vera tutor him?"

"I saw he was having trouble. I didn't want the burden to fall to you. So I made a suggestion," Semyon said.

"His last resort."

"His best chance, actually," Semyon said. "Like he said, she's one of the best students in his class." He lit up his cigar and lounged back in the chair, deceptively relaxed. "But it sounds like Petya's not the only one enjoying the benefits of her attention. What's going on between you two?"

"Nothing," Gennady said.

"Genna," Semyon chided. "You kissed her, and then you fought with your own brother about her. That's not nothing."

Semyon knew about the kiss. Gennady didn't need to ask how. Too well, he remembered the KGB agents, his uncle's agents, stationed outside her apartment building.

When he was kissing Vera, Gennady had momentarily forgotten that anyone else in the world existed, until the agents' laughter had broken the spell.

He should have wondered why they were there, who they were watching. He hadn't connected the agents with her or her family, but if what Petya said were true, it made sense the Soifers were under heavy surveillance. "Is Vera in trouble?"

"Vera? No."

"Then why the interest?"

"Because of your interest," Semyon said simply and blew out a plume of bitterly fragrant smoke. "What interests you interests me."

"Are you concerned I might like her?—Because of her family?" He voiced some of his own earlier doubts.

"She's her own person and should be judged on her own merits, just like you said," Semyon said, easing his mind. "If you like her, then I trust your judgment. I wouldn't be lamenting your future in the military so much if I didn't."

"It doesn't matter anyway. She ran away," Gennady admitted, knowing that his uncle probably already knew that, too.

"Of course she did," Semyon said with a chuckle.

"What do you mean?" Gennady asked, suddenly feeling terribly insecure. He still had no idea why Vera had rejected him, but his uncle found the rejection humorously predictable.

"Think about it," Semyon said. "You heard what Petya said about how she's treated by her peers. And it's probably worse than he let on. The girl's like a beaten dog."

"You think she'll run from any hand that reaches in her direction." The insight relieved some of Gennady's self-doubt. Maybe he hadn't done anything wrong. Maybe she hadn't rejected him specifically.

Vera would run if anyone tried to get too close too fast.

Semyon nodded, eyes twinkling, as if he could see the thoughts coalescing in Gennady's mind. "Human nature is a powerful thing," he said. "Once you understand the patterns, people are entirely predictable."

Semyon leaned forward as if about to impart a secret. "If you can win the girl's trust, she'll be entirely devoted to you."

Human nature. Vera's rejection wasn't about him. She wouldn't trust anyone's compliments or kisses, wouldn't let anyone too close, not until he proved himself to her.

But if Gennady could gain Vera's trust, he thought, he would hold her heart forever.

The challenge and the precious reward both called to him.

"Am I so predictable?" Gennady asked. "The boy abandoned by his faithless mother grows to be a man who wants a woman who'll be loyal and constant in her affections?"

"Not so predictable. That description could be applied to Petya as easily as you, and he's not interested." Semyon tapped the end of the cigar into the ashtray on the general's desk. "No, knowing you and knowing you want this girl, what's predictable is that you'll win her."

Semyon lifted his glass as if in toast and took a generous gulp of brandy.

CHAPTER SEVENTEEN
ARTUR

ARTUR WAITED IMPATIENTLY in the Office of Visa and Registration. What was taking so long? The boys in the back office had been told to grant the Jew bastard his exit visa but not why, and he hoped they weren't having too much fun with him.

Or rather, he hoped they were having just enough fun with him to make Artur's job easier.

Finally, Edik emerged from the back office. Edik's ghost-white skin was pastier than usual, and his thick hair stuck up in spikes from where he had undoubtedly raked it with his hands.

Artur stood as soon as he saw his target. "So what did they say?"

Edik shook his head. He held a piece of paper in his shaking hands.

"Don't tell me they called you down here to deny you again," Artur said.

The bureaucrats in the back office better not have screwed this up. Their job was the simplest one in the whole scheme. They merely had to give the man his paperwork.

"They… They… They…" Edik stuttered, and Artur's self-righteous fury grew.

His fellow agents at KGB headquarters already questioned whether he should have been given this assignment. Artur would make sure heads rolled if someone else's incompetence sabotaged his opportunity to prove Semyon's faith in him wasn't misplaced.

"Edik, tell me what happened," Artur insisted. After a few tense moments of stretched patience, Edik still hadn't managed to put two coherent words together.

Artur snatched the letter and read it for himself. Edik's visa had been approved. Edik was scheduled to leave the country in two weeks, exactly as planned.

Artur clamped his hand on Edik's shoulder. "I don't understand. This is great news. Why are you so shaken up?"

"Sofia," Edik mumbled feebly.

Artur resisted the urge to roll his eyes. After nearly a week of boozing the man up and pretending to offer a sympathetic ear to his self-made misery, Artur hadn't developed even an ounce of sympathy for Edik.

He couldn't comprehend the man's ridiculous obsession with his cousin. His *married* cousin.

"What will she do without me?"

"Didn't you say her husband came home?" Artur reminded him. He had mentioned the fact at least twenty times today.

"Yes," Edik grumbled.

"I'm sure he'll take good care of her," Artur said.

"That's because you don't know him," Edik said glumly. "Sofia might need me now more than ever."

Artur couldn't imagine anyone needing Edik. At thirty, the man was an easily distracted, overgrown child. No wife. No child. No career. Not like Artur. Though a couple of years younger than Edik, he had already started his family and was on the fast track in his career.

The hapless Edik still lived with his father and would leave his apartment without a coat and hat if his father didn't remind him to bundle up for the chilly Moscow weather.

Artur expected the truth of the matter was that Edik wasn't sure how he would function without Sofia.

He hooked his arm around Edik's neck. "This is a miracle. It's wonderful news," he said. "In two weeks, you'll be in a new country with a whole new life."

"But why now all of a sudden?" Edik asked. "After all of these years of denials?"

"What does it matter?" Artur said. "You've got your freedom."

Edik's slow-churning thoughts gathered momentum, though. "First Mendel gets released, and now this right after. Too many coincidences. There's a conspiracy," he said.

"What conspiracy?" Artur tried for a hearty laugh but only managed a muddled sound, tinny and weak. Edik seemed too absorbed in his own viciously cycling thoughts to notice. "That's ridiculous," Artur said. "You sound paranoid."

"Paranoia doesn't mean they're not out to get you," Edik said.

Sometimes he made an infuriating amount of sense, leaving Artur to worry how much Edik truly knew or suspected and how much his conjecture might rile up his compatriots.

"A change of luck doesn't mean a conspiracy," Artur countered.

He had two weeks to get his hooks into the people in Edik's inner circle before the Jew departed. He couldn't risk that Edik might reject the precious visa that had been granted him or worse, that he might render worthless Artur's careful stratagems with his suspicions of conspiracy.

"You're just scared because things are finally, finally going your way, my friend," he said. "I for one am happy for you. Let's go celebrate." Any question Edik might harbor over this sudden change of fortune, Artur would drown in mighty quantities of vodka.

He led Edik out of the OVIR waiting area and into the chilly Moscow night. He pulled on his fur hat and gloves and waited for the shell-shocked Edik to follow his example.

Edik actually had his hat with him tonight, and Artur wondered whether the listening device was still lodged in the cuff where he'd hidden it last week.

"We should splurge tonight," Artur said. He grabbed Edik's upper arm and dragged him to a restaurant, a place that represented a true indulgence for two allegedly out-of-work Jews.

They ate thick borscht and split a plate of *pilmeni,* but Edik remained listless and depressed as he downed the shots Artur insisted the waiter keep pouring.

Artur's best attempts to coax Edik out of his taciturn shell yielded almost no result. Shaking his head in misery, Edik only raised his glass, "To my dear, dear friend."

Artur supposed the toast in itself resembled progress, a quick promotion given that they'd only met last week, but he worried that Edik's stubborn devotion to his own misery could botch his careful plans.

The bill came and should have represented a staggering amount for the unemployed Edik, but he didn't flinch, and he refused to accept any of Artur's money.

Edik pushed away from the table. "I've made up my mind," he said. "I need to go talk to Sofia."

"But, Edik, you're drunk."

"No drunker than you." A little unsteady, Edik nonetheless managed to move with determined strides, and Artur hurried to keep up with him. "I'm going to her apartment. Don't try to talk me out of it," Edik warned.

Artur wouldn't dream of trying to talk Edik out of visiting his cousin. Sofia Reitman was near the top of his list of people central to this investigation. The fool would make the introductions, leading the wolf straight into a pen of unsuspecting sheep.

This was almost too easy.

CHAPTER EIGHTEEN
ARTUR

TENSE WITH ANTICIPATION, Artur climbed into the backseat of the cab Edik had drunkenly hailed. So long as Edik fell in line with his plans, he would now begin to embed himself more deeply in his undercover alias as the newly arrived Yosef Koslovsky.

Semyon would be pleased. Very pleased.

"What are you going to tell Sofia?" he asked. The introduction and even the visa plot could go all wrong if Edik started spouting about government conspiracies.

Perhaps, even if Edik expounded on his theories, Sofia would dismiss them as the ravings of a drunk man. Or maybe not. Aside from the loud belch that accompanied his instructions to the cab driver, Edik managed to sound clear-headed.

"I'm going to ask her what she wants me to do," Edik said.

"Isn't it your decision?"

"It affects her," Edik said.

"But won't she want you to go? You've been trying to emigrate for so long."

"So have a lot of people," Edik said. His eyes took on a glassy sheen, and he fell silent for a long moment, but his lips moved soundlessly. Artur wasn't sure whether Edik had fallen into a drunken stupor or was carrying on a full conversation with his cousin in his head.

Finally Edik said, "Some things are more important."

"You mean like love?" Artur asked.

Edik frowned at him but didn't answer, and Artur worried he'd inadvertently alienated Edik by not showing the appropriate sympathy for his situation. He really couldn't bring himself to understand Edik's unnatural devotion to his cousin.

"Are you going to tell her how you feel?"

"How I feel about what?" Edik asked. His obtuseness couldn't be an act, Artur decided, but it was confusing. Edik seemed so perceptive about some things and so dim about others, making him dangerously unpredictable.

The cab pulled to a stop in front of a stark, concrete apartment building. Edik threw some money at the driver and jumped out of the car, and Artur scrambled to follow.

Edik tripped over his own feet, and his knee touched down in a crusty snow bank left over from the last big storm. He popped back up, as if after a lifetime of cowardly surrender nothing could hold him down any longer. Across the street from the entrance, two agents nursed coffee thermoses and watched the building from an unmarked car. Tonight's visit would make for an interesting scene. Artur wondered if the agents would be able to hear the whole drama play out on their radios.

Edik barreled into the lobby. He jabbed at the button for the elevator and then turned on his heel, grumbling, "Out. Again. And she lives on the seventh floor."

Edik found his way to the stairwell and started to climb. He swayed a little and hung to the rail, and he was winded by the time they reached the second landing. Still, he kept on, swaying slightly and losing momentum with each consecutive floor.

By the fifth floor, Artur worried Edik might pass out from the combination of intoxication and exertion.

He couldn't let Edik fail at this, the way he suspected the man had petered out and failed at so many other points in his life. Not when Artur needed the introduction for his mission.

Artur wedged himself between Edik and the rail and half-carried the pathetic man up the remaining two floors. Edik pulled free when they reached the seventh floor.

Panting, Edik staggered down the hallway and stopped at a door in the middle of the row. He pounded on it with his fist. "Sofia," he yelled. "Sofia! Sofia, open up damn it. I have to talk to you."

Sofia didn't open the door. Her husband did.

Mendel Reitman was a rangy man, bordering on skeletal. His dark eyes were haunted and his cheekbones gaunt. His pajamas bagged on him, and it was likely he had been in bed before Edik had started banging on his door.

Though he looked like a tattered scarecrow, he had a fierce and imposing presence. His eyebrows cut harsh slashes over his eyes. "Edik? What the hell do you want with my wife?"

"I need her advice," Edik said.

"Advice about what?" Hands on his hips, Mendel blocked the entrance. Edik tried to look around him into the apartment.

"Is she here? I have to talk with her. I have to—" His words died on a belch.

His breath stank of bile and rich food. Mendel wisely took a step back.

"Mendel?" a female voice called softly. "Is everything all right?"

"Sofia, Sofia, Sofia," Edik lamented.

"Everything's fine," Mendel said gruffly. "Your idiot cousin is here."

There were soft footsteps, and then Sofia appeared behind her husband. Her photograph hadn't done her justice.

Artur's vision tunneled, and the details of the hallway,—the stale air, the worn carpet, the nicks in the plaster and chipped paint on the walls, the burnt-out light bulbs, the drunken man wobbling beside him—faded away, and she filled his awareness.

She wasn't beautiful.

She was compelling.

There was something absolutely captivating about her in person.

Her gaze slammed into his, and the force of that collision shook him.

Maybe Edik wasn't a complete fool. Or maybe Artur had been more affected by tonight's vodka than he had credited.

"We haven't met," she said to Artur. She pinned him with a clear-eyed gaze.

For an instant he was convinced she could see right through his guise, that she instinctively knew he didn't belong. He stumbled over his alias. "I'm Yosef. Yosef Koslovsky."

"My friend. My dear, dear friend," Edik said drunkenly, and he started to cry.

"Edik, what's wrong? Are you sick?"

"He doesn't deserve any pity," Mendel said. "He got himself drunk and then decided he had to see you."

She cut in front of Mendel to get to Edik, who chanted her name like a mantra. She pulled him into the apartment and Artur followed, crowing to himself over his won success.

Housed in one of the buildings quickly constructed in the post-war era, the Reitman's apartment was small and utilitarian. The short front hall opened to a main living area that might have qualified as modest were it not also bisected by a bookcase to make a sleeping nook.

"What's happened?" Sofia asked.

Edik took her hands in his and started to bawl.

"Is it your father? Has someone been arrested?" She peppered him with questions.

Edik tried to talk to her through his loud, hiccuping sobs, but his words were unintelligible. He belched loudly again and then ignominiously vomited all over his beloved's foyer.

"Goddamn it!" her husband cursed.

Sofia ignored him and kept her focus on her cousin. "Come in the kitchen. Let's get you cleaned up. Maybe you want some water."

She led him away, toward the kitchen, while Mendel groused about the mess and unwanted visitors making a racket in the middle of the night.

Artur followed Sofia and Edik, and just like that, he was in!

CHAPTER NINETEEN
SOFIA

SOFIA GUIDED EDIK, still bundled in his coat and hat, into the kitchen. He was unsteady on his feet, and he reeked of vomit. She pushed him into one of the chairs and then took a healthy step away from him. She heard Mendel grumble and curse as he cleaned the mess Edik had made in the hall.

"Breathe," she urged Edik. She waited for his drunken sobs to subside enough for him to speak again. Mendel joined them in the kitchen. Arms crossed, he glowered at Edik, but Sofia knew something had to be terribly wrong. It was unusual for Edik to reach this level of agitation.

"Tell me what's wrong," she urged. "Is it your father?"

Edik pulled a crumpled letter form his pocket and handed it to her. She read the letter over twice in shocked disbelief. The Office of Visa and Registration had granted Edik's request to emigrate to Israel. "This is wonderful news," she said. "A miracle!"

Mendel snatched the paper from her and scanned the page. "You big fool," he scolded Edik. "Why would you need Sofia's advice about this?"

"Should I go?"

"You shouldn't have come in the first place," Mendel said.

"No, I mean to Israel."

"Of course, you should go, you moron," Mendel said, not giving Sofia a chance to speak. "I don't see what there is to discuss."

Edik ignored Mendel. He took her hand and clutched tightly. "How can I leave you?"

"There's no choice. You know that," she said. "You can't pass this up."

He was such a sweet man, so earnest and dedicated. Also, at the moment, a damp, sweaty, and stinky one. She extricated her hand from his clammy grasp and patted him comfortingly on the back, using the rhythmic taps that she knew helped ground him. Her cousin wasn't like most people. Sometimes he had trouble regulating his emotions, feeling too much or too little. He could get caught in the stickiness of big feelings, and he sometimes needed a little help to find his way back.

"Who'll take care of you?" Edik asked.

Behind her, Mendel snorted with impatience. He had never understood their connection.

People regularly misjudged and underestimated Edik, even the KGB, which had determined he didn't need his own tail, unlike the other men in her family. People tended to focus on how socially awkward he was, how unnervingly direct and simple in his interactions. They imagined that if he was a social idiot then maybe he was one in the rest of his life, too.

But Edik was no fool. He had a remarkable memory and a talent for numbers. He'd used those skills for his own benefit to make a small fortune counting cards, and for hers to be an invaluable partner in crime. He kept track of their black market stock and sales and calculated all of the ledgers in his head. No paperwork trail. Less chance of discovery. His lack of social graces sometimes kept him from reading the cues of his clients, and Sofia could often command better prices on the same batch of goods than he could. Nonetheless, he had built up a dependable network of buyers, and, like her, he could come and go without constant harassment from the KGB.

She would miss Edik terribly when he left for Israel. He was one of the few people she let herself depend on. But he had a chance to be free, and she desperately wanted that for him—for all of them.

"You have to go," she said.

"But what about—"

"We'll talk when you're sober." She cut him off before he could say more.

His friend, Yosef, stood in the corner, watching their exchange with avid fascination. His hazel eyes sparkled with keen intelligence, and he seemed to be stockpiling every detail.

He made her uneasy.

She couldn't risk that Edik would accidentally let anything slip in front of him. Or Mendel.

"But, but, but," Edik protested.

"Hush. Calm down." She tried to preempt one of his fits. When he got too wound up, it was hard to settle him again. She spoke soothingly, in the tone of voice she'd learned best calmed him. "I'll visit tomorrow, and we'll talk it through."

"I don't fucking believe this." Mendel threw his hands up in the air. He marched toward Edik and towered over him. "Grow the fuck up!"

Sofia gasped at the harshness in his tone. Edik began to rock in the chair. He was in distress, and Mendel was only making things worse.

"Stop! You're upsetting him," she warned, but Mendel talked over her. "Pull yourself together. You think you take care of Sofia? You think she needs you?" Mendel shouted at Edik, "Look at yourself! Showing up in the middle of the night, crying like a baby and looking to her to wipe your spit. You're pathetic."

"That's enough." She planted herself between them to shield Edik. "You're being cruel."

"No, I'm telling it like it is."

She tried another tactic to shut Mendel up. He wasn't helping matters at all with his tirade. "You're going to wake Kolya."

Mendel didn't heed her warning. His voice rose with anger until he was yelling, this time at her. "You don't need some depressed man-child hanging on your shoulders. He's leaching off of you. Just like your parents. Having you run their errands and hold their hands. Like your mother can't get her own damn sugar!"

Edik crumpled under the weight of Mendel's censure. He buried his head in his hands and sobbed wretchedly.

"It's not true," she tried to reassure Edik. Her own anger swelled. She had been making allowances for her husband, tried to be understanding, but there was a limit.

The man she had married would have shown compassion. He wouldn't have gone after Edik like this. Her cousin wasn't capable of defending himself.

Mendel rounded on Edik's friend. "And you! What the hell's the matter with you? Why'd you bring him here?"

"He got it in his head that this was where he needed to be." Unlike Edik, Yosef wasn't ruffled by Mendel's temper. He spoke confidently, as if he were accustomed to having authority and instantly commanding respect. He didn't seem like the kind of man who would ordinarily befriend her cousin. Edik tended to attract oddballs, who were as awkward as he was.

"There was no stopping him," Yosef said. Yet Yosef was taller and broader than either Mendel or Edik, and he stood with a straight posture that suggested he might be fit and strong under his coat. He glowed with vitality, the way Mendel once had. Certainly, he should have been able to wrestle Edik into a cab and get him home.

"I came along to make sure he got here safely," Yosef explained.

"You should have taken him home," Mendel scolded, voicing her thoughts.

"I don't have the address."

Her gaze snagged on Yosef's thick lashes, on his firm chin, his wide shoulders. She found him attractive and wished she didn't.

"I thought you said you were 'dear, dear' friends," Sofia quoted Edik's words back to him.

"Dear friends. The best of friends," Edik moaned in agreement.

His color was a little green. He liked his liquor, but he usually stuck to a strict limit, and he wasn't one to deviate from his routine.

She had never seen him so sick with drink. Had the news from the OVIR so unsettled him, or was this Yosef's influence? She regarded Edik's new best friend with sharpened suspicion. She didn't want to push Edik while he was in this state, but she needed to ask. "Then why doesn't he know where you live?"

"I just moved to Moscow. From Leningrad," Yosef answered before Edik could. "We met last week at a bar."

His answer was plausible.

Maybe Edik had overstated their relationship, and Yosef had been too polite to contradict him. Maybe Yosef was simply a newcomer, just like he said, who had latched onto the first friendly person he had met.

But what if he wasn't?

"I'll write the address down for you." Mendel was obviously eager to eject both men from the apartment. He scribbled the address using the pen and pad of paper she kept on the counter by the phone. When he was finished, he shoved the slip at Yosef. "Take the fool home."

"I'm sorry, Sofia. I'm sorry. I'm sorry. I'm sorry," Edik repeated, over and over again, like a broken record caught in a groove. He started to rock again.

"Hush," she said. "It's okay. You didn't do anything wrong. He didn't mean it."

"I did mean it," Mendel contradicted her. "Every word. She's done taking care of you."

"Don't talk to him like that." Her own temper exploded.

"Stop coddling him," Mendel said. "He needs to grow up. Be a man. All this time, he should have been taking care of *you*. Not the other way around. You were all alone!"

"I wasn't alone."

"You were alone!" he shouted. "And no one—no one!—took care of you. Protected you. I was trapped in hell, and you were alone. And they never let me forget it."

She wasn't quite sure who "they" were. She hadn't asked him about his experiences again after his request their first night, and he had remained completely close-lipped.

"I'm fine. Everything's fine," she said, trying to soothe him now, too. "You're home now, and it will all be okay."

She wrapped her arms around Mendel and embraced him tightly. His ribs poked against her chest.

He pushed her away as if her touch were unbearable.

"I'm home now." His voice softened, as if to soften the blow of his physical rejection.

But it hurt. Even if she could understand it, even if she knew she needed to be patient and give him time, it still hurt.

Edik rocked harder in the chair, back and forth, as if he sensed the depth of her own distress, and it fueled his.

"Edik, stop," she warned, but she was too late.

The chair pitched too far back. Edik tipped over. He windmilled his arms. His feet kicked in the air. And then his head thumped against the linoleum.

The fall knocked him out of his fit. He fell momentarily silent.

She rushed to his side to check him over. He grabbed her hand, and his grip was strong. She helped him to his feet.

His hat had fallen off. He ran his hands through his sweaty hair and gave a shake, the way a wet dog might.

"I'm okay," he said, but he swayed unsteadily on his feet.

She pushed him into another chair. Mendel muttered under his breath, and she was glad she couldn't make out his undoubtedly toxic words.

He set the tipped chair back on its feet and scooped up Edik's hat. Then suddenly, he froze. "What the hell is that?"

On the floor, near where Edik had toppled, there was an all too familiar object.

Black, the size of a kopek.

A listening device, just like the one she'd found in Mendel's *mezuzah*.

CHAPTER TWENTY
ARTUR

"**I**T LOOKS LIKE a listening device, but how did it get in Edik's hat?" Artur pretended to be as stunned as the rest of them.

"Are you sure that's what it is? Have you ever seen one before?" Sofia asked.

There was a testing quality to her question. He could tell from the way she had earlier interrogated Edik about their friendship that she didn't wholly buy his cover. He needed to assuage her suspicion.

"Yes," he said. "My friend Boris once found one in his pocket after riding the subway. He put it in a glass of water to disable it."

"Does that work?" Sofia asked. "What if it's waterproof?"

"Good question," Artur said.

Mendel rolled the device between his fingers thoughtfully. "Better I think to flush it down the toilet. That way, even if it's waterproof, it will be far from here."

Before anyone could protest, Mendel marched out of the kitchen. A moment later the toilet flushed.

"I knew it," Edik said to Yosef. "I told you there was a conspiracy."

Sofia went to the sink and ran the water, but she didn't wash anything. To muffle their conversation? The tactic would have thwarted the bug in Edik's hat, even at this close proximity. Smart.

"What conspiracy?" she asked over the noisy spray of water.

"Edik thought there was something suspicious about OVIR granting his request now when your husband's just been released," Artur said.

Sofia glanced sharply at Edik and pressed her lips together. Some silent communication passed between the cousins, and Artur suspected Sofia wasn't so quick to dismiss Edik's concerns.

He really couldn't understand her seeming soft spot for Edik. Her husband's account of the man's shortcomings had been right on the money.

Artur shrugged. "It sounded crazy to me. The only reason I'm crediting it now is that someone put that thing on him."

"Do you think they planted the bug on you while you were at OVIR?" Sofia asked Edik.

"Maybe," Edik said.

"Maybe they planted others then, too," she surmised. "Take off your coat."

Edik obediently shed his coat. Mendel came back into the room and berated him, "What the hell are you doing? You're not staying. Don't get comfortable."

"We're searching him for other bugs," Sofia said. To Artur, she said, "You were with him at OVIR. It's possible they placed one on you, too."

"Yes, you're right. I didn't think of that," he said. She wouldn't find anything on him. He had planted the bug on Edik, but he played along. He took off his coat and turned the pockets inside out.

Sofia took the coat from him and took over the inspection, a sign of her lingering mistrust.

When she didn't find anything of interest, she stepped up to him and, without asking, reached for his hat.

The move brought her into close proximity. He looked down into her face as she looked up into his. He felt an unaccustomed sense of connection, of longing, a desire to sink deep into her gaze and look and look.

Her large, almond-shaped eyes widened. Did she feel the same draw toward him that he felt toward her?

She looked abruptly away and inspected his hat. She pressed the material between her fingers.

"You have one, too," she said.

"I do?" He didn't believe her, but then she ripped the seam and pulled a listening device out of the lining.

Victor was spying on him. The nerve of that guy!

Artur hadn't known. He hadn't even suspected. And he wasn't sure what rankled more—that Victor was spying on him or that he'd been caught unaware.

Artur should have expected that his fellow agents would ply the tools of their trade for their own personal benefit and not only, or even primarily, for the Soviet Union. After all, human nature was greedy, lustful, and selfish, which was what made handling informants so easy.

But Artur had believed what he'd been taught, namely that he and his fellow agents held to a higher standard. They harnessed their base urges and rose above them for the cause.

Hoarding and stealing information from him, Victor had shattered that belief, that trust. *They're not all patriots, like you.*

Mendel took the bug from her and headed once more to the bathroom. Artur dropped heavily into the kitchen chair beside Edik and removed his shoes.

"What are you doing?" Edik asked.

"Checking the soles of my shoes," Artur said. "That's another well-known hiding place. Isn't it?"

He was suddenly as motivated as his targets to ferret out any other bugs. He didn't like the idea of Victor monitoring him without his knowledge. Of the unfair advantage it gave his new rival.

He heard the toilet flush, and he was glad. He wasn't about to let Victor sabotage him.

"Do you have a knife?" he asked.

Sofia handed him a sharp paring knife, and he dug the tip into the edge of the shoe's heel. She hovered by his shoulder. She smelled faintly of lemons.

"It looks solid," she observed. There was nothing in his shoe.

"Why's the KGB so interested in you?" Mendel asked Artur. His words brimmed with blame and accusation. Mendel's earlier fury at Edik seemed to have reignited and now extended to Artur, as well.

"How should I know?" Artur shot back.

He was disgruntled that he'd been under surveillance and hadn't realized. He could imagine the way Victor would laugh at him for being so clueless, when he himself had done the same thing to Edik.

Artur picked up his second shoe and inspected it, finding nothing inside the heel of that one either.

"Take off your shoes," Sofia instructed Edik. He moved slowly, laboriously, as if removing his shoes was a complex and highly difficult process. She knelt down and sped the process along, pulling his shoes from his feet as if he were a child.

She handed the shoes to Artur, trusting him with the operation, although she kept glancing over his shoulder to check his progress, while she emptied Edik's pockets.

Neither of their searches turned up any additional surveillance. But Artur realized that from now on, so long as he was working with Victor, he should always expect there was a spider watching him as it spun its web and contemplated how to catch him in a messy tangle.

He didn't like the feeling.

Mendel leaned against the kitchen doorway, arms crossed over his chest, and glared at Artur and Edik as if his eyes were shooting death rays.

Finally, he said, "I want you both out."

CHAPTER TWENTY-ONE
SOFIA

"**Y**OU'RE BEING INEXCUSABLY rude," Sofia told Mendel. She pressed the heel of her palm to her forehead to push back the headache ready to explode behind her eyes.

The last fine thread of her patience threatened to snap. In her head, she recited the litany of reasons for cutting Mendel some slack.

"These two show up in the middle of the night, bringing all kinds of trouble with them, and you're going to tell me I'm being rude," Mendel said.

"So, it's their fault?" she said. "Are you serious? Do you even hear yourself?" She threw her hands up in the air and stalked from the kitchen and into the hallway.

Having no safe outlet for her own mounting rage, she threw open the hall closet, stepped inside. Mouth opening wide, fists clenching, nails digging into her palms, she unleashed a silent scream.

Then she yanked their coats from the hangers. She snatched up hats and shoes. She shut the closet door with a vicious kick and marched back to face her problems.

The bug in Edik's hat changed everything.

She hadn't guarded her words with Paul. So long as no one was nearby and they spoke softly, she'd thought they had safety in the open air. But what if there were listening devices in her own hat or her coat? What if the KGB had been riding along for her conversation, not even several paces back, but right there?

She dumped her haul in front of Yosef.

"What are you doing?" Mendel asked.

"What does it look like?" She was so frustrated with him for the way he'd attacked Edik. For the doubts he wouldn't dispel about whose side he was on.

"We have an infestation," she said. "What if Edik's right, and there's a KGB conspiracy? It stands to reason we might all be targets."

"Why would they be interested in me?" Mendel asked. "I've been in prison for five years." Was her husband being deliberately obtuse?

"Seriously? You're the one with two KGB agents following you everywhere," she said.

"You served four years five months and fifteen days," Edik corrected with his usual precision.

"No one asked you," Mendel sniped.

"But he has a point." She was done tiptoeing around Mendel. "You were released more than six months early. Why?"

She handed the shoes to Yosef to pry the heels open as he had done for his and Edik's shoes. She emptied out her coat pockets, laying the odds an ends on the table—a few crumpled tissues, her gloves, her bottle of pepper spray that she carried for protection, a few stray kopeks—and then inspected the coat pockets and lining. Then she moved onto Mendel's coat.

"You think I made a deal with the KGB?"

"How should I know what to think? You haven't told me a single thing."

Mendel blanched. "How could you ever think I'd cooperate with *them*? Ever?"

"I don't know you anymore!" she cried out, giving voice to all of her frustration with him.

"You see?" Edik asked Yosef.

She became aware of them in a way she hadn't been before, another audience for what should have been a private moment. They both had pity in their eyes.

She had let them see too much.

"Mama?" Kolya poked his head into the kitchen. He pushed past Mendel and scampered to her. He threw his arms around her and burrowed into her side.

She seldom raised her voice, seldom lost control of herself the way she just had. By the way Kolya clung to her, she knew their argument had frightened him.

She wrapped an arm around him and locked down her raging emotions. "Were we making too much noise? I'm sorry," she said. "Let me put you back to bed."

She steered him out of the kitchen, across the living room, to his bed nook.

"Why were you and Papa screaming?"

She stroked his hair and worried what he might have overheard, even with the water running. They couldn't trust Kolya not to repeat their words to his friends or his teachers.

"Edik came by for some advice about a problem, and your papa got angry because it's so late," she said.

"A bug problem?" Kolya asked.

"Yes," she said. "A little bug rode in on his hat."

"A cockroach?" Kolya climbed back into his bed. She pulled the covers up to his chin.

"Maybe. I'm not sure," she lied. "But it was big and black and ugly."

"Dangerous?"

"No. Not dangerous," she said, not wanting to scare him. "Just disgusting. I don't like bugs."

"Me neither," he agreed.

He seemed satisfied, and she was pleased to have an innocuous cover for their argument, one a little boy could understand, one that didn't involve her suspecting his father of being a KGB informant and planting listening devices in their home.

She could scarcely imagine what it would be like to live her life without having to censor every word that came out of her mouth. To be able to rage or cry or love without an uninvited audience.

She had once shared this musing with Paul. He had told her he lived that way all the time in America.

"It's not Edik's fault that the bug picked his hat," Kolya said.

"No," she agreed.

"So why was Papa so mean?"

"He's been through a rough time." The excuse felt stale, even though Mendel had only been home a week.

"I don't care," Kolya said. "He was mean to Edik, and he made Auntie Vera cry. And he yells at you. I want him to go back where he came from."

"Don't say that," Sofia chided. "He came from a very terrible place, and we're lucky he returned to us."

"Then he's lucky, but we're not," Kolya said with a stubborn lift of his pointed little chin. "I don't like him. I want *Dedushka* to be my papa again."

She rubbed at a sore spot in the middle of her chest. How many times could her heart break in one week?

"We just need to give it a little more time," she said.

"And then what?" Kolya asked, but she didn't have an answer for him.

"Then we'll see," she said. She smoothed the unruly hair away from his face and kissed his cheek.

She returned to the kitchen to find Edik staring listlessly at the table while Yosef and Mendel squabbled.

"You should check them. They're the perfect place to hide a bug," Yosef insisted.

"No. Absolutely not," Mendel said.

"What's this about?" Sofia asked.

"We should check those box things on your doors. They're suspicious," Yosef said. "And Mendel said he put them up recently."

"There's no conspiracy!" Mendel argued. "Those were gifts from the rabbi."

"In the past, that in itself would have been enough reason for you to check them." Sofia opened the kitchen drawer and pulled out the hammer.

"What are you going to do?" Mendel asked with horror. He lunged to grab her arm, but Yosef stopped him.

For a moment, she was tempted to swing at the religious article with all of her might, knock it off the wall, and shatter it to pieces.

But she checked her temper and turned the hammer around. She used the curved end to pry the *mezuzah* carefully from the doorframe.

The *mezuzah* came loose easily. She brought it to the kitchen. The faucet was still running, and the white noise seemed to envelop them.

Mendel looked ready to rip it from her hand, and Yosef stuck close, as if to give her cover. She flipped the rectangular case and slid off the back, the way she had earlier.

"Satisfied? There's nothing there," Mendel said.

She ignored him and pried out the parchment.

"Be careful with that!" Mendel moved closer. "The rabbi gave it to me. To protect us. It has God's name."

She didn't unroll the scroll. She held it to her eye like a telescope. "That's not all it has."

She handed Mendel the scroll. Handling it reverently, he held it up to his eye, just as she had. "*Bozhe moy!*" he cursed, as she confronted him with the truth she'd known for days.

He placed the scroll carefully on the table and then picked up the hammer. He stalked from the room. She heard him go to the front door and then stomp through the apartment to their bedroom. He returned with a *mezuzah* in each hand.

"Check them," he said, laying them before her.

She opened each one carefully, the same way she had the first. Small black bugs dropped into her palm from each of the scrolls.

Mendel scooped them into his own palm and stormed to the bathroom. He slammed the door, and she heard the toilet flush. Then there was the sound of banging—his head or his fists?—against the door.

She left Yosef and Edik alone in her kitchen and went to check on him.

"Mendel?" she called tentatively.

"Leave me alone."

She could hear the unmistakable pain in his voice.

"Talk to me," she pleaded.

"No."

She pressed her hand to the door and felt the vibrations as he pounded the door under her palm. So much pent-up rage and pain, and she had no clue how to make things better for either of them.

CHAPTER TWENTY-TWO
ARTUR

"RISE AND SHINE," a grating voice sang out. Artur lurched out of a deep sleep.

His body protested his waking with a series of unfamiliar aches and pains. He had a sharp headache and a crick in his neck. His legs were cramped.

As he stretched, he realized he had contorted to wedge himself onto a too-short sofa, upholstered in ugly brown velveteen with large bright flowers.

Where was he? He suffered a keen sense of disorientation.

A shadowy figure pulled open shades on a large picture window. Artur blinked and covered his eyes. The sudden onslaught of light made his head pound. He couldn't hold back a groan.

"Sorry, Yosef. I would have let you sleep, but I need you up and out of sight," his tormenter said.

Yosef. In a flash, the details of his undercover alias and the events of the night before cut through Artur's fog.

"I waited as long as I could, but I've got visitors coming any minute," the speaker said, and Artur supplied the details that had been missing a moment earlier.

The man before him, an older replica of Edik, was his father, Ruben. They'd met last night when Artur had dragged in a distraught and still intoxicated Edik. It had been very late. Artur had crashed on the sofa in the living room.

"You want some coffee?" Ruben asked as Artur sat up. "Or maybe a cigarette? I know I'm supposed to quit, but there's nothing like starting my day with a good smoke."

"Coffee," Artur croaked. "*Pozhalsto*." He listened for other sounds in the apartment. He didn't hear anyone else moving around, and he suspected Edik hadn't yet risen.

Wintry sunlight poured through an open window and highlighted a swarm of dust motes. He blinked his eyes, scarcely believing he was here and this man was talking to him as if he really were Yosef Koslovsky.

How strange to be inside the apartment he'd had under surveillance for the last week!

The garbled audiotapes of conversation hadn't picked up the musty smell or the manufactured feeling of depression and desperation.

The room seemed to be furnished to highlight the family's supposed poverty, but over the past week, Artur had seen Edik throw around enough cash that he knew the Soifers were flush with money.

"Come in the kitchen," Ruben invited, and Artur shuffled behind him, feeling like an old man himself. Ruben set to preparing a large percolator to brew.

"You don't need to make so much. I'll only drink one cup," Artur said.

"My guests are American. They like their coffee," Ruben said. "They'll be here soon."

He scrutinized Artur and then, without asking, reached out and finger-combed his hair. Artur tolerated the grooming. He would be as accommodating as necessary to make Ruben like him.

"By any chance, do you speak English?"

"A little," Artur lied; he was fluent in English.

"Stay," Ruben decided. "You're a good-looking fellow. They might like you. Even if you can't speak English."

Americans were coming to the apartment? Now? And Ruben wanted him to stay and meet them? Despite his pounding headache, he was suddenly giddy with anticipation.

The Jews had been meeting with foreigners and passing secrets, and now he had a front row seat. He could discover what else the KGB's surveillance had been missing. He would hear and see everything, no matter what tricks they used to outsmart surveillance.

There was barely time to slug down a few sips of coffee before the Americans arrived. Maybe he could return to KGB headquarters with a report of real significance. He had something to prove today, especially to Victor.

Ruben threw open the door to the apartment and gave the strangers a warm, jovial greeting, as if they were long lost relatives. They came bearing a large suitcase full of gifts. Artur didn't get to see what was inside the heavy luggage, but he bet guests like these were the source of the cigarettes and anything else Edik was selling on the black market. The source of so much cash in his wallet.

Ruben ushered them into his living room and hobbled through introductions in broken English.

Artur observed everything from the door of the kitchen, where he drank his coffee. The loud animated chatter seemed to stab at an aching point above his right eye. When Ruben pointed him out to the guests, he waved, pretending to be shy. He wasn't ready to join them yet.

Ruben asked him to serve coffee. He retreated into the kitchen, grateful for the momentary reprieve from the sound. He needed a few more minutes for the caffeine to work its hangover magic. In the meantime, he snooped through the cabinets and drawers in the kitchen as he set up a tray with milk, sugar, spoons, and napkins. He didn't find anything of note, but he hoped to have many more opportunities.

Eventually, he would convince Ruben to accept him as a boarder when Edik left for Israel.

He set to filling mugs for the two middle-aged couples sitting side by side and hanging on Ruben's choppy, pidgin English.

There was another knock at the door. Ruben sent him to answer, and Artur smiled to himself at how easily the old Jew might come to rely on him.

He would be a fixture in this apartment in no time.

CHAPTER TWENTY-THREE
VERA

"WHERE'S MENDEL?" VERA asked when Sofia greeted her. Having arrived a few minutes early to pick up Kolya, Vera ordinarily would have come into the apartment, but today she lingered by the door, ready to make a speedy exit.

"I don't know," Sofia said. "But he's not here."

Vera breathed out a gusty sigh, but Sofia frowned, not sharing in her relief. Vera noticed that Sofia's forehead showed lines that usually weren't there, and her eyes were puffy and red, as if she'd been rubbing them. Or crying. Had Mendel made her cry?

It couldn't be easy to have Mendel home.

"Do you need me to babysit this afternoon?" Vera didn't leave her spot by the door. She fidgeted with the strap of her satchel and didn't meet Sofia's eyes. This wasn't a casual question.

She wanted Sofia to say yes, that they needed her, despite what Mendel had said earlier. She wanted her older sister to give her an excuse so that she wouldn't feel compelled to help Petya. So that she wouldn't have to go anywhere near Gennady.

"You're always welcome to visit if you don't have other plans,"

Sofia said.

Insulted, Vera straightened her spine, lifted her chin. Mendel's return might have left her at loose ends, but she refused to be an object of pity, a burden.

"I have plans," Vera said. "I'm tutoring a classmate after school."

"That's great," Sofia said.

"But I could cancel," Vera added, trying to sound nonchalant. She leaned in and whispered, "I'm worried. About Kolya. He doesn't want to come home after school. I've had to drag him onto the bus. He says he wants to come home with me."

Truly concerned for Kolya, she told herself she was obliged to report what had happened, but that didn't keep her from embellishing her point. "He doesn't want to be with Mendel. He says Mendel's mean."

She only spoke the truth, but it gave her a vindictive rush. She was the one—had always been the one—doing the favors. How many afternoons of her life had she given up to take care of Kolya, only to have Mendel discard her now?

"Mean to Kolya?" Sofia yelped and then lowered her voice. "What has Mendel done?"

Her sister's wide-eyed alarm made Vera backpedal. She felt suddenly guilty. She didn't want to add needlessly to Sofia's worries. She only wanted her sister to know that Kolya was unhappy. And to recognize Vera's importance.

"I don't know," Vera said. "He hasn't said anything specific."

"He's still upset about how Mendel treated you. Maybe that's all?" Sofia asked.

"Maybe," Vera said, but the hopefulness in Sofia's eyes made Vera want to say more to ease the concern she'd just kindled. Surely Kolya would have told her if Mendel had bullied him in any way. She thought back to the day before, when Kolya had so fearlessly confronted Gennady. She added more confidently, "Yes. That must be it. Little man. Always trying to be my defender. You should have seen him with Gennady."

"Who's Gennady?" Sofia asked, and Vera quickly realized her

mistake.

"No one. A boy I know." She could feel her face heat, and she knew if she saw herself in the mirror it would be an unattractive, blotchy red. She could never hide her emotions. They were always so close to the surface.

"A boyfriend?" Sofia probed.

"No. It's not like that."

"Why isn't it like that?"

"Because it's not," Vera said, unable to hide her embarrassment and pain. She yanked open the door.

In her last year of high school, she was told she looked much the way Sofia had in her teens, slim—almost coltish, with lean legs and a long, graceful neck. She should have had a string of boys chasing her, as Sofia had. But she didn't.

Instead, they seemed to fall over themselves for the chance to make a fool of her. Why?

"Come on, Kolya. It's time to go," she called, even though there was no need to rush. Sofia would see right through her hasty departure, but Vera wasn't ready to confide her newest heartache to her older sister.

It still hurt too much, and she couldn't stand the pity. Or the shame.

Backing out into the hall and calling for Kolya to hurry up, Vera nearly crashed into Mendel.

"Hey!" Mendel recoiled and jerkily shoved her out of the way.

Vera stumbled. Sofia took a half-step into the hall, calling, "Vera, are you all right?"

Light on her feet, Vera recovered almost instantly. She dodged around Mendel, putting as much distance between them as possible in the narrow corridor. She gave Sofia a reassuring wave and then, without another word, rushed to get away.

"Have a good day at school," Mendel said. Was he taunting her? She hazarded a glance over her shoulder. Mendel wasn't paying her any mind. He gazed longingly at Kolya, who stopped before him in the hall.

Kolya glared up at him and answered his father's greeting with censorious silence. Then he hurried after Vera.

When Kolya caught up to her, he grabbed her hand and squeezed tight, saying all of the things in that one gesture that no one else ever said to her.

CHAPTER TWENTY-FOUR
SOFIA

SOFIA STEPPED ASIDE as Mendel came into the apartment. He closed and locked the door behind him.

There were so many things she wanted to say to him. Scream at him. What was that painful scene in the hallway with Vera and Kolya? Why had he been so unforgivably cruel to Edik? And was he a spy?

She bottled up her roiling emotions and settled on asking her most immediate question. "Where'd you go this morning?"

"Out," he said.

Out? That was all he had to say to her? She dug her fingernails into her palm. Mendel hadn't spoken to her since he'd locked himself in the bathroom and supposedly flushed the bugs down the toilet. And now he offered her only the one word? No apology. No explanation of where he'd gone or what he'd been doing. No reassurances that he would never knowingly plant listening devices in their home.

He wouldn't look at her.

She couldn't stay another minute in the apartment with him. She wasn't ready to make another excuse for the pain he was causing, and she couldn't be the one trying to pull words from him that he didn't want to give her. Words she might not welcome.

She tugged on her boots and grabbed her coat and scarf and pushed past him.

"Where are you going?" he asked.

"Out," she almost replied, giving him exactly what he'd given her, but that would be childish. "To see Edik," she said.

"I'll come with you."

"Don't." She walked away without looking back. She lost time waiting at the elevator, which apparently was still not working, and he caught up with her in the stairwell.

"I'm not a spy," he said.

Her steps faltered, but she kept going, down one flight and then another.

Maybe he wasn't. Maybe he hadn't known about the listening devices. His surprise had seemed genuine. But he was acting guilty. If not of that, then of something.

She reached the lobby and strode out into the bright spring morning. He followed, but he lagged behind, as if he were having trouble keeping pace with her.

She snuffed out any pity she might feel and walked faster. His agents, parked on the bench, sprang to attention as soon as they saw him.

Soon she had a procession. Herself. Then Mendel several feet behind, with the gap between them widening. Then his agents.

"Sofia, wait," he said.

She didn't slow.

"We need to talk."

She kept going, pumping her arms and legs, nearly running.

"I'm sorry!" he called after her.

The apology was enough to stop her, but not enough to make her forgive him.

Still, it was a start.

When he caught up to her, he was panting from the exertion. "I'm sorry," he said again.

"Sorry about what specifically?"

"You're not going to make this easy for me, are you?" He wiped at the beads of sweat on his forehead. She noticed he was wearing his *yarmulka*, despite the unavoidable evidence that the other items the rabbi had given him offered no protection whatsoever.

Just the opposite.

"Why should I make anything easy for you?" she demanded. "You've been a total beast, and I've been tiptoeing around you, trying to give you the space you asked for. But you're the one who screamed at me for coddling Edik. So you tell me, exactly how much slack am I supposed to cut you?" She screamed at him in a whisper, not wanting to put on a show for the agents.

Mendel stayed silent. She shouldn't have been surprised. His non-response fueled her anger.

She averted her face and stared at the windows of the buildings they passed. She couldn't bear to look at him. She sped up her walk again, not caring when he fell behind, especially when he offered nothing to draw her back to him.

Edik's friend Yosef answered the door when she arrived. He was still in his clothes from the night before, and scruff shadowed his face.

"What's happened? Are you all right?" Yosef pulled her into the apartment, and his hands were on her shoulders, and he was looking down at her in a way that no one had in a very, very long time.

Then he pulled her into his arms and cradled her head against his chest, and his musky scent surrounded her. And that's when she realized she was crying.

It had been so long since someone had held her the way he was, since she had cried to anyone but her pillow.

And he was solid and warm and so very handsome.

This was wrong.

She pulled away and dashed at her tears. "Where's Edik?"

"Still sleeping," Yosef said.

"Ah, Sofia, it's good you're here," her uncle shuffled into the hallway. He kissed her on both cheeks. "Is everything okay?" he asked and smudged away the remnants of her tears with his thumb.

"Fine," she lied.

He kissed her forehead, offering her his quiet sympathy, but he didn't press her. "Are you up to entertaining?" he asked. "We have an American contingent, and I'm not as fluent in American as you are." Her uncle spoke some English, but he had difficulties with American accents.

"Not nearly as pretty, either," Yosef mumbled.

"Too true," Uncle Ruben chuckled. "Would you mind?" he asked her. She agreed to play hostess, and she slipped into the bathroom to splash some water on her face. When she came back out, she heard Ruben instruct Yosef, "Don't forget the coffee."

Ruben pulled her with him into the living room, where two couples squeezed together on the sofa.

She wasn't surprised he had company. He often did. His apartment had an excellent location for visitors to find—the building at the end of the block on the square, 2nd floor, number 18.

Ruben pointed her to one of the folding chairs he'd set up in a circle around the sofa and his armchair. Hands resting on his round belly, he resembled a fat, happy Buddha.

The apartment was unusually gracious in its dimensions, fitting a large number of people in the main room, even if her late aunt's poor interior design choices made it feel small.

Sofia's grandparents had been members of the Communist Party, and this apartment in the city center had been one of the many trappings of a privileged life.

Until Stalin had decided to execute them because they were Jews.

These accidents of location and size had conspired to make the apartment a hub for foreign visitors seeking to help Soviet Jews, and her uncle reveled in his role as host.

With the TV playing at full volume on a station full of static, Ruben resumed a story in English, one he must have started before he'd been interrupted by her arrival, about his KGB entourage.

"So, the agents, they all get into taxi with me. I say, 'You split bill, or get own cab.'"

His listeners laughed heartily as he delivered the punchline.

When the laughter died down, he made the introductions. Today's visitors were married couples, about the same age as her parents, visiting from New York. Their accents made her think of Paul.

Yosef brought out a tray with coffee and cream and sugar. Mendel arrived as the visitors settled back into place with their hot drinks.

"Mendel Reitman? You were in prison for teaching Hebrew. Right?" one of the visitors said when Ruben introduced him.

Mendel stared at him, not understanding the words, and Sofia translated. Mendel shifted uncomfortably.

"Ask him to tell us about his time in prison," the visitor said.

She translated, and Mendel stiffened.

"He doesn't like to talk about it," she told them.

"I'll tell you," he said. "But I need a cigarette."

Ruben drew a pack out of his pocket. "Don't tell your mother," he told Sofia with a wink.

Mendel tapped a cigarette out of the pack and rolled it between his fingers. "Tell them, in prison men will kill over something as small and worthless as this cigarette."

He waited for her to translate and paused a little longer. He trained his gaze on the cigarette.

"I realized that we are separated from animals by the finest of threads," he said. "I didn't want to be an animal—reacting, following my basic instincts, killing, fucking." She flinched at his harsh use of language. "Tell them," Mendel urged her, and she translated.

The American couples leaned forward in their seats, drawn by his words, and Yosef hovered beside them, watching her and Mendel both with a disturbing intensity.

"Every day I was tempted. In prison, they tried hard to make us forget we are men," Mendel said. "And mostly they succeeded."

His voice cracked, and he fell silent for a moment. She quickly translated his words for the audience, and he continued.

"I had a book of psalms with me," he said. "Weeks would go by when those words were all I had for company. And they slowly seeped into me, word by word. 'The Lord is my shepherd,'" he quoted. "And one day I realized that no matter what I did, God was with me and watching. God was what separated me from the animals. And following God's rules would protect me from the worst in myself and set me free."

He touched his hand to his *yarmulka* and gave her an imploring look.

Please understand.

Please forgive me.

Why couldn't he have given her these words, this truth, when they were alone?

Why couldn't he have pulled her into his arms the way Yosef had?

CHAPTER TWENTY-FIVE
ARTUR

ARTUR WATCHED THE whole meeting with morbid fascination. The Americans listened eagerly to Mendel's story, gobbling up every word, savoring the horrid details, looking at him like he was some kind of hero.

"How awful," said the woman who'd asked for the story, and her eyes were bright with admiration.

"Yes, we're very lucky he's home now," Ruben agreed. "But there are others."

He nodded at Sofia, her cue to tell another story.

"Mendel's sister and her family are still in prison. We don't know where." She launched into the story of the Abromovich family, Max, Irena, and their daughter, Nadia. "They sent Max to the gulag for speaking out against Soviet nuclear policy."

Sofia cast Max's activities as noble, his arrest as unwarranted, a deviation from the facts in the file Artur had read at the Lubyanka. He couldn't hold back from saying, "He confessed to spreading anti-Soviet propaganda."

"Yes," Sofia agreed and then twisted the truth for their audience. "He was coerced. He was forced to name his wife and daughter as co-conspirators. Nadia was only fifteen years old," Sofia said.

"Fifteen!" The guests were horrified, and Artur found himself wondering how old Max's daughter had truly been and what had actually become of her. He didn't believe a girl that young would be sent to the gulag. But the story as told was a powerful one for playing on the Americans' emotions.

Was this then the whole of the conspiracy? Visitors came, heard the stories from Reitman's families and friends, and then beat the drum about human rights abuses when they got home?

"The Soviets don't tell the story this way," Artur interjected for the Americans' benefit.

"Of course they don't," Sofia said as if they were in complete agreement, as if he were feeding her lines for this farcical show for the American audience instead of trying to correct her. "They don't worry about the truth. They own the newspapers and the TV stations. They have the power to make any story they want the official one, even when it's a complete lie."

"I thought you didn't speak English." Ruben issued his challenge in Russian.

Too late Artur realized he'd been caught in a lie. He recalled that earlier he had told Ruben he didn't speak much English, but his comment in English showed not only that he could speak but that he had followed Sofia's stories. He shrugged and said, "I understand more than I can speak. I'm not fluent like Sofia."

Sofia seemed to ignore their interchange. She fixed the Americans with an earnest gaze. "They can make people disappear," she said. "I believe the reason Mendel made it home is that we made sure no one forgot his name."

Could it all be so simple, Artur wondered. Had he found their traitor?

He recounted her words later when he returned to KGB headquarters that afternoon. He presented the details to Victor, hoping his partner would easily see what he could offer in solving the case.

"Congratulations," Victor said sarcastically. "You watched the same people we've been watching in the same apartment we've been watching having the same damn conversations we've been listening to for months."

Artur sat in his chair at the cubicle. Victor stepped in close and hovered over him, filling Artur's vision with his beak nose and squinty eyes. He resembled a hawk about to snap a field mouse up in its beak and crack its spine. "You sabotaged the investigation and brought back nothing to show for it."

"Sabotage?" Artur asked, anger rising. Victor was a fine one to bring up sabotage. He had withheld vital information from Artur when he sent him out to interview Edik.

Artur rose from his desk chair. He was taller than Victor and turned his own tactic back on him, standing too close and forcing Victor to look up at him.

Victor took a step back, but he didn't back down from his angry tirade.

"You stupid, inexperienced rube. You've bungled this whole thing. What devil possessed you to make them check the apartment for bugs?"

"Zhukhov. Gregorovich. In my office. Now," Kasparov, their immediate supervisor, hollered to Victor and Artur from his office. Likely he had heard every word of Victor's diatribe.

Victor had a vicious gleam in his eye. He bumped Artur as he shoved past him to get to the office first.

Artur took an extra moment to collect several of the files from Victor's desk and his own typed report. He projected an outward confidence, covering over his nervousness. Had he accomplished enough?

He had thought witnessing the conversation this morning a coup, but Victor had been entirely dismissive. He had denied Artur any credit for contributing to their case.

Victor stormed into Kasparov's office. Standing at his own cubicle, Artur couldn't make out what Victor said, only the harsh, urgent tone. He had no doubt Victor was giving Kasparov an earful about Artur's gross incompetence.

"Artur!" He turned to see his father-in-law striding down the hall.

He waited for Semyon to catch up to him and then continued toward Kasparov's office. "Maya's been worried," Semyon said. "She said you didn't come home last night."

Artur hadn't given a thought to Maya, and now he imagined how she might have waited up for him and how worried she must have been when he hadn't come home.

He hadn't expected to spend the whole night out with Edik, but he had grabbed the opportunity to stay.

"Should I have called her?" Artur asked.

Semyon chuckled and slapped Artur on the back as if he'd made a clever joke. "Call her? In the middle of an undercover assignment. 'Hi, darling. I'm going to be late tonight. Don't wait up.' Haha. Good one."

Artur manufactured a smile to match Semyon's jovial mood, but he doubted Maya would see things the way her father did. If Artur didn't manage this confrontation with Victor, he was going to be out on his ear on more than one front.

"What did you tell Maya when she called you?" Artur asked.

"That she needed to remember her place," Semyon said. "You're a KGB agent. Not a schoolboy. You don't report to her."

Maya must have loved that, Artur thought. He decided he better arm himself with a bouquet of flowers before returning home.

"How's the case coming?" Semyon asked.

They were right outside Kasparov's office now, and Victor's voice carried clearly to them now. "He told them where to look. Set them right on the trail! And now I've got nothing."

Semyon's eyes narrowed. "Did I hear Victor say you've got nothing?"

"Not nothing," Artur said. He feigned a smug smile. "Else I would have been home last night."

"I'm eager to hear all about it."

Artur thought Semyon meant later. Later, after work. Later, when they could drink cognac and smoke cigars. Later, when Victor wouldn't be there to spoil the story with his doubts and criticism.

But Semyon gestured for Artur to precede him into Kasparov's office.

The moment he entered, Kasparov confronted Artur. "Victor tells me you helped the Jews find and destroy four listening devices."

Kasparov sat behind his desk. He spoke to Artur, but he looked to Semyon, as if trotting out proof that Artur didn't belong on the case.

"Five. There were five listening devices," Artur corrected. He cast a sideways glance at Victor who didn't even have the good grace to look embarrassed. "The first one fell out of Edik's hat."

"Because you did a sloppy job planting it," Victor accused.

Artur shrugged. "And then they started searching. When they found the one in my hat, I played along."

"You didn't play along," Victor said. "You pushed them. Argued with them. Reitman wouldn't have looked inside the religious articles if you hadn't forced the issue. Do you have any idea how much work went into getting those bugs in position?"

"They're very suspicious people," Artur said. "It was a way to make them trust me."

"Trust you! You think having them trust you was so important you could risk all of *my* hard work? Can't you see how much damage you've done to the case?" Victor gesticulated wildly with his hands, flapping them in the air like wings. "I have Reitman exactly where I want him. But you've made them distrust him. They'll think he planted the bugs."

"There's already a lot of tension between Reitman and his wife."

"That you've made worse!" Victor threw his hands up in frustration.

"A brilliant move if you ask me," Semyon offered. He stood beside Artur in solidarity.

"Brilliant? How? He's undone months of work," Victor complained.

"Has he?" Kasparov asked, spearing Victor with a disapproving look, either because he now doubted Victor's version of events or because Victor had the poor sense to contradict the Spymaster.

Semyon said to Artur, "Tell us what you know so far about the wife."

"You think the wife knows something?" Victor asked, as if he hadn't considered the possibility and didn't believe it now.

"She definitely knows something," Artur said. "She might even be our traitor. I watched her dish out propaganda about Reitman and his brother-in-law, Max Abromovich, to American tourists. In English."

"You're going to have to do better than that," Semyon said.

Artur's confidence deflated. Victor cast him a superior glance, as if Semyon had validated his criticism.

Had Artur really contributed nothing of note?

"The Jews are up to more than talking with a few tourists," Semyon said. He opened his folio and pulled out two stapled packets. He handed them to Kasparov, who asked, "What's this?"

"Information from an American contact," Semyon said. "The first is names and addresses of Jews for whom the Israelis are manufacturing family connections. The second is names and locations of Jewish political dissidents we've arrested." He poked at the paper and glared at Victor. "These are the sources our enemies are using as proof we violate human rights."

"It's too detailed to be from the conversations with tourists," Artur concluded miserably.

Even Sofia's translation for the Americans this morning only included Mendel's story and three names: Max, Irena, and Nadia Abromovich. But the packet went on for pages and pages.

"Someone is curating this information and smuggling it to the Americans and who knows who else," Kasparov said.

"Exactly," Semyon said. "And the Jews have either been outsmarting our surveillance, or we've been looking in the wrong place."

"So what do you suggest? We bring the wife in for questioning?" Kasparov asked.

"You do so love your interrogations," Semyon said.

"They're effective," Kasparov said.

"Are they?" Semyon asked. "Victor had Mendel Reitman under interrogation this whole last month. At his mercy day and night. Pumped full of your darling truth serums. Subject to every torture technique available. And what did you learn from the lowly Hebrew teacher?"

Semyon hadn't raised his voice, hadn't made any direct accusation, but the rebuke filled the air like a stink bomb. Beside Semyon, Artur stood a little straighter. Victor had aggressively attacked Artur, when his own competence was clearly in question and for real failures.

"He's not a lowly Hebrew teacher." Victor's neck turned a telltale red, making him look even more like a puffed up hawk. "He's one of the ringleaders. That's why the Americans were so eager for his release. And why they mention him by name. And he's doing exactly as I predicted. Leading us straight to his associates."

Semyon didn't contradict Victor, but he held the silence long enough to signal his doubts.

"I've got him under my thumb," Victor protested.

"Well, now we have another avenue if Reitman doesn't cooperate. Informants aren't always reliable. It's always good to have our own man inside," Kasparov said.

"But Artur's never been undercover before!"

"And yet he did admirably," Semyon said.

Kasparov tilted his head and studied Artur, seemingly reassessing him. "Tell us what else you know about Sofia Reitman."

"I'll tell you what's not in the file. She's lonely," Artur said. He flashed to an image of her locked outside the bathroom, her hand on the door that wouldn't open. He said, "Five years of separation is a long time, and the man who came back to her isn't the one who left. He's become suddenly religious. And he's distant and angry. And she knows he's keeping things from her."

"You think you can get her to open up to you?" Kasparov asked.

He remembered her tearful arrival at Ruben's and the way she had, for just an instant, burrowed into Artur's embrace for comfort.

"Yes." Lonely people were prone to unburden their secrets to *anyone* willing to listen.

"Indeed," Semyon agreed. "In a case like this, I expect seduction will work far better than torture."

"If I go back undercover, I can befriend her," Artur said.

"Befriend her?" Semyon barked out a laugh. "Sometimes you are too funny."

He hadn't been joking.

"He wasn't joking," Victor said. "He's never done this kind of thing before."

Semyon shrugged, but the gleam in his eyes belied his indifference. "Every good undercover agent has a first time."

Artur had been slow on the uptake. When understanding caught up to him, he felt as if he'd been tackled to the ground after a hard run. He was breathless with shock. "You want me to seduce Sofia Reitman?"

"Of course," Semyon said.

Artur's stomach knotted and roiled the way it had when he had spied his first dead carcass as a child, a rotting bird with broken wings.

The idea of seducing a target was all well and good when it was Lilya or another dangle on the hook.

With tremendous self-control, Artur schooled his features to make himself seem confident and intrigued.

"You're showing real aptitude for undercover work," Semyon praised. "You'll need this notch in your belt if you want to join the club. Who knows? Maybe we'll even be able to implant you in America as an illegal."

His words were laced heavily with the promise of more and greater opportunities, of a reassignment from the domestic First Directorate to foreign intelligence with the Second Directorate, all the things Maya wanted for him, for them.

But she wouldn't like this at all.

Victor regarded Artur with what seemed a newfound respect, but whether due to Semyon's clear interest in him or his own merits was impossible to tell. "So Artur will go deep inside—haha!—while I continue to work on Reitman?"

His pun pulled a smile from Semyon that seemed to please Victor greatly. "I'm counting on you both," Semyon said, giving Victor the recognition he seemed to crave, too.

"This could work. This really could work," Victor decided.

"I'm counting on you," Semyon said, addressing all of them, but Artur felt the message was for him alone. "I know you'll do whatever you have to do to catch our traitors."

CHAPTER TWENTY-SIX
SOFIA

SOFIA CHECKED HER tote bag carefully before leaving her house. The piece of clear tape she'd hooked across the top hadn't been disturbed that she could see.

That meant she'd survived another day when Mendel hadn't tampered with her things, hadn't searched her tote bag, hadn't found the lipstick-shaped camera currently stowed in the pocket.

He hadn't yet tried, not that she was aware. Maybe he wouldn't.

He had denied he'd come home to help the KGB. But so would she if that had been her aim.

She could hear him and Kolya in the throws of another disagreement as Mendel helped with homework. They seemed to be constantly at odds. Kolya seemed to regard every move his father made with sullen disapproval. Usually so quiet and polite, Kolya could be frequently heard grousing, "No, Papa. That's not how Vera does it."

"I don't care how Vera does it." Mendel's temper, always hardy, erupted. "I'm here now, and this is how I do it."

"Don't fight," she called from the hallway as she buttoned her coat.

The screaming made her uncomfortable. She'd talked to Mendel about it, but he didn't seem able to control it. Still, as unpleasant as it was, she didn't believe he'd actually hurt their son.

She didn't want to believe it.

She didn't want to believe he might betray her to the KGB, either. But her fear hadn't abated.

His hair trigger didn't prove he had sided with the KGB, but neither did it prove he hadn't, and it was wholly unfamiliar to her. Her husband always could be stubborn and pigheaded, but he had never been impulsive and easily riled.

She opened the apartment door and saw the *mezuzah* Mendel had hung once more. Without the bug, he had claimed, but she hadn't seen for herself, and she hated the persistent doubts she couldn't help but harbor.

"I'll be home at the usual time." She called out her farewell and headed to work. She might worry about them both, but she didn't hesitate to leave.

Not once had her commitment to her cause wavered, but right now it consumed her.

The elevator, constantly on the fritz, was out again. She marched resolutely down the seven flights of stairs to the ground floor. She walked out the door, past Mendel's two agents, and straight to the subway.

She was vigilant as ever, but she worried less and less about the risks as she went about her business.

She entered the subway station and headed down the stairs to catch the train to the university. She kept her tote bag close by her side as she navigated her way through the turnstile.

The Kremlin would pay for everything they'd done to Mendel, for everything they'd taken from her, for all the victims the Soviet system chewed up and spit out, for the countless lives destroyed.

One day, the Soviet government would wake up and find itself powerless to continue terrorizing and oppressing people, all of its sharp and deadly fangs removed.

She didn't have to wait long for the train. She found an empty row and sat with her bag in her lap.

Maybe the KGB was closing in on her. Maybe Mendel was helping them. The heightened sense of threat only spurred her, giving way to a heady anticipation. She would do as much damage as she possibly could before the noose tightened around her neck.

She looked around her at the people, but didn't notice anyone out of the ordinary, anyone watching her too long. All clear, for now.

She felt powerless in so many ways, but here was a way to strike back.

When she finally arrived at work and stopped at the guard desk, Grisha spent more time than usual inspecting her things. He stared too long at her chest. She was uncomfortable around him. She wanted to speed along to her work—and her revenge—but waited, hands held loosely at her side, her posture and bearing deceptively demure and patient.

Grisha's hand curled around the pocket to her work pants, and her breath caught.

He dug out the Tropel she'd hidden there and held the silver tube up to the light. "What's this?"

"Lipstick," she said through the sudden dryness in her mouth. Her heart pounded wildly. If Grisha opened the tube, he would know there was no lipstick inside.

"I've never seen you wearing lipstick." His beady eyes fixed on her lips, and her skin crawled.

"No," she agreed. "But things are different now. My husband's come home."

Grisha fingered the tube, rolled it thoughtfully in his hand. She couldn't tell what he was thinking, but she didn't like the speculative look in his eyes.

"I heard about that," he said cryptically.

What had he heard? From whom?

"You're surprised I know this." He lifted his chin as if she had challenged his pride. "You think I'm only a lowly night guard."

"I don't think anything. I clean toilets," she said. She had never had such a long conversation with one of the security guards, and his attention made her uneasy.

"Do you know what they do here?" he asked slyly, and she couldn't help feeling he was trying to bait her.

"I know what they do in the bathroom, and it's the same as in any other," she said with a nonchalant shrug.

"This is a high security building," Grisha boasted. He still held her camera, and she had a stab of fear that he knew exactly what information was contained upstairs and what he held in his hand. "Full of military secrets."

"Military secrets?" She pretended to be surprised.

He smiled wolfishly. "I assure you that they wouldn't send a lowly night guard to watch over this place."

"Oh." She didn't have to pretend this time. She hadn't given much thought to the guards who had worked here, other than inventing ways to avoid being caught by them.

Was he telling her he was with the KGB? Or was this an attempt to exaggerate his own importance and impress her?

She considered the way he struggled each night to find the right keys. If he was a KGB agent, he couldn't be a very good one, she decided.

Maybe she had nothing to worry about. Nothing more than usual, anyway. Maybe this was all bravado.

He cupped her hand with his moist palm and gave her back the lipstick tube. The metal was warm from his touch. He seemed to stare intently into her face.

He was new, and he seemed to have a stronger interest in her than the other guards had. Was he flirting, or was he trying to intimidate her?

She closed her fingers tightly around the Tropel.

"I should get to work," she said.

He released her hand, and she headed to the supply closet to change. She locked the door behind her and leaned against it, breathing deeply. That was close!

She changed her clothes and gathered her supplies, pretending for Grisha, and perhaps for herself, that this was a normal night.

Grisha led her, like usual, to the office suite upstairs, but he marched down the hall with uncustomary swagger. He stopped in front of the door to the laboratory suite and wave his hand with a flourish.

"What's this?" Sofia asked, trying to swallow back her alarm. The lock had been replaced with an electronic keypad, an oversized gadget with a number pad and blinking lights.

"Increase in security," he said. "I told you this was an important place."

"I've worked here for years," she said. "How come they're only becoming concerned with security now? Did something change?"

"That's classified information," Grisha said after a long hesitation and puffed out his chest.

She hoped he had bluffed his answer and didn't know anymore than she did.

He covered over the buttons on the keypad with one hand while he entered the code. His thick lips moved as he punched in the numbers. She didn't catch all of them, but she expected that if she paid attention, she might be able to decipher it after a few more nights.

Inside the office suite, there was a new, large desk. "See this?" Grisha said. "Now they make everyone sign in and out during the day."

During the day. Maybe they were increasing security overall, and this didn't have any direct connection to specific suspicions about her.

Grisha lumbered to the second set of doors. They also had a keypad. He crouched over this one too, again shielding his fingers from her view.

He was frustratingly conscientious. Did he think someone was watching them? Or was he making a show of his special knowledge to impress her?

Sofia glanced around for cameras. She didn't see any obvious signs, any new fixtures or additions to the ceiling or the walls, but that didn't mean they weren't there.

Did the new security precautions extend into the hallway? Would there be cameras? What about the locks on the doors? What if she could no longer access the office?

Once they were through the inside door and into the hallway of offices, she noticed that none of the doors had the clunky electronic keypads.

What she couldn't tell from her quick, cursory inspection as she shuttled down the hall with the cleaning supplies was whether the locks had been changed or any other precautions taken.

She unloaded her supplies by the doorway and deliberately fumbled for her own keys. She dropped them on the floor and took the time as she retrieved them to look around for cameras. Unlike the keypad and the new guard desk, there was nothing obvious.

She pretended to search her keychain, the same way Grisha usually did. Eager to test her keys on the locks in Max's office, she hoped Grisha would leave before she unlocked the bathroom.

He didn't.

He lingered, watching, making her increasingly nervous and uncomfortable. Did he suspect her? Or was he waiting for her to give him a sign of approval.

After his groping last week, she didn't dare encourage him.

She propped the door open with her hip and took most of the cleaning supplies in with her, but not all of them.

She waited a long moment, ear pressed to the door, and listened. She heard Grisha's heavy footsteps, heard the door open and shut.

But tonight, she decided she would wait.

She arranged her cleaning supplies and then carefully crept back to the door and eased it open. She peered into the hallway.

"What are you doing?" Grisha demanded.

She startled and gave a little shriek. Yet somehow she wasn't completely surprised to find him lurking in the shadows. "Oh!" She put her hand to her heart. "You scared me."

"Why aren't you in the bathroom?"

She pointed to the bottle of bleach she'd deliberately left on the floor beside the door. She had gotten adept at leaving trails of plausible excuses for most of her activities. "I needed the rest of my supplies."

"I see," he said, but she suspected he hadn't noticed the bleach by the door. He leaned against the wall and watched her go back inside.

What was he still doing out there? Why hadn't he left? What was he expecting her to do?

She turned on the faucet and filled the bucket with water and bleach. She went through the motions of mopping and scrubbing the bathroom, all the while considering her next move and listening for sounds of Grisha's movements.

Before Grisha, no one had ever questioned Sofia or even watched her that closely. No one had paid any mind to the lowly woman who scrubbed the bathrooms before. In the past, the guards had left her to herself.

Did someone now suspect her?

She heard the hallway door close once more, but she couldn't be sure Grisha had actually left. She bided her time and did a perfunctory cleaning, left the bucket and mop in one of the stalls, and tiptoed back to the door. She eased it open and peered out into the hallway. The lights were off, and there was no sign of Grisha now.

She did a second quick check of the hallway and listened hard for any sounds from the security area in the office suite. Nothing.

The hall was so quiet that she could hear the sound of her own heartbeat. She swallowed, and the sound seemed to be magnified in the stillness.

She ached to rush into the laboratory, steal the file, and continue with the painstaking work of photographing the pages.

But she feared being discovered.

CHAPTER TWENTY-SEVEN
ARTUR

"WHAT CAN YOU tell me about Yosef Koslovsky?" Artur asked his father. He needed as many details as he could get if he was going to go deep undercover.

"Why on earth would you want to know about him?" Artur's mother asked. They sat at the dining room table, under an imported chandelier of Austrian crystal, and ate on the fine, gold-rimmed china. Maya had insisted on treating his rare appearance for dinner like a special occasion.

"I have an assignment," he said. "I'm going undercover."

"Undercover? Since when do you go undercover?" his mother asked uneasily.

"That's not your usual job," his father added. Yana and Mikhail Gregorovich had never been completely comfortable with Artur's choice to have a career in the KGB.

"Artur's moving up in the ranks," Maya said with a barbed smile. His ambitions had always been a source of tension between them and his parents.

He wasn't sure how pleased Maya herself would be about if she knew what "moving up in the ranks" seemed to entail.

Yana abruptly turned to Aleksei, avoiding the minefield around Artur's career. They boy had eaten the fried potatoes on his plate and nothing else. "Sweetheart, have a little soup," she suggested.

"No." Aleksei turned his nose up at the rich, thick vegetable soup Artur's mother had lovingly prepared, a food staple that had been one of Aleksei's favorites until recently.

"Then some asparagus? I'll cut it for you." Yana reached over and began to slice the tender spears of asparagus, the first of the season.

"No," he said. "I only want potatoes."

"You can't eat just potatoes," she said. "You need to grow up big and strong, like your papa. You need to eat your vegetables and the *kutletka*."

"No," he said.

There was a miniscule amount of food on the boy's plate, two spears of asparagus and half of an untouched chicken cutlet.

"If you don't eat your dinner, you won't get to have any of the cake I made," she wheedled.

"I want cake," Aleksei said.

"Good. Then eat up." She gestured with her fork to the food on his plate.

"No," he said petulantly. "I just want cake."

"Not until you finish," she said calmly, but Aleksei rolled out of his chair as if she had struck him.

His face turned bright red, and the relative peace of their dinner, possibly Artur's last at home for a long while, shattered. Aleksei let loose a blood-curling shriek. He screamed. He cried. He pounded the floor with his fists and feet.

Artur threw down his napkin and rose from his chair. "Stop it. This instant."

His child paid him no heed, rolling on the ground as if he'd been overtaken by a demon spirit.

"If you don't stop right now, you won't eat anything else tonight," Artur threatened.

Aleksei only wailed harder. Artur rounded the table, prepared to haul the boy to his room and leave him there until peace was restored.

"Aleksei, honey, stop." Maya also rose. "You can have whatever you want. Come sit in Mama's lap."

"Let him be," Artur's mother said over the tantrum. "You can't appease him every time he starts to cry."

"Don't tell me how to raise my own child," Maya said. In response, Yana pursed her lips but didn't say another word.

Maya pulled the shrieking child into her lap, and he almost instantly settled. She gave them all a smug look, saying, "I'm his mother. I know what he needs."

She proceeded to feed Aleksei the potatoes on her plate and nothing else. Artur knew he should intervene, but guilt kept him silent.

His parents had moved a year ago to Moscow. At the time, Maya and Artur had been expecting a second child. When tragedy struck, his parents had stayed to help, moving into one of the bedrooms in the spacious apartment. While Maya wasn't thrilled to have her mother-in-law under the same roof, even she couldn't deny they needed the help. She'd lost two more pregnancies since then, and Artur was hardly ever home.

It was only going to get worse now. He was going undercover. He might not be home for weeks or even months. He was going to seduce a target, to sleep with another woman.

Maya had the right to feel the queen in her own domain.

His mother looked like she would protest, but his father put his hand on her shoulder to stay her.

His father, Mikhail, a natural appeaser, returned to their original discussion as if nothing had happened. "Why do you want to know about Yosef?"

"Funny story," Artur said. "I didn't expect to engage with our target directly, but he didn't respond to the woman I sent in." He didn't specify what Lilya was supposed to do with Edik, but the adults at the table all caught the gist. "When I tried to salvage the situation, we ended up talking. I pretended I was Jewish, and we had instant rapport. But

I hadn't prepared for it, and when he asked me my name, I gave him the only Jewish name I could think of."

"You're pretending to be Yosef Koslovsky?" Yana put down her fork, as if she'd lost her appetite.

"Yes," he said. "Newly arrived from Leningrad. Ready to be their partner in crime."

"What crime?" Yana asked. "Is it dangerous? Could you be hurt?"

"No, no. Don't worry," Artur said. "I have to stop my targets from spreading lies to foreigners about the plight of the Jews."

"Are you sure they're lies?" Mikhail asked.

Maya snorted. "Of course they're lies. Do you think the KGB would send a high status agent undercover if they weren't our enemies?"

"Enemies change with the wind," Yana said quietly. "With the regime."

Artur's father nodded his agreement. "When Chernenko dies, the new leader might change his mind and let the Jews leave."

"Never tell me you believe their propaganda about human rights violations," Maya said.

"You're too young to remember life under Stalin," Mikhail said. "The Leningrad case. We watched friends, Party members, tried and executed. The city's leaders exiled. And then, years later, Khrushchev came along and renounced it all."

"Well, right now, these Jews are traitors, and that's all that matters," Maya said. She petted Aleksei's head. He leaned against her, getting drowsy.

"They're people!" Yana protested, with a passion at odds with her usually calm and patient demeanor. "With dreams. And people that they love."

She got up from the table. The dishes and cutlery clattered and clinked as she cleared away the dishes. She didn't look at Artur, and he sensed this assignment unsettled her in a very deep way.

"Since when is Yana a friend to the Jews?" Maya asked.

"You don't know the story," his father said. "This is sensitive for her. Yosef Koslovsky was a very important man in her life."

"In *her* life?" Artur asked. "But I thought he was your friend." His father had often reminisced about Yosef. Artur had seen the photograph of them standing arm in arm, smiling in their military uniforms.

"He was important to both of us," his father said. "It's how your mother and I met. Yosef was my best friend in the Army, like a brother to me. And your mother was madly in love with him."

"Mama was in love with Koslovsky? With a Jew?" Artur could scarcely believe it. "You're joking," Artur accused. "She's never talked about him."

"They were engaged," his father said, his voice serious and steady.

His mother had planned to marry a Jew? A Jew!

The room seemed to be spinning. Artur closed his eyes and waited for the world to right itself. But when he opened them again, he still felt dizzy.

"How did you make her come to her senses?" Maya asked.

"I didn't," his father said. "Yosef died."

Artur lifted his glass with a shaking hand and choked back a large gulp of water. His parents had a strong, stable relationship. Artur had never doubted they loved each other deeply. He had never suspected his father might have been his mother's second choice.

"What can you tell me about the—about Yosef?" Artur caught himself at the last moment and called Koslovsky by his name.

Yana returned to the table. She poured tea and then cradled a cup in her hands. "Yosef was *like you*," she said, her words full of emphasis. "Confident. Brave. Devoted."

"A good man. A good friend," his father added. They exchanged another weighted glance, and Artur sensed his parents had years of secrets. Secrets they had never shared with him. Secrets he had never even suspected were there.

It was too much to take in all at once. Artur glanced over at Maya. Aleksei had fallen asleep in her arms. "Let's put him to bed," he said.

He got up from the table and scooped his son into his arms. Warm and pliant, the boy nuzzled into him in a way he never did when awake. Artur carried him to bed, and Maya joined him. Together, they undressed Aleksei and tucked him into bed.

"I should have said good-bye to him," Artur said. "I don't know when I'm going to be home again."

"I'll explain things to him. I'll tell him about the important job you're doing. About how his father's a hero," she whispered, turning to him. She cupped his cheek with a soft hand, and kissed him sweetly, seductively on the mouth.

"Don't let your parents get into your head," she said. "They don't understand what it is to have real ambition."

He couldn't disagree. After a long career in the military, Mikhail Gregorovich was still only a major, an accomplishment, but one well below his potential, and he didn't seem interested in advancement. On the few occasions they'd discussed the matter, his father had never quite understood Artur's drive and was prone to question his choices, although never outright. Just like he had at dinner, suggesting Artur question the rightness of his assignment.

"You know you're doing the right thing. This is a matter of national security. You can't afford to be soft-hearted. To have doubts."

"I know," he said. Intellectually, he knew carrying out this assignment was a job and nothing more.

He couldn't afford to think of Sofia Reitman as a person. There was no room for the well of sympathy that could too easily flow in her direction, saddled as she was with Edik and Mendel. Or for the guilt he felt for Maya's sake.

Artur was already physically attracted to Sofia. Anything more would give the woman far too much power. He had to remember she was a target, a job.

"The sooner I can deal with her, the sooner I can come home to you," he said.

"Her?" Maya asked.

"Them," he whispered. "I meant them." He kissed Maya before she could question him further, not wanting to sully her with his concerns, with the underhanded methods his job required.

He backed Maya out of their son's room, down the hall, and into their own bedroom.

He kissed her hard and long, intending to take enough to last him through this next phase of assignment, enough to inoculate him against any feelings for Sofia and successfully complete his assignment, enough to remember all that he might lose if he failed.

CHAPTER TWENTY-EIGHT
VERA

VERA MET KOLYA by his cubby when school let out for the day. He sat on the floor, his arms wrapped around his knees, curled up in a little ball. Her heart beat fast. She hurried toward him.

"What's wrong?" She had a sinking feeling she knew. Lively and charismatic, Kolya usually had a small ring of friends gathered around him, but now the children from his class gave him a wide berth, as if he had the plague.

And he did. The same one she did. The same one that made her a pariah day after day, year after year.

He didn't answer, and she crouched beside him. "Were the kids mean to you?"

"The teacher," he said.

She hugged her schoolbooks to her chest with one arm and put her other hand on his shoulder. "Don't let it get inside you," she whispered, even though she had never succeeded in putting that advice to use.

"I didn't," he said, and Vera wondered if she were the only one in her family who didn't have a tough shell.

"I'm just thinking," Kolya said. Elementary school children buzzed around them, pulling on coats and woolen hands and stuffing their hands into mittens. Kolya made no move to gather his own things. Yesterday Vera had cajoled him and rushed him out the door, but she didn't have the heart to hurry him along today. Petya could wait.

"Thinking what?" she asked.

"How it's not fair," he said. "My teacher can be as mean as she wants, and I'm not supposed to talk back."

"Did you?"

He held up the back of his hand for her to see. His knuckles were red. "She hit my hand with the ruler," Kolya said. "To teach me a lesson."

"Does it hurt?"

"No," he said, but he winced when he flexed his fingers. In him, she could see the model of what her family wanted her to be, the mark from which she would forever fall short. Resilience came so naturally to him, and she was so, so deficient.

"But I'm so mad," Kolya said.

"I know," Vera said. Having Kolya with her at school this past year had eased some of her loneliness. She appreciated not having to sit or stand all alone and having someone to talk to, even if he was only seven. But she hated that he was now suffering, too. She had only a few months of school left, but he faced several more years of the same torture she had endured.

"Is my father really a criminal?" Kolya asked.

"Well, that depends," Vera said. She put down her books and sat beside him on the cold, hard floor. She tucked her skirt around her legs and leaned toward him.

She spoke softly, even though the hall quickly emptied of any stragglers as everyone left to catch the buses and return home. "He was arrested for a crime. He didn't do it, but the court decided that he did. And he went to prison."

"For five years," Kolya supplied. He pressed his lips together, but she couldn't tell whether he was angry his father had been sent away or that he had returned.

"Yes, and that's a big punishment. So people think he's guilty."

"But it wasn't fair," Kolya said.

"No, it wasn't," she agreed.

"He didn't do anything."

"He taught Hebrew," she said. "And the government didn't like that."

"The government hates us," Kolya said, parroting Vera's father.

"Shhh." She put her finger to his lips and whispered, "Never say that here. We don't talk about the government. Or we'll get in trouble."

He nodded, showing he understood. "When I grow up, I'm going to make things fair."

"How are you going to do that?" she almost asked him, but he was too young to be faced with the impossibility, and so she nodded instead, leaving him to his dreams.

"How are you going to do that?" a male voice asked. Vera looked up quickly. She hadn't noticed Gennady's arrival.

Was he taunting Kolya? She put her arm around the boy to shield him.

Kolya shrugged away from her arm and jumped to his feet. "I don't know yet," Kolya said. Although a few feet shorter than Gennady, Kolya faced him, shoulders squared, with a confidence she wasn't sure she'd ever felt. "But I'm going to do it."

Gennady looked him over, and she scrambled to her feet, ready to intervene. She wasn't going to let him say something cruel and grind Kolya down into a pulp.

"You're small, still," Gennady said.

"Hey!" she said.

"It's the truth," he said. "You're not big enough and strong enough yet to fight with your fists. Are you a good student?"

"Yes," Kolya said without hesitation.

"Smart like your aunt," Gennady said, and she scowled at him. "Smart and tough," he amended. "That's good. You can learn to fight with your head," he said. "Maybe you'll be a lawyer or a judge. And work in the courts. Make sure their decisions are fair."

How cruel of him, she thought, to suggest something so impossible. He might as well have encouraged Kolya to become a prizefighter.

Stuck in the Soviet Union, Kolya faced the same miserable prospects she did. He wouldn't be heading for college, either. Plus he would have to go to the military. And then he might never come home. Like cousin David, Edik's brother.

"Maybe," Kolya said with a shrug. "We'll see." But he had the look of intense concentration he often got when he was puzzling and planning.

Vera bit her tongue and kept her dark thoughts to herself. Kolya didn't need to hear them, not now.

"Why are you here?" Her question was blunt and rude, and she didn't care. Gennady had no worries for his future. He was already a student at Moscow State University, and as the son of a general, his fast promotion through the military ranks was assured. He would never have to fear that his fellow soldiers might decide to shoot him.

"I was waiting for you at the bus stop, but everyone else came out, and you didn't. I got worried."

"Worried I'm not coming to help Petya," she said. She crossed her arms. "I said I would."

"Worried about you," he said, and she didn't dare believe him. What was his game?

"Nothing to worry about. I'll come after I take Kolya home. You don't need to bother about me."

"You're no bother, Vera." He smiled at her, the kind of smile she had fantasies about, as if he cared.

She could hardly stand to be in Gennady's presence now. Why couldn't that kiss have been real for him? It had been real for her. Perfect, until the ridicule had started.

She wanted to scream. She wanted to pound her fists against his chest. It was all so, so unfair. The way all good things were just out of reach. The way her peers and teachers sought ways to hurt her and never suffered the consequence. And now they would do the same to Kolya.

"Maybe you bother me," she said, surprising herself with her own strength. Gennady made her so angry! She didn't want him anywhere near her. Anywhere near Kolya.

"You'll hardly know I'm here," Gennady said.

"You could just go away, and then we won't have to pretend." Vera crossed her arms and pursed her lips.

"What fun would that be?" He flashed that soft smile at her again, his blue eyes twinkling, as if he enjoyed sparring with her. Rankled, she turned away.

"Come on Kolya. We need to go," she said. Kolya didn't protest. He gathered his coat. Vera picked up her bag and school books, and headed toward the door, leaving Gennady behind. But his legs were long, and he quickly caught up to her.

"Let me carry your books," he said, as if he were her boyfriend.

"No." She didn't dare indulge that daydream again. She'd come too close and been burned too badly. She hugged her books to her chest. "You said I wouldn't know you were here."

"So I did," he said with a chuckle. He let her walk ahead of him and fell into step behind her, with Kolya.

No one was at the bus stop when they arrived. "I'll meet you two here every day. You'll wait for me," Gennady instructed.

"No," she said, but he raised his hand, silencing her.

"You've made your feelings clear," he said. "But this isn't a game. You're traveling all over the city as a favor to my family. I'm going to make sure you get back and forth safely."

"I go around the city all the time by myself," she said. "I can handle myself."

"I'm sure you can," he said, irritatingly agreeable.

What was his game? Why couldn't he leave her be? "But now you have me to keep you safe."

"Moscow isn't nearly as dangerous as you seem to think."

"Don't be stupid," he said. "It's not smart for you to walk home by yourself after dark. A young woman. Alone." He turned to Kolya. "What do you think, Kolya? Does that sound smart to you?"

"No." Kolya said.

"Your mother does it. Every night," Vera said. "She comes home from work when you're asleep."

"Because she has to. Because there's no one to take care of her," he said softly, revealing worries she hadn't known he had. "But you have Gennady."

"I told you you were smart," Gennady praised him, and Kolya seemed to stand a little taller. "Can we make a deal? Will you make sure she waits for me?" He stuck out his hand for Kolya to shake.

"Deal." Kolya grasped Gennady's hand and shook once.

"Nice grip," Gennady said, admiringly. She searched him for any signs of mockery but saw none.

When Kolya smiled for the first time in a long while and Gennady smiled back, she wished it were just a little easier to continue hating him.

CHAPTER TWENTY-NINE
ARTUR

"COME ON, EDIK," Artur wheedled. "You should go."

"Ugh," Edik moaned. He threw his arm over his face to block out the light. "Leave me alone."

"You don't want to miss one of your last chances to say good-bye to everyone before you leave for Israel."

Today was Saturday, the Jewish sabbath. While most of Moscow's Jews did not observe any religious rituals related to the weekly holy day, they reportedly gathered in great numbers outside the Moscow Choral Synagogue on Archipova Street on Saturday afternoons. Artur had great hope that Edik would introduce him around at this large gathering and help him insinuate himself into the Jewish community.

"No one cares. They're glad I'm leaving," Edik whined. "They all think I'm a useless failure."

"That's not true," Artur said, playing the loyal friend. "Don't let what Mendel said get to you. He was just jealous of how much time you spent with Sofia when he was locked up."

Mendel's harsh words seemed to have decimated Edik. He hadn't wanted to leave his room, let alone socialize. Much to the detriment of Artur's investigation, Edik had taken to his bed.

"No," Edik said. "No, he was right. I'm an overgrown child," he repeated Mendel's insult with cloying self-pity. "I should have been a man for her. Taken care of her." He looked plaintively at Artur."

Artur threw his head back and blew out a frustrated breath. He was quickly losing patience. Edik's moping threatened to derail his case, and he couldn't go back tainted with the stink of failure. He needed Edik to fall in line with his plans and introduce him around.

"If you don't get up out of that bed, I'll call Sofia over here to help me. She didn't agree with what Mendel said, but she could change her mind if she sees the sorry state you're in now."

"You wouldn't do that to me," Edik said.

"Watch me." Artur turned on his heel and stomped to the phone in the next room. He lifted the receiver and paused when he heard the dial tone. He didn't actually know Sofia's number. "How long has it been since you showered?" Artur called. "I want to let her know what to expect."

Edik came flying out of the room and grabbed his arm. "Don't!"

"Then go get showered and let's go," Artur said.

"Fine," Edik mumbled. He shuffled to the bathroom and slammed the door.

"You'll thank me for this," Artur called after him, but he had to concede that Mendel's criticism had been spot on. Edik did behave like an overgrown child.

When he heard the shower running, Artur snooped around Edik's room. He hadn't observed the passing of any goods the other morning, but he had a strong hunch that the American visitors typically smuggled the family objects of high worth.

He surmised there must be a hiding place somewhere in the apartment. He had managed to check the kitchen and the front hall, but he hadn't found a stash of cigarette cartons or anything else of interest.

Nothing of interest under the bed or in the drawers. The narrow closet yielded nothing unexpected either.

Think!

Then he noticed the scuff in the parquet floor next to the dresser, as if that piece of furniture had been moved frequently. He grabbed the corner of the dresser and dragged it along the scratch until the foot met the rug in the center of the room. Behind the dresser, he found a short door with a latch. He crouched down, unhooked the latch, and eased the door open.

Inside was dark. He peered into the shadows. Jackpot!

The door opened on a full-sized walk-in closet that spanned the length of the room. He had to enter on his hands and knees, but once he'd crawled inside, he could stand.

A stockpile of American cigarette cartons lined the back wall from floor to ceiling. Boxes upon boxes of Marlboros and Virigina Slims. Next to those, he found a bookcase with shelves heavy with cameras, rolls of unused film, batteries, tape casettes and other items that could intermittently be found in Russian stores, but more frequently were out of stock. Such luxury items carried a premium on the black market.

The government had moved to curtail the financial support the Jews were enjoying from abroad. The law now required that recipients of packages pay the hefty Customs taxes before they could receive their goods. Most people couldn't afford the taxes up front before turning a profit on sales, and so the shipments had dropped off sharply.

Yet Edik, simple childlike Edik, had a secret closet full of western goods that could only have been smuggled into the country.

Artur didn't have time to explore further. He'd solved the mystery of where Edik had gotten his cash, at least. Most likely, the guests who visited the apartment smuggled in the goods, and their sale kept the Jew bastards flush with money.

He ducked out of the closet, just as the water from the shower shut off. He hurried to shut the door and slide the dresser back into place and then skidded out of Edik's room. He threw himself onto the sofa in the living room, crossed one leg over his knee, and managed, he hoped, to look like he'd been sitting there, perhaps dozing off, through the duration of Edik's shower.

Mercifully, Edik returned to his room and got dressed without any further protest, and in a few more minutes, they were on their way.

Although sober, Edik moved at lumbering pace. He plodded beside Artur, head down, limbs heavy, as if he were an exhausted pack mule climbing a mountain with an untenable load on his back, instead of a healthy and relatively young man on his way to a social gathering.

Artur refused to chance that Edik might lose steam before they could reach his chosen destination. He needed to gain introductions to as many of Edik's associates as possible before Edik left. He had a limited window to make the most of the gathering on Archipova Street, which promised a windfall of opportunity to make himself known. He hailed a taxi.

"Do you think we'll meet any pretty girls today?" Artur asked.

"None prettier than Sofia," Edik said glumly, and Artur abandoned his weak attempt to make conversation. They passed the rest of the short ride to the synagogue in sullen silence, and Artur found their arrival a relief.

Up ahead, he saw a large butter-yellow building with white columns. A large white dome with a gold six-pointed star was affixed to the steeple, instead of a cross.

"That's it. There," Edik told the driver, who dropped them at the end of the block.

"Is it always so crowded?" Artur asked. He'd read reports of the weekly gatherings, but he hadn't anticipated this throng of Jews.

"On Saturday, yes," Edik said.

"It looks like everyone's out."

He wasn't sure he had realized there were so many Jews in Moscow. Or at least so many who would identify themselves in public.

The KGB had arrested a score of Jewish activists and Hebrew teachers and harassed and intimidated others. They had installed obvious surveillance and assigned escorts to likely troublemakers.

Yet, here the Jews were, talking and laughing, matchmaking, trading books, passing money, conducting all manner of business, boisterous and unabashed.

The presence of the KGB agents standing at the fringe of the crowd and monitoring their activities didn't sober them. Rather, these Jews seemed to be thumbing their noses at the Kremlin, defiantly pursuing their agenda, putting his country in danger.

Artur hated all of them.

CHAPTER THIRTY
ARTUR

"**I** SEE MENDEL," EDIK said to Artur. Edik pointed to the lanky man standing on the synagogue steps, surrounded by a knot of loud, gesticulating Jews. Five years in prison had left Mendel slightly bent and sallow, but obviously not defeated. By rights, he should have been lying low and spending time with his wife and child, not playing to an audience from the synagogue steps. Not blatantly repeating the crimes they'd stopped him for in the past.

Unless Victor had put him up to it.

Artur had precious few details about Victor's side of the investigation.

Artur searched the crowd for Sofia but didn't spot her. His reports said she was a regular at these gatherings outside the synagogue. She, at least, had more sense than her husband, keeping a lower profile.

Where was she now?

Edik tugged on his sleeve and pulled him into the crowd. He headed toward the steps. "Ilya," he called out, and a portly man turned in their direction.

Artur recognized his fleshy face. Ilya Soifer, Edik's uncle, Sofia and Vera's father. The man had a voluminous file. He'd had a KGB tail for the past several years.

"Uncle Ilya, I'd like to introduce you to my friend, Yosef Koslovksy," Edik said.

"Koslovsky," Ilya repeated and rubbed at his double chin. He cocked his head and regarded Artur with a hint of suspicion that made him wonder if he'd done something to give himself away. "I don't know that family. Where are you from?"

"Leningrad," Artur said. He'd created a truth-tinged legend around his cover. Artur had indeed grown up in Leningrad. "I just arrived in Moscow."

"Well, welcome to Moscow," Ilya said, but unlike his words, his gaze stayed sharp and slightly suspicious. Unlike Edik, Ilya wouldn't easily extend his trust to an outsider.

Mendel's voice rose over the hubbub. "You claim you are Jews," Mendel said.

"No, the Russians insist we're Jews," someone shouted back. "They stamp it on our passports and hold it against us."

Catching the trail of the propaganda he'd been sent to stop, Artur marked the speaker's face in his memory. He would discover his identity, perhaps with the help of the other agents lined up on Archipova Street, and track him down later.

"Judaism is more than a nationality," Mendel said. "Jews are the Chosen People. Identified and chosen, not by the Soviets, but by God. The God of our ancestors. And we have an obligation to do as God commands. To live as God commands. So that we will be blessed and not cursed."

A few onlookers seemed to be engaged with Mendel, but most of the crowd ignored the would-be prophet in their midst. Mendel raised his voice to carry above the animated chatter. "When we embrace God's teaching, no matter where we are—in Moscow, in the holy city of Jerusalem, even in the gulag—we will be truly free."

"How come the KGB agents aren't stopping him?" Artur asked. "Wasn't he arrested for teaching?"

"He was arrested for teaching Hebrew," Ilya said. "But now he's preaching."

"Isn't that the same thing?"

"Not according to Mendel. Hebrew is the language of the Jews and Israel. It's vocabulary and conversation. But this is different. This is religion. Mendel says he found God in the labor camp, and now he's spouting nonsense about rules and rituals," Ilya said with disdain, as if Mendel had contracted a nasty, infectious disease. Artur shuddered with shared sentiment. "I guess five years in prison with nothing but a book of psalms for company will do that to a man."

"How come he's not inside the synagogue then?" Artur asked.

"No one goes inside," Edik said. "Except the synagogue elders and the rabbi."

"He was there earlier, too," Ilya said. "The old men finished their mumbling in there about ten minutes ago."

"But isn't he afraid of the KGB?" Artur asked. "He just got back from prison, isn't he worried they'll arrest him again?"

"He insists they've never bothered with the religious zealots." Ilya shrugged. "Maybe he's right. Maybe they don't mind if the Jews have a little opiate of the people, eh? Maybe they think we'll quiet down if they let us observe our holidays and eat special food. And then the new guy—Chernenko—can pull the strings of his puppet rabbi, and the man will say the Jews have it good in Moscow. No problem here."

Ilya's analysis was a bit too piercing. The man was shrewd and outspoken and, obviously, a dangerous radical. He already had a detail of two KGB agents assigned to him, but Artur would put in a request to have that number increased. Odds were good Ilya himself was one of the traitors he hunted.

"But what do I know?" Ilya said as if he perceived the shadows of Artur's gathering suspicions and sought to disperse them.

"They also could be superstitious, like all good Russians," the bright-eyed Jewess beside Ilya said. Artur also recognized her from the file, Ilya's wife, Renata. "And they don't want to mess with anything mystical."

Was that how these Jews saw the KGB—as backward and

superstitious? Did Mendel actually think he could get away teaching Hebrew again if he said he was teaching religion instead?

"He does look like a mystic, doesn't he—with that ugly beard and big black skullcap? A modern day Rasputin. Poor Sofia," she clucked.

Poor Sofia. Any dissatisfaction Sofia felt over her husband's religious awakening was bound to help Artur's bid to seduce her.

"He could be the rabbi's agent." Edik offered an unexpected insight. "After all, he installed those listening devices on the rabbi's say-so."

"What listening devices?" Ilya asked sharply.

"In the—what do you call them?—things that go up on the doors," Edik said.

"*Mezuzot?*" Ilya supplied.

"Yes. I think that's what they're called. Mendel put up three of them that the rabbi gave him, and every one had a bug inside."

"Ah, that must be what Kolya was talking about. He was going on and on about bugs the other day," Renata said. "We thought he meant a different kind."

"Do you think Mendel knew they were in there?" Edik asked.

They all shrugged, not knowing, but Artur noticed that none of them jumped to Mendel's defense.

Perhaps Victor and the rabbi were pulling Mendel's strings, doing exactly as Ilya had suggested, and trying to shunt the community's rebellious tendencies into less dangerous directions.

Ilya and Renata moved on, leaving Artur alone once again with Edik, whose avid gaze remained fixed on the synagogue steps, where Mendel continued to wax on about God and Jewish heritage. Artur followed his line of sight, straight to Sofia. Of course.

She stood at the fringe of the crowd near the steps. Artur hadn't noticed her at first, hiding as she was in plain sight. Her long, curly black hair was tucked up in a wool hat, and she wore a bulky coat that easily lent the appearance of an additional twenty pounds to her slight frame. Despite what seemed a brilliant disguise, he now recognized her bold ethnic features, almond-shaped eyes, full lips, and a long nose.

He shouldn't have found Sofia attractive, especially now with her frumpy, shapeless coat and the bemused frown that wrinkled her forehead as her husband's speech increased in intensity and conviction.

As if feeling Artur's eyes on her, she turned and glanced in his direction. She started walking toward him, and once again he was captivated.

He loved his wife. He had never once considered having an affair. But now he imagined what it would be like to kiss her, to undress her, to take her to bed. His thought flowed freely in directions he wouldn't have let himself contemplate before, now that he knew he had to seduce her.

Sofia walked past him and embraced Edik. "Edik, you came."

She gave Artur a cursory acknowledgment, enough to be polite, but not overly friendly. If she felt the same atraction he did, she didn't show any sign.

She focused on Edik. "I'm glad to see you up and about. Are you feeling better?"

Edik's face flushed a deep red. He stammered an unintelligible response. She gave him an understanding smile, and an answering smile bloomed on Edik's face, as if all was once again right with his world.

"How are the preparations coming?" she asked. "You must have a lot to do to get ready to leave. Let me know if you need any help."

Edik shifted his eyes toward Mendel, as if seeking permission that would never be granted, and then back to Sofia. "I don't. I won't."

In the past, Edik would undoubtedly have leaned on Sofia to make arrangements for him. Whether or not Edik could handle the preparations on his own, he would likely have embraced the excuse to spend time with her. He might even have manufactured more tasks for her to do on his behalf. But Mendel's tirade the other day had suitably shamed him.

"I'm heading home," she said. "I'll see you later." She started to walk away.

"Wait!" Edik said. "What about Mendel?"

"He'll catch up with me when he's ready," she said. Her smile was brittle. Artur could almost taste her discontent with her husband, and it made his mouth water.

"But you shouldn't walk alone," Edik said.

"Edik, I know Mendel said all of those things about my needing protection, but trust me, I'm fine. I go all over the city by myself. And have for years," she said. "Besides, I have my pepper spray if anyone gives me trouble."

"I'll walk with you," Edik insisted and hustled to her side, completely forgetting Artur.

No matter; Artur fell in step behind them as if he'd been invited along. He wondered when he would have the opportunity to be alone with her and make a move. He considered how he might arrange to meet her without Mendel and Edik.

A block beyond the gathering at the synagogue, Artur noticed four youths milling on the street corner. Rangy teenagers, tall but not yet filled out, they passed a cigarette back and forth between them.

His training kept him alert to them, but he didn't register any threat, even when one of the boys made a shrill whistle and called out, "Look, *tovarishi*, here come the dirty Jews."

Then suddenly he realized they were talking about him.

CHAPTER THIRTY-ONE
SOFIA

S OFIA STUMBLED AS Edik pushed her in front of him. Likely, he meant to shield her from the teenagers trailing behind them. They catcalled insults and hurled empty threats. Mischief makers, Sofia thought, the kind that talked big and pounded their chests and thought they were tough.

"Just ignore them," she said. She had never before encountered any trouble near the synagogue. Close to the Kitay Gorod Metro station, the area was densely populated and, though less so on a Saturday, busy with cars and buses. The buildings, older and shorter than her cement block tenement, sprang out of the wide sidewalk, and their painted facades were clean and well-maintained.

The anti-Semitic heckling came as a small, unpleasant shock. She didn't anticipate any real danger from these rough boys, but she was glad Kolya wasn't with her.

She tugged Edik along by his sleeve. Her cousin had a hopeless knack for making any touchy situation worse, despite having the best intentions.

"Don't make eye contact. Keep walking," Yosef agreed, showing the street sense her cousin undoubtedly lacked. Left to his own devices,

Edik would either play tough and engage the boys, or else he would show fear and invite further mischief.

Either way, his responses would be all wrong. The most prudent course involved showing no reaction and getting away as swiftly as possible.

"Don't worry, Sofia. I'll protect you," Edik said, ignoring them both. He threw back his shoulders, puffed out his chest, and strutted forward like he had something to prove. Perhaps he felt he did, after Mendel's tirade, but she wouldn't ever have chosen him as a protector had she actually needed one. Slow-moving and clumsy, Edik got winded easily and would make a horrible bodyguard. For his own sake, she hoped he didn't make a spectacle of himself.

She stuck her hand in her pocket and wrapped her fingers around her can of pepper spray. She'd used it once before when a thief had tried to steal back his cash after she'd sold him several cartons of cigarettes. One shot had debilitated him, and she'd walked away from the incident unharmed and confident in her ability to defend herself.

She could handle these young thugs herself. They would meet their match if they came too close and compelled her to retaliate with her spray.

Her smug sense of safety abandoned her when six more teenagers poured out of the building ahead of them. No coincidence, she realized, and not mischief. An ambush.

The new group was older, taller and more meaty, men rather than boys. This group cracked their knuckles and bared their fists and teeth.

Pepper spray wouldn't be enough to defend them if the gang attacked. They were outnumbered ten to three, assuming Edik could even hold his own.

"This is bad." Her cousin could always be depended upon to state the obvious.

"What do we have here?" The leader wielded a long wrench. He slapped the metal menacingly against his palm.

"We don't want any trouble." Yosef drew himself up and addressed the leader.

"I'll bet you don't," the leader said.

"Let us pass," Yosef said. His voice and stance threatened that the thugs would be the ones facing trouble if they didn't move aside.

Sofia hadn't before appreciated what an imposing figure he cut. Taller than Edik, Yosef wasn't a big man, but he carried himself with strength and grace. He might be a good person to have on her side in a fight, but she doubted they could best a mob intent on harming them.

His command seemed to do the trick, though. The gang in front parted to let them pass.

Then, as if on signal, they lined up in a gauntlet on either side of the sidewalk. The gang harassed them with taunts and shoves. Edik tried to grab her and move her out of harm's way, but one of the thugs tripped him.

Edik flailed and fell. He pushed her down to the ground with him and landed on top of her. His body weight crushed her flat against the hard concrete. Her hands and chin stung from the impact, likely scraped. Edik quickly recovered from the fall. He scrambled to get off of her and kneed her in the kidneys.

Hampered by Edik's struggle to find his footing, she'd managed to rise to her knees when one of the thugs kicked her in the side. She fell again on the concrete.

"Don't you touch her!" Edik hollered. He surged up toward the offender. He shoved hard at the teen who had kicked her and sent him stumbling toward the others, only to face off with another eager bully.

"Check out this tough guy," someone taunted. "You going to take on all of us?"

Edik windmilled his arms. He got in two good punches and sent his opponent reeling backward.

Then the leader swung the wrench and hit him in the gut. Edik doubled over with a groan and clutched his stomach.

"Stop!" Yosef shouted. "Leave us alone." His militant tone made the gang momentarily freeze, until a chorus of voices from the balcony egged them on.

"Teach the Zhidi a lesson," a *babushka* yelled from her balcony.

Sofia had regained her feet, but Edik was surrounded. She couldn't get to his side.

"Finish what Hitler started!"

Encouraged by the neighbors, the leader swung his wrench again and clocked Edik in the back of the head.

"Edik!" Sofia shrieked.

She watched him fall down hard, this time without a mew of complaint. He didn't get back up. He didn't move at all. Blood welled from the back of his skull.

Was he dead?

The leader's lip curled into sneering smile, a terrifying mix of hatred and delight. He raised the wrench to strike Edik again while he was down.

"No!" she yelled in horror. She couldn't get to him, and he was defenseless.

If he wasn't dead already, another strike with the hefty wrench would finish the job.

Yosef jumped in and blocked the blow. He engaged the leader and drew him away from Edik. The rest closed in and circled her and Edik like a pack of hungry sharks frenzied by the scent of blood in the water.

Fingers trembling, she pulled the pepper spray from her coat pocket and flipped the release. She crouched protectively over Edik's prone body and threatened their attackers with her spray can.

"Stay back." She waved the can at them and hoped it would be enough to deter them.

One ventured closer. He lunged and tried to grab her. She pushed down on the nozzle and sprayed him in the eyes.

He jumped back, cursing and rubbing at his face. One of his fellows tried to take his place. She sprayed him, too.

A third ran at her. She pivoted toward him and took aim with her spray, but he kept his head low and shielded his eyes with his arm. He knocked into her and lifted her off of her feet. He threw her over his shoulder with a whoop.

His fellows gathered around. She kept her finger on the nozzle, and they gave her a wide berth, until the steady stream trickled and died out.

"Let's teach this Jewish bitch a lesson." They swarmed her then.

She kicked and fought, but they only laughed and handed her from one to the next, like a playground ball.

Their rough hands were everywhere. They pinched and grabbed at her and passed her around.

"Let's see what she's hiding under that big coat." They lifted her off the ground, holding her hands and legs, and laid her on the hood of a car parked in the street. She thrashed and twisted, but four of them held her down.

"Help! Help!" She screamed at the top of her lungs, even though she expected no help from the audience on the balconies, hungry for violence.

She had never known fear like this. This wild gang had killed Edik, and now they were clawing at her. Did they mean to rape her here on the street?

She lifted her head but couldn't see Yosef. Had they taken him down, too?

Someone tore open her overcoat and pushed the flaps aside.

Cars went by. No one stopped to help.

The boys laughed as she struggled and kicked.

"Help! Someone, please help us," she sobbed.

One of the boys clamped his hand over her mouth. She bit him, and he smacked her hard across the cheek. The tang of blood filled her mouth.

They ripped her blouse apart. The buttons popped and rolled. Cold air hit her naked skin.

CHAPTER THIRTY-TWO
ARTUR

ARTUR FOCUSED ON the kid with the wrench, the only one with a weapon. He would neutralize him first.

He expected to be the kid's target, but the gang played dirty. They went after Edik, who lay where he had fallen, defenseless. Hopefully unconscious and not dead. Artur still needed him.

The leader hefted the wrench and made to bash Edik's skull. Artur blocked the blow with a swift chop to the forearm. He heard the crack of bone and the bell-like clang as the metal hit the sidewalk. The leader howled in pain and cradled his arm against his belly.

Artur lunged for the wrench, but one of the troublemakers reached it first and came up swinging. Artur dodged the blow.

The kid charged him, waving the wrench. He was vicious and angry, but not a trained fighter, not like Artur. Artur ducked and feinted, confusing his opponent.

Sofia deployed her pepper spray and held her own. She diverted the pack's attention, leaving Artur to contend with only their wounded leader and two others.

He needed to get the wrench.

He heard a war whoop and glanced over to Sofia. One of the boys had managed to get close and lift her off the ground. His buddies closed in around her.

Artur's reflexes and instinct took over. On the next swing, he grabbed the wrench with both hands and used his opponent's momentum to throw him to the ground. The kid hit the pavement, and the impact dazed him. His grip on the wrench went slack, and Artur easily claimed the weapon, while the kid blinked at him in surprise.

The hoodlums swung Sofia back and forth by her hands and feet. Then they threw her onto the hood of a car parked up ahead of them on the street.

Artur caught the leader around the neck with the wrench. Cars slowed and stopped on the street to watch the drama, but no one got out. No one tried to stop what was happening.

"Tell them to leave her alone," he growled.

"You tell them," the leader said defiantly. His two friends held back, waiting it seemed for direction.

"The militia will be here soon," Artur warned.

"Yeah, just see whose side they take, you worthless Jew," the leader said, still full of piss despite the beat down Artur had delivered. "My dad's on the force."

Artur could have trumped him, could have arrested him then and there himself, but he maintained his cover.

"You killed my friend."

"He's a Jew. No one cares," the boy rasped as he struggled in Artur's hold. "And anyway, you broke my arm," he said as if the two crimes were equivalent.

"Let's see what she's hiding under that big coat," someone shouted, leading the charge as the gang descended on Sofia.

Artur was going to end this. Now.

"You're a coward." Artur pulled the wrench tighter against the thug's windpipe. "Will your papa care about that? How will you explain how I beat the crap out of you when you had all your friends here for backup?"

"Fuck you," the kid shot back.

"Bet he'll be real proud. Won't he? To see what a sissy he raised."

He jerked the wrench up and down and shook the hothead. "Call them off, or I'll break your other arm before the police get here."

He heard fabric tearing and the excited panting of young men aroused by violence. He didn't look in Sofia's direction, but he could tell they had ripped away her blouse.

He was out of time. He had to get them away from her now.

He released the gang leader and shoved him with enough force to send him flailing. The kid stumbled and struggled for breath, face pale from the pain of his broken limb. He narrowed his eyes and threw a death glare, still not ready to concede defeat.

"You want it the hard way. That's your choice." Artur adjusted his grip and brandished the wrench. The kid flinched back, not as fearless as he pretended.

"Your knees will be next. Walk away now, or you won't walk at all." Artur smiled grimly and prepared to take a bone-crunching swing.

"Militia's coming. Let's beat it," the leader called to his comrades. He flipped Artur the bird and turned on his heel, but the only ones to join him were the other two who had been sparring with him. The rest remained fixed on Sofia.

Artur gave a war cry and charged toward the car where they had her pinned. They had laid Sofia out on the car like a sacrifice, legs and arms spread wide. They had torn her blouse open, and now they groped at her breasts.

"Hands off!" he yelled, feeling like a caveman with a club. Sofia was his prey, his prize, and he wouldn't share her with these idiot street thugs. He reached the two holding her legs, swung twice, and clubbed them each in the face. Bone crunched. Blood spattered. They released Sofia, cupped their hands over their noses, and howled in pain.

"Who's next?"

The gang swiveled their heads from him back to their freshly wounded comrades. He stalked toward the pimply-faced punks still holding her arms.

"Let's get out of here. He's crazy," one said, and his partners in crime agreed. They released her and scurried after their leader.

Sofia dismounted from the car. She was breathing hard, shaking. Her frightened gaze met his, and he felt a jarring jolt of connection, same as he had that first night they'd met.

He opened his arms, expecting she would throw herself at him now that he had saved her, savoring in advance the way she would feel when he held her close and she showed her gratitude. He imagined it would be so easy to seduce her now, and his gaze dropped to the skin exposed by her torn shirt.

She pulled the sides of her coat closed to cover herself. She turned from him abruptly and rushed to Edik. She knelt beside her cousin and touched his neck to feel for a pulse.

In the excitement of the last few moments, Artur had spared no thought for Edik, who lay motionless on the sidewalk.

He slumped his shoulders, feeling not the glory he'd anticipated, the victory of his strategies and prowess in bringing him to this new point where his targets would undoubtedly trust him and invite him into their confidences.

Instead, he suffered a cold lick of shame.

CHAPTER THIRTY-THREE
SOFIA

EDIK LAY SPRAWLED on the sidewalk where he'd first fallen. Face down on the ground, he hadn't moved since he'd been hit in the head. Dark blood matted his hair. Was he dead?

Buses and cars drove down the street. Some of the drivers slowed to gawk at them, but no one stopped. No one got out to help. People walking on the street crossed to the other side or stepped around them.

Their blatant apathy scared her almost as much as the gang's violence.

She lived in a city that hated her, full of people who, if they didn't wish to inflict harm themselves, would nonetheless stand by while others did.

Sofia knelt beside Edik. Her hands shook with rage and fear, and she couldn't find his pulse.

She hated feeling so damn powerless.

She had never thought this neighborhood unsafe, never been concerned about walking here. She hadn't known the violent hatred staring out at her from behind the closed windows. The neighbors had been screaming for blood from the balcony. They saw Jews as less than human, not worthy of basic respect and dignity. Those boys had been stripping her on top of a car, possibly intending to rape her right there in the middle of the street, and people had cheered. Drivers had stopped to watch.

She positioned her fingers a little higher up on Edik's neck and felt a sluggish beat under her fingertips. "Sla va Bogu!" *Thank God.*

"Edik, wake up. Come on, Edik," she urged, but she couldn't rouse him from unconsciousness. They needed help.

Yosef had scared off the gang. For now. Any moment, more trouble could come their way.

She felt Edik over for injuries with her palms. She wasn't a doctor like her mother, but she didn't think she felt any broken bones. "We need to move him," she told Yosef. "We have to get out of here and get him to the hospital."

Before the authorities arrive, she added silently. The authorities had no love for Jews either. If they didn't attack with fists and weapons, they attacked with legal falsehoods. Given the chance, they might charge Yosef and her with "attacking innocent Russian children," or maybe with hooliganism because they'd stopped traffic, or public indecency because her breasts had been exposed. The KGB could make any charge stick, no matter how untrue.

Sirens blared, her fears being realized. What could she do? She couldn't leave Edik, and she couldn't move him fast enough to get away.

But it wasn't the authorities. It was an ambulance.

The ambulance screeched to a halt where they stood. She glanced up again at the windows. Someone had helped them. The whole world wasn't against them. Good people could be found even in the most inhospitable places.

The paramedics examined Edik, and Yosef pulled her aside. He took off his wool coat and handed it to her. Then he pulled off the sweater he wore underneath. "Here," he said. "Cover up. You can't go to the hospital like this, and I know you want to ride with him."

"Thanks." She fumbled to shed her own coat and pulled the sweater on over her ruined blouse. The sweater wrapped her in heat from his body, but she couldn't stop shivering. She shoved her arms clumsily back into her coat, and then he pulled her into the shelter of his embrace.

Ah, she had been here once before, her cheek pressed to his broad chest, his strong arms holding her gently.

"It's going to be all right," he said. "You're safe now."

She didn't feel safe with him, though. He exuded danger and virility, the way he fought with such lethal grace, the way he stared at her now so intensely, with something that looked like desire in his hazel eyes.

She felt herself straining toward him, toward all of the things he offered that she had been denied for so, so long.

She didn't let herself linger in his embrace. She stepped out of his arms and patted him awkwardly on the shoulder. "You're a good man," she said.

He ducked his head, as if he didn't feel he deserved her praise.

Her parents and Mendel appeared at the end of the block, taking the edge off of her fear, even though the four KGB agents assigned to her husband and father followed. There was strength in numbers, and between the ambulance's arrival and her family's, she could trust Edik would get the help he needed without further incident.

When he caught sight of her, Mendel ran toward her. His agents jogged to keep up.

"What the hell happened?" She longed for him to gather her in his arms and hold her close, the way Yosef just had, but he kept his distance.

He didn't touch her. He never did anymore.

"We were attacked." Sofia kept her voice low and spoke quickly before the agents came into earshot.

Mendel's gaze roamed over her. He seemed to take in the missing buttons on her coat, and she didn't know what else he saw. Maybe in that moment he satisfied himself that she was unharmed because all he asked was, "Where's your hat?"

"My hat?" She lifted her hands to her head. She hadn't given a thought to her hat. She must have lost it in the tussle. His question disturbed her. He'd wasted the precious seconds they had before the agents were on them to ask about her hat, when there was so much else, so many more pressing matters.

Who cared about her hat?

Mendel turned from her and scouted the area, as if finding the hat would magically solve all of their problems.

Taking in the scene, her mother bypassed them and joined the paramedics, taking charge of Edik's care. Whether or not they appreciated her interference, the paramedics deferred to her mother's medical expertise. Good, that was good.

Her father came to her and caught her by the shoulders. "Are you okay? Were you hurt?"

He asked the questions her husband hadn't, and the contrast made her eyes burn with tears. Her father shook his head and hugged her tightly to him. She buried her face against his shoulder and greedily accepted the comfort her husband hadn't offered, the comfort she hadn't been free to accept from Yosef.

"They're putting Edik on the stretcher now," he told her, and she could hear the simmering rage beneath his words. "Your mother will go with him. We'll clear out and meet them later." Her father easily read all of the nuances of the situation without needing any explanation.

"Here." Mendel shoved her hat at her. "Put it on," he ordered.

Her father bristled at his tone. "What will that solve?"

"She's a temptation to any man who sees her," Mendel said. "She invites their attention."

"So the gang of boys that attacked us, it's my fault?" she challenged. "That's ridiculous, and you know it."

"It's not your fault," he said quickly. "You're a beautiful woman. You can't help it that God made you this way. But you must do your part to keep men's animal instincts at bay. You must cover your hair," he said.

"Right. Because my hair sent them into a frenzy. And that's why the neighbors joined in and cheered them on."

"You were wearing the hat when they attacked us," Yosef said, asserting his presence for the first time since her family's arrival and once again offering her support. "It didn't stop them."

Mendel ignored their arguments, ignored the fact that they were still on the street and that KGB agents stood scant feet from them. "I need you to do this for me," he said. "God demands it. God demands modesty." His voice rose, and he scrubbed agitatedly at his arms. "I can't keep you safe if you don't do this."

His talk of God, of religion, here, on the street, after everything that had happened, when she was still shaking from the aftermath, when they still didn't know how Edik fared, seemed the height of selfishness. She had no patience or tolerance left. He'd pushed her past her limit.

"Keep me safe?" she nearly shrieked. If Mendel hadn't shamed Edik for not protecting her, the whole violent episode might have gone differently. Edik wouldn't have thrown those punches, and maybe they would have all walked away with little more than an uneasy feeling.

"You didn't keep me safe now. Yosef did," Sofia said.

Maybe it wasn't right to blame Mendel, but she couldn't help it. He had wanted to stay at the synagogue, spouting his faith, rather than walk home with her. "Not with your hats and prayers. He used strength and guts and wits."

Those were the tools they needed to fight the evil all around them.

Faith and hope would only get them so far and offered no protection on their own.

If there truly was a God and if God helped them, it would be because they had taken the fight into their own hands. Which was what she planned to do, what she had been doing.

The paramedics rolled Edik's stretcher up to the ambulance. Her mother said, "He has a head wound, and he was knocked unconscious. I won't know how bad it is until we run some tests."

Her mother narrowed her eyes at Mendel. "Go ahead and pray to your God if you like," she said, and it was clear she'd overheard their entire argument. "I'll put my faith in medical science."

CHAPTER THIRTY-FOUR
ARTUR

ARTUR TRACKED SOFIA'S every movement as she paced the hospital waiting area. Arms crossed, she made a circuit back and forth, back and forth, like an exotic fish in a tank, gliding with graceful agitation within its confines.

"Sofia, stop." He rose and took her hand. He tried to lead her back to the row of chairs, but she seemed unwilling to sit, unable to relax her vigil.

The hospital waiting room had other people waiting, like them, for news, but they kept to themselves. For now, Artur and Sofia were relatively alone. Her mother was with Edik, and the rest of the family had yet to arrive.

He didn't know how many opportunities he would have to get her alone. He knew he had to exploit every advantage right now and establish a connection, a foundation for seduction.

He pulled her into his arms. He hugged her to him, the way he had the morning after they'd met, when she'd burst into tears at Edik's apartment. "Edik's safe now. You're safe now."

He stroked his hand up and down her back in what was meant to be a soothing gesture, but she didn't melt into him the way she had the other day. She pulled away.

"Thank you for what you did today," she said, but she backed away as if eager to put as much distance between them as possible. "I don't want to think what would have happened if you hadn't been there."

She didn't look up. She kept her gaze averted from him. She crossed her arms over her chest as if hugging herself and resumed her pacing.

She wore the wool sweater he'd given her after the attack. The sweater had fitted his form, but it draped on her and swallowed her slender frame. She had such a strong presence that he hadn't realized she was actually rather small.

The collar of her blouse peeked out at the neckline. No one would have suspected the blouse was ripped apart underneath, but Artur knew. He had glimpsed her skin, her breasts, round and full, her soft, inviting shape.

Her body was hidden now, but he knew what was there, and he wanted her. Wanted her secrets.

"You're going to wear out the floor," he said.

She gave him a brittle smile, as if she were losing patience with him. Perhaps she'd been grateful for his assistance earlier, but she didn't seem to want him around now.

She chewed her lip and made her circuit. Not talking to him. Not looking at him. Perhaps wishing he weren't there.

Her seeming indifference riled him. He was all the more eager to corner her, alone, in a place where he could command all of her attention, where he could strip her bare and seduce her.

What would it be like? He would taste her olive skin and the dusky nipples he'd spied through her bra when her shirt had been torn. Salty or sweet? He would run his fingers through the mass of springy curls that Mendel wanted so desperately for her to hide from sight. Silken or wiry?

She looked sharply at him, as if she sensed his prurient thoughts, as if she sensed how he undressed her with his gaze. For a moment, their gazes locked. He felt that odd sense of connection, and he thought, *Yes, she feels it, too.*

Then abruptly, she cut her gaze away. She turned her back to him.

Edik's father arrived, putting an end to Artur's attempts to stoke her desire for him. Two KGB agents, Ruben's tail, accompanied him. The men positioned themselves across the room with their backs to the wall and watched them dispassionately.

Did they know he was undercover? When they reported back to headquarters, would they also send details about his performance, about her unresponsiveness to his advances?

Ruben was pastier looking than usual, and Sofia stopped her pacing and fussed over him. "Don't worry," she said. "Mama's with Edik. He's going to be fine."

Artur recognized that the words were solely for the older man's benefit, an effort to calm him when she hadn't been able to calm herself.

"I can't lose another son," he said.

She shed her earlier agitation and took the chair beside him, angled toward him, and squeezed his hand. Could she give comfort but not receive it? Or was her problem with Artur?

The precariousness of his status hit him with sudden force. He had no place in this scene. He wasn't a family member. He'd had only the barest association with Ruben. And, so far, he'd failed to build any real rapport with Sofia.

This shortfall wouldn't be immediately apparent to the KGB audience that now watched from across the room, but he didn't know how to remedy it.

He started to feel a mild panic. His access to Ruben, Sofia, to the apartment, all of it hinged on Edik. What would happen if Edik didn't wake up? If he didn't go home?

Artur had yet to secure his place. His undercover career could be over before it began, before he had anything useful to report.

Ruben's breathing was a little unsteady. He rubbed at his chest as if he had pain there. He turned to Artur. "I know what you did today. For Edik," he said. "Ilya told me everything. Thank you."

"It was nothing," he said, but Ruben dismissed his humility.

"Bah! It wasn't nothing. If he survives, it will be because of you."

His gruff voice rose with his adamance and drew the eyes of the others in the waiting room.

Sofia urged him to quiet down. He cleared his throat, and when he spoke again, he heeded her advice. "I've been thinking. Edik said you didn't have anywhere to stay. I think you should move in with us. If—when—Edik leaves for Israel, you could rent his room."

"I'd like that." Artur didn't have to hold back his broad smile. For over a week now, he had been building toward this moment, laying the foundation for this very request. All the better that Ruben thought the idea his own.

"I think you should take some time to think about this," Sofia said. "Edik's only known Yosef a couple of weeks. He's still practically a stranger."

She was still suspicious of him. Because he was new? Or because he had done something to give himself away?

Perhaps Kasparov had been right, and he was too green for such an important assignment.

"Nonsense," Ruben said. "He might have saved Edik's life."

Sofia bristled at the brusque dismissal of her concerns, but she didn't push the issue. She only asked, "Where are you staying now?"

"At my girlfriend's. Ex-girlfriend's," Artur quickly amended. "I moved here for her, and then it didn't work out. She's seeing someone else."

"And she's letting you stay in her apartment?" Her question rang with suspicion.

There were holes in the story. He hadn't started with a well-planned alias. He had improvised on the details, and the lack of forethought haunted him now.

"She feels guilty. She convinced me to move from Leningrad to be with her and then took up with another guy," he explained in an effort to assuage her worry. "She's letting me stay with her until I find something else."

"I see," Sofia said in a way that suggested she didn't buy the story at all.

Dealing with her would be so much easier if he could get her to stop thinking so hard, if he could take her in his arms and kiss the sense out of her.

He didn't know if he could even accomplish that much, though. She didn't seem to welcome his attention, and he didn't know how he would get her alone.

Maybe he was approaching this all wrong. What would Yosef Koslovsky, if he were real, be saying and feeling?

He replayed the last half hour in the emergency room and could see his missteps. He shouldn't have been trying to touch her or tell her everything was fine when they didn't know for certain. He should have been sharing in her anxiety over Edik.

He needed to fully become Yosef Koslovsky if he hoped to be embraced by this family, by Sofia.

"Don't worry so much," Ruben scolded Sofia. "This is a good idea. It'll be good for everyone. You know my health isn't the best. I've been leaning on you too much to play hostess, and I know Mendel doesn't appreciate it."

"He told you that?"

Ruben ignored her question and kept talking. "Yosef could help me. He speaks English. He could talk to the guests when they come."

"My English isn't that good," Artur said. Yosef Koslovsky would be a little modest, and he wouldn't want to appear too eager.

"Meh," Ruben said. "The visitors will like you. You're young and handsome. Not like me."

Sofia's gaze bore into him, and he sensed her taking his measure.

He couldn't afford to come up wanting yet again, to have her dismiss him and turn away. Indoctrinating Ruben's visitors with anti-Soviet stories was the last thing he wanted to do, but he said, "I'm happy to help."

"This is dangerous," she said.

"I trust him," Ruben said.

"That's not what I mean," she said. "This is dangerous for him." She nodded her head toward Artur, but her gaze fixed on the KGB agents standing by the wall.

"Sofia," her uncle chided. "What would you have him do? Bury his head in the sand? There's danger everywhere here. Not just from them." Like her, he inclined his head to point to the agent. "Look at what happened to you today. Look at what happened to David."

"David?" Artur asked.

"My older son," Ruben said sadly. "He was the victim of a Jewish accident."

"A 'Jewish accident?' What's that?" Artur had never heard the term.

"You know, when Jewish soldiers get 'accidentally' killed in the army by friendly fire. During field exercises or on missions," Sofia said. "David was killed when a gun *accidentally* misfired."

"Surely you've heard of this. Maybe you know someone," Ruben probed.

"My father died in the army." Artur exploited the limited details he knew of the real Yosef Koslovsky's life. He was unhappy to realize he had scant few of them to share. "But no one ever said he was murdered."

Yosef had died while serving in the army with Artur's father, but Artur didn't know more than that.

"Because it was an accident?" Ruben suggested with heavy cynicism.

Artur imagined how a new initiate—how Yosef Koslovsky's son if such a man existed and had actually been sitting here—might respond to the connection these Jews were drawing. Would Koslovsky conclude that his father had been murdered for being Jewish?

"So, you're saying his death was because he was Jewish?" Rationally and logically, Artur rejected the whole notion. No one had ever intimated the Jew—his mother's fiancé—had been murdered.

"I don't know the details of your father's death," Ruben said. "All I know is that a disproportionate number of Jewish men die in the Soviet military. Due to so-called 'accidents.'" Ruben drew finger quotes in the air.

This was merely another example of the anti-Soviet propaganda he'd been sent to silence, all the more dangerous since Ruben seemed wholeheartedly to believe it and could point to the example of his own son. Worse, this personalized fable of Jewish oppression could be used to warp the mind of someone already feeling like he was on the fringes of Soviet society and recruit him to the cause.

That was obviously Ruben's intent. To recruit Yosef Koslovsky.

So why was Sofia against it?

"I understand the risks, and I want to help," Artur said, as if Ruben's story had swayed him.

This was a better opportunity than he could have imagined. More than merely claiming a place as a tenant, he would now join the family enterprise and worm his way into understanding the entire setup.

Sofia looked like she was about to launch another objection, but her mother appeared in the waiting room. As she approached, Renata's face broke into a wide smile. "He's awake, and he's going to be fine. No signs of lasting damage. Just a concussion and a few stitches."

Everyone murmured their relief. Ruben levered out of his chair and threw his arms around Artur. "You saved him, Yosef. You saved him."

"I didn't," Artur said. He gave Ruben an awkward pat on the back and wished Sofia had been the one to wrap him in a tight embrace. "But I'm glad he's all right."

Sofia stood apart, her arms wrapped around herself, her head bowed as if she were deep in contemplation.

They couldn't all go to see Edik at once, and Renata took Ruben back to visit him first. Once they'd left, Sofia turned to Artur.

Spontaneously, she touched his arm. Her voice dropped to an urgent whisper. "You have to understand what you're getting into. My uncle is watched all the time by the KGB."

She inclined her head the slightest fraction, indicating the agents, who had stayed in the waiting room rather than follow Ruben onto the hospital ward. "His apartment is watched all of the time, too. When my uncle has foreign visitors, the KGB follows them to their hotels. They'll follow you, too. Just visiting makes you a person of interest, especially if they think you talked to foreigners. And the men in my family all have KGB tails."

"Edik doesn't," Artur said.

"Are you so sure? Maybe he doesn't have agents following him, but someone put the listening device in his hat."

"And in mine," Artur reminded her, glad now for the fact. It gave him that much more credibility with her. He moved closer to her so that he could whisper, too. "Let's face it. I'm already part of this."

"No," she said. "You don't understand. They might really come after you. Target you. Make it impossible for you to get a job, like they've done for Edik. Or arrest you on trumped-up charges like they did Mendel."

Trumped-up charges? Artur bit his tongue to keep silent. The report on Mendel's arrest said the investigators had found several kilos of hashish in the apartment. After finding the contraband in Ruben's secret closet and seeing Edik's reserve of cash, Artur had no doubts about the report's credibility. After all, what was to stop the Jews at selling cigarettes and blue jeans? Surely, drugs were more lucrative.

As if she sensed his doubts, she said, "I saw the investigators bring the bags of marijuana into our apartment. They planted them and then lied, and they sent him to the gulag for five years. Five years, Yosef, just because they didn't like that he was meeting people and teaching them Hebrew." She shook her head. "And what they did to Max was even worse. All he did was give a speech. And for that they went after him and his wife and child."

She believed the story she was telling him, that the KGB had gone after innocent people. This wasn't deliberate propaganda, a performance for an American audience or an attempt to recruit someone to the cause.

She was trying to warn him off.

Her hand clutched his arm. Her eyes were full of fear and concern. He wondered if he had misread the signals earlier. Maybe she wasn't suspicious. Maybe there was a bond forming between them.

Maybe she actually cared.

Maybe his assignment—her seduction—was progressing exactly as it should.

CHAPTER THIRTY-FIVE
SOFIA

KOLYA WAS STILL awake when Sofia got home from the hospital. "I wanted you to put me to bed," he said.

She went through the familiar evening ritual with him, while Mendel sat and brooded, his palms pressed together at his lips as if in prayerful contemplation. But there was nothing peaceful or calm about the way his eyes tracked her.

She hadn't been home since the attack. They hadn't spoken since he'd made his demand that she cover her hair.

"Is Edik going to be okay?" Kolya asked the question that Mendel should have.

"He has a very big bump on his head," she said. "But the doctors say he'll be fine."

"What does *babushka* say?" Kolya asked. "She's the best doctor."

"She said he needs to rest, and he might have a very bad headache for a while."

She tucked the blankets around him. She was so grateful he had gone to visit a friend and hadn't accompanied her to the synagogue today, the way he often did. He hadn't seen Edik's still body or his blood or the way the gang had attacked her and ripped her clothes.

He hadn't been in danger today.

But he could have.

Sofia kissed Kolya's head. *You're a mother, Sofia. You've done enough if you're ready to stop. You should give some thought to exfiltration.* Paul's words tumbled through her mind, leaving her restless and unsettled.

Kolya propped himself up on his elbows. "It's not fair."

"No," she agreed. "It's not."

"But it can change. Right?" he asked.

She could say the word and get her husband and little boy out of this country that hated them. She could keep her son safe and give him a good life in Paul's America.

But she would only be helping her own little family.

"It can change. It will change," she promised. She would continue to do her part if she could. If her keys still worked. If she could still gain access. If the KGB hadn't already figured out her role.

The risks were multiplying. Kolya could be left without a mother.

But if she succeeded, she could help a lot of people, a lot of children, and not only Kolya.

"Now go to sleep," she said. She turned off the light and headed for the bedroom. Mendel stirred from his corner to follow her. She could feel him watching her as she undressed.

She pulled the sweater Yosef had lent her over her head. The wool was scratchy but warm, and it still held the faint scent of whatever cologne or soap Yosef used, something fresh and clean.

She resisted the urge to bury her nose in the fabric and inhale deeply to identify the scent, to remember the feel of strong arms wrapped around her, of strong shoulders to share her burdens.

She shouldn't be thinking about Yosef at all.

She folded the sweater and put it aside to return to him. Then she slipped on her nightgown.

"You're a temptation to any man who sees you," Mendel said, revisiting his newest preoccupation.

"What about to you? Am I a temptation to you?" she asked, coming to him. She wanted him to touch her, to hold her the way Yosef had been more than willing to do.

She wanted to lose herself in passion with him, the way she once had.

"Go to bed," he said gruffly.

She felt his rejection like the twisting of a knife.

She crawled into bed, but he didn't join her. He nestled into a pile of blankets on the floor.

He hadn't wanted to be close ever since his return. The passionate dreams that had sustained her through the years of his absence seemed a farce. There were no tangled limbs or heated caresses. No kisses that lasted for hours. No chance of another child.

He punched at his pillow. Little white feathers floated in the air. Then he rolled away from her on his side, moving as far from her in their cramped bedroom as possible. He had come back to her so prickly and distant. She stared in frustration at the ceiling.

"Why don't you want to be near me? To touch me?" she asked finally, even though she didn't expect to get an answer this time, either.

"You wouldn't want me near you if you knew what I'd done," he said.

What had he done?

She sat up in bed, alert and wary. She couldn't bring herself to believe he had sold out her family and sided with the KGB, that even now he was spying on them and awaiting just the right moment to stab them in the back.

But he had done something.

He was silent for a long time. She slid out of the bed and curled herself around him, but he shrank from her touch. He rolled away from her, taking the blanket and all the warmth with him.

She thought of what he had told Ruben's visitors, about how the prisoners had been treated and demeaned in the gulag.

"Whatever happened in prison is in the past," she said.

She wasn't even sure she could blame him if he had made a deal in order to escape the horror of where he'd been.

Finally, he said, "There was a woman." His voice cracked. "Masha."

She closed her eyes against the unexpected stab of pain.

"She looked like you. Reminded me of you. Her hair," he said. Then he was quiet for a long time, likely remembering. The floor was unforgiving against her back, and she shivered with cold.

Sofia might not blame him for anything he'd done to survive in that terrible place or to escape it, but that didn't mean it wouldn't hurt.

She had lost him in so many ways.

"She was also a dissident," he said finally. "And the prisoners, some of them were hard men, *Vor v' Zakone*, mafia, the worst kinds of criminals. The guards let them run the prison. They thought it was funny to watch them terrorize the rest of us, especially the political prisoners."

Mendel drew his knees into his chest and curled into a fetal position. She waited out his silence, afraid any sound from her might scare away the confession.

She didn't know what he might say. She almost didn't want to hear it. Her heart ached for what he must have suffered and with the premonition of what more he would now confess.

"She kept her hair in a tight braid. Because of the lice," he said. "But one night, I asked her—begged her—to take it down for me. It was so dark and thick. Like yours."

Maybe she should be glad he'd found comfort in another person during his sojourn in hell, but she couldn't help her possessive jealousy.

His voice cracked when he continued with his story. "That night, the *Vory* saw us together—saw her. And then they wanted her."

He started to cry. She had never once seen her husband cry, not even at his sentencing. Now his body shook as he told her, "I couldn't protect her. And they took her. Sofia, they took her, and they... and they."

He broke down crying and couldn't continue.

"Hush." She stroked his hair, his face. "Hush," she said, but she had no words of comfort.

She wanted to ask if he loved this woman, this Masha. If she was still in the prison.

He stopped all of her questions with two simple words. "She's dead."

Her eyes welled with tears. She mourned the terrible fate of this woman, who had reminded him of her, who could have been her.

She slid her arms around him and gathered him to her, as if he were a small child. He didn't mold into her the way Kolya would, though. He held himself apart.

"I couldn't protect her." His voice was ragged, haunted. "And I can't protect you."

"I don't need you to protect me," she said at the same time he said, "Only God can protect you."

He continued, "I won't be able to hold onto you if they come for you. Not if they see you."

"Not if they see my hair?" She guessed at where he was steering the conversation, back to his tokens and talismans, to special hats and protective pieces of paper.

To his God who made him feel free in the tightest and worst of confines.

She didn't believe the same things he did, but she could no longer dismiss his beliefs as mere superstition. She respected the power of his faith, the strength it gave him to survive, to keep going despite the horrors he had faced.

Despite the dangers they all still faced.

"Please," he pleaded. "Please, Sofia. Please cover your hair when you go out."

His experiences in the prison had scarred him deeply. He harbored terrible anxiety over protection, and today's violent events could only have made things worse.

Would covering her hair be so terrible if it gave him a measure of peace?

It seemed a small price if it would bring the man she loved back from his too-long exile.

"I'll cover my hair," she said, but her concession didn't ease his pain. Or her own.

While he didn't shrink from her touch this time, he also didn't turn toward her. The distance was still there, a little less perhaps, but still too far to cross.

"Mendel, what if we could escape?" she whispered. "Just us, you and me and Kolya? Leave the Soviet Union?"

Maybe it was what he needed. Maybe running as far and as fast from this terrible place, from all of the nightmares that haunted him, would help him heal.

"Wishful thinking. Useless wishful thinking. We're never getting out," he said.

"Edik's leaving."

"It's a cruel trick."

"You don't think they'll let him leave?" she asked.

"They'll let him go," Mendel said. "They'll let one man leave for every ten thousand who want to get out so they can give us hope and then dash it. They'll do their best to turn us against each other, if only for sport."

"Like they did in the gulag?"

"Like they're doing right now," he said bitterly. "Releasing me early and in this condition so you'll suspect me or trot me out in front of tourists. Planting bugs inside sacred scrolls so that any religious thing seems tainted and we don't trust the rabbi. For all I know, they even sent that gang after you today."

"To what end?" she asked.

"To rile us up. To stoke our desire to leave. To fight." He rolled over toward her now. He propped up on his elbow and leaned over as if he were about to kiss her, long and slow, the way he used to.

His voice was a thread of a whisper. "They know," he said. "They know about the lists and the communications. They questioned me about them for a full month before they finally let me go. They're trying to flush out the activists."

He moved closer and pressed his lips to the shell of her ear, but this was no kiss.

In one breath, he confirmed all of her worst fears. "They sent me home so they could catch you."

CHAPTER THIRTY-SIX
ARTUR

THE SOIFERS' APARTMENT was only a twenty-minute taxi ride from Artur's own. As he crossed the threshold to the familiar building, he felt himself crossing over into another world, leaving Yosef Koslovsky far behind him.

Maya greeted him at the door. Her beauty struck him a sharp blow. With her porcelain skin, delicate features, and shining blue eyes, his wife exemplified Russian beauty.

How could he fantasize about Sofia, when he had Maya waiting for him at home?

He took her in his arms, backed her up against the door, and pressed his body close to hers. He drew out the kiss and tried to banish the thoughts of another woman's kiss, a kiss that hadn't happened yet and couldn't mean anything when it finally did.

He clung tightly to the knowledge of who he was in this life.

Artur Gregorovich and not Yosef Koslovsky.

She pushed him away. "Careful," she warned, and she graced him with a soft smile. "I'm pregnant."

He cupped his hand gently over her still-flat belly, but tempered his elation. "How are you feeling? Is everything all right?"

He'd learned to be cautious. They'd been trying to have a second child, only to face a stillbirth and later not one but two miscarriages.

"This time is going to be different," she said with effervescent optimism. "I had a dream. I saw a little girl with dark hair and eyes, just like yours."

His wife liked to believe she had a little bit of witch in her. He put no stock in such things, but he knew better than to say so. He preferred to sidestep any potential conflict, especially when he only had this single evening at home. "This is a wonderful surprise," he said.

"Why are you home? Is the case over already?"

"No, love. But it's going well. They invited me to move in. I'm here to pick up some things so that I can make it look good."

"They've accepted you. That's wonderful. I never doubted you'd make a wonderful spy." She glowed with happiness, about his achievement, about the pregnancy. She threw her arms around his neck and sighed contentedly, "Oh, Artur, we are going to have the perfect life."

He basked in the soft sweetness of the moment, the weightless feeling that he was flying and all of his dreams were within reach.

"Aleksei, stop it this instant." Artur heard his mother chastise Aleksei. Reluctantly, he disentangled from Maya's loving embrace to investigate.

He found Yana and Aleksei in the living room. Spry and young for her years, Artur's mother sat cross-legged beside Aleksei on the colorful Turkish wool carpet in his living room.

"No! You can't make me. I hate you. I hate you. I hate you," Aleksei chanted, and he tore pages from his workbook and pelted Yana with them.

Yana batted the paper away and grabbed both of Aleksei's wrists. She held him in place and in the quiet voice that used to always freeze Artur in his tracks, she said, "This is *not* how good boys behave."

Aleksei burst into loud noisy tears, and Maya pushed past Artur to intervene.

"What's wrong? What did you do to make him cry?" she demanded, even though she had witnessed the scene.

"He doesn't want to do his homework," Yana said. She gripped Aleksei and didn't release him.

"Yana! Why are you holding him like that?" Accusation dripped from Maya's voice.

Aleksei tore himself out of his grandmother's grasp and threw himself at Maya, burying his head in her waist. "She hates me," Aleksei cried. "She said I'm not good."

"Of course you're good, honey," Maya soothed. "You're the best boy in the whole world."

Artur cleared his throat. "Aleksei, apologize to your grandmother, and clean up the paper you threw on the floor."

"Do I have to, Mama?" Aleksei looked to Maya, while Artur's own mother closed her eyes as if she willed herself anywhere but here. The quiet gesture spoke volumes. A teacher and lover of children, she had so looked forward to being a grandmother. While she could easily manage a roomful of children, she could scarcely manage Aleksei.

"Yes," Artur said at the same time Maya said, "No."

"Yes," Artur repeated. "You don't talk to your grandmother that way. Apologize now."

Aleksei's face reddened. He fisted his little hands at his sides. Sound exploded out of him in a dramatic, "I'm sorry!"

His mother covered her heart with her hand and took an involuntary step back, as if the apology had been an attack. Aleksei took off and ran from the room without cleaning up the paper. He slammed the door to his bedroom.

Maya rounded on Artur, eyes full of anger and accusation instead of the warm acceptance of only moments ago. "Look what you've done! You haven't been home for days, and suddenly you're going to be a father? You have no idea how to handle him."

Somehow Maya was the only one who did. As time went on and Aleksei's behavior became worse, Artur put increasing stock in his mother's diagnosis. Maya indulged him too much.

"I know when he's being a monster," Artur said.

"You think a fit of temper is such a bad thing? It shows will and spirit. I'm raising our son to take his place in Russian society."

"What place?" Artur's mother asked indignantly.

"Look around you, Yana," Maya said with a lift of her chin. "We're not like other people. We're royalty."

"This isn't tsarist Russia. There's no such thing as royalty here," Yana said.

"No? Your own son has had every advantage. A fast track in the KGB, this beautiful apartment, all the right connections, money. Because his wife is the daughter of a KGB Spymaster. If Artur follows *my* father's example, he could be the General Secretary of the Communist Party one day. We're not like other people."

Whenever she felt threatened by Yana, Maya would allude to the differences in the family's status. She never came out and made the point directly, but they were all aware of the subtext.

Marriage to her had brought him everything. He would never have risen so high on his family's own connections.

"Royalty or not, Aleksei's not going to get far if he throws a tantrum every time someone tries to make him read. He's going to flunk kindergarten," Yana said.

"He'll never flunk. His teachers wouldn't dare," Maya said. "Everyone knows who his grandfather is."

This barb was more pointed than usual, and Artur couldn't abide the unnecessary dig at the difference in station between Yana and Semyon.

"He needs to learn how to read," Artur said. He couldn't let the jab at his mother stand.

"He'll learn when he's ready," Maya said with a careless shrug. "We need to make allowances for him. You've been away on assignment. He misses you. And now, in the two minutes you've been home, all you've done is side with your mother against me and call him a monster."

She turned on her heel and headed for their bedroom, making as dramatic an exit as Aleksei.

"She's impossible," Yana complained.

"She has a point," Artur's father said as he entered the room from the study, carrying a newspaper and pipe. No doubt Mikhail had been eavesdropping the whole time and waiting for the coast to clear. He always claimed that sound strategy depended on knowing when to enter and when to leave.

But Mikhail's strategies amounted to little more than avoidance and appeasement.

"The words coming from her mouth sound like sense until you really listen to them," Yana grumbled, but Artur couldn't take his mother's side.

"She's pregnant," Artur said.

"Is that supposed to be an excuse?" Yana asked.

Artur found he didn't appreciate the challenge in her stance. It was as if he had somehow encouraged her criticism of Maya by taking her side earlier. But with him away and with Maya pregnant, it was more important than ever to keep peace in their home. Maya might not be able to handle the extra stress of conflict with his parents. He didn't want her to lose another child.

"She might have a point," Mikhail said again gently, as if he too saw the need to keep the peace. "Imagine how different your life would have been if you'd married Koslovsky instead of me. If Artur had been his son instead of mine."

His mother gasped. "Why would you even say such a thing?"

Artur scowled at his father. After all these years keeping the secret of Yosef's engagement to Yana, Mikhail now invoked him freely?

"I think about it often," Mikhail admitted. "But especially since Artur asked about him. I think about what your life would have been if Yosef had lived. If you had married him. Had children with him. There are a lot of disadvantages to being a Jew in this country," he said.

Artur saw through the seemingly innocent conjecture. His father wished to continue their last conversation, to push his views once more, this time pretending he agreed with Maya. Did he think Artur was so easily led?

"I think about that, and it keeps me humble." Mikhail spoke his words in a gentle tone, but it didn't take the challenge out of them, the ever present question of Artur's path, of the values he shared with Maya.

"That reminds me," Artur said. He thought he might relish confronting his self-righteous father with the propaganda Ruben had wanted to use to recruit him. "One of my targets—"

"People," his mother corrected.

"People," Artur conceded for the sake of her civilian sensibilities. He could temper his use of depersonalized terms when he spoke about work with her. But it didn't change what he did, what he would do.

He turned to his father and baited him. "One of the men I'm investigating mentioned 'Jewish accidents' in the army. That's not real. Is it?"

He already knew the answer to his own question, and he waited smugly for his father to confirm that Ruben had tried to indoctrinate him with lies, that things weren't as bad as the Jews claimed, that the questions his father wanted him so badly to ask would offer only empty answers.

"What do you mean?" Yana asked, while Artur savored his father's hesitation.

"He claimed Jewish soldiers get killed by our own side. By friendly fire or maybe in training exercises. That such accidents happen frequently," Artur explained.

"Those things happen," Mikhail said on a heavy sigh, "but not by accident. Almost never by accident."

Yana swayed as if she might faint. Artur caught her and lowered her to the sofa. Usually quiet and sensible, his mother was never one for melodrama, and her reaction alarmed him. "Are you all right?"

She pressed her fist to her mouth and shook her head. Artur had an uncomfortable feeling in his chest.

"Let me get you a drink," Mikhail said. He crossed to the sideboard and poured her a generous snifter of cognac.

Artur gestured for him to fill a second glass. If Ruben's stories weren't lies and paranoia, then he needed his own stiff drink.

"You said it was an accident." Yana's voice came out high-pitched and reed thin. "When Yosef got shot in training. An unfortunate accident."

Mikhail passed Artur a glass then turned his attention to Yana. "I lied to you. And I'm sorry." He pressed the snifter into Yana's hand. "I didn't have a choice back then," he said. "I couldn't tell you the truth. I couldn't tell anyone."

Artur poured the cognac down his throat, but he didn't feel the usual warmth. He felt cold inside.

He had never seen his mother touch a drop of alcohol, but like him, she greedily drank down the cognac Mikhail offered. She placed the empty snifter on the coffee table with a soft clink.

"They killed him," Yana choked. "You never said so, but that's what happened. Isn't it?"

"Yes." Mikhail sat down heavily beside her on the sofa and pulled her into his arms. "It was murder."

"They killed him," she repeated and then burst into tears. Artur couldn't remember ever seeing his mother cry, and the sight unsettled him deeply. "I loved him, and they killed him." She sobbed against Mikhail's shoulder, weeping for a man she had never discussed with Artur.

All these years, why had his parents avoided mention of her engagement to Koslovsky?

"I loved him," she repeated.

"I know." Mikhail rubbed soothing circles on her back. He kissed her head tenderly. "So did I."

Artur turned away, giving them a little privacy. He struggled to gather his own scattered thoughts, but they slipped out of his grasp.

He didn't remember moving to the sideboard, but he found himself there pouring more cognac into his glass. He stared out the window at the prized view of Moscow. Everything looked strange and unfamiliar tonight. The Moscow River was a dark stain cutting through the lights of the city.

Artur sipped his cognac. When his mother's crying wound down, he reluctantly turned back to them. He had too many questions, and he didn't know when there would be other chances to ask them. He was due back at Ruben's soon.

"Was there an investigation? A trial?" Artur asked. He couldn't wrap his mind around his father's story. He had no reason to doubt Mikhail, but he resisted believing.

It couldn't be true.

Ruben's propaganda couldn't be true.

"No. There was no trial," Mikhail said with a bitterness Artur had never heard before. "I pushed, but no one wanted to listen. They forced me to let it go."

Artur could almost feel the weight of his father's frustration and regret, the secret he had been forced to keep for so long. He understood now why Mikhail seldom talked of Yosef, except to share a fleeting, happy memory.

"My superiors didn't think it mattered," Mikhail said, and Yana buried her head in his shoulder. "They didn't think Yosef mattered."

Artur abandoned the protest on his own lips, the cross-examination he was conditioned to give to get the answers he wanted.

Unlike Ruben, Mikhail had no reason to lie about this.

The story made a horrible kind of sense. It explained why Mikhail was always so cynical, why he constantly pressed Artur to open his eyes to the weakness and hypocrisy in the system.

But why the secrecy for all these years? Why had he never shared this story with Artur? Why was Yana's engagement to Koslovsky such a closely guarded secret?

Artur swallowed another mouthful of his second drink, trying to wash away the taste of answers he didn't want. The warmth flowing down his throat didn't ease his growing insecurity, this doubt about what was true and what wasn't.

He felt compelled to ask about things he had once confidently taken for granted. The questions were unthinkable, and yet he couldn't stop thinking them. He went to drink some more and found his glass empty. It hardly mattered. No amount of alcohol would let him escape the thoughts roiling in his mind.

"Am I Koslovsky's son?" Artur was glad Maya wasn't in the room to hear him utter such blasphemy. But he had to ask.

There was a moment of stunned silence, when all of them froze. His parents looked at him and then back at each other, and there were secrets in their eyes, a lifetime's silent conversation passing back and forth between them.

No fast protestation. No reassurance.

Was Artur a lowly Jew? An impostor?

He hurled his glass across the room. It crashed against the wall and shattered. Yana gasped.

"Am I?" he demanded again.

"You're my son," Mikhail said fiercely.

Was that the truth? It had to be the truth. But Mikhail had hesitated, and that brief hesitation, that moment between one breath and another, left room for a world of doubt.

CHAPTER THIRTY-SEVEN
ARTUR

EDIK WAS DISCHARGED from the hospital with a mild concussion and several stitches in the back of his head. Artur had little patience for his moans and groans or for his existential whining about how he could ever leave Sofia.

Then Sofia arrived to visit, and Artur gained an appreciation for Edik's artful complaining. Sofia, much to Artur's disbelief, fussed over him and told him how brave he had been. She showed endless patience for addressing the aches and pains he doubtlessly manufactured, just so he could milk every ounce of her attention.

Artur gathered Mendel had prevailed in their argument about covering her hair. Today she hid her abundant hair under a floral kerchief tied under her chin, in the style of Russian *babushki*. He longed to pull the silly scarf off of her head and see her hair spill free.

She caught him looking at her. Her forehead wrinkled, and she cut her attention away from him. She didn't seem to be able to stand the sight of him, and Artur wasn't sure what he had done wrong.

She tucked Edik into the corner of the sofa with pillows and a thick blanket, while Ruben sat in his armchair and observed the proceedings with uncharacteristic sobriety.

Almost as soon as Sofia got Edik settled, there was a knock on the door. Artur, taking on what he assumed would be his new duties in the apartment, opened for a couple, likely a husband and wife.

Artur guessed them to be in their early forties. He led them into the living room, where they performed introductions. The visitors had brought a single shopping bag with candies, a sort of hostess gift, but no contraband for Edik's closet.

"Sofia, I'm not feeling well," Ruben said. "Would you mind bringing out the tea? Yosef can help you. And maybe you should call your mother."

Sofia led the way and pushed through the swinging door into the kitchen. "Get the cups and saucers," she said.

She stood at the faucet and filled the electric kettle, her back to him. Artur imagined pressing in close behind her, whispering in her ear, making her come undone right here, right now, while the sound of the running water would muffle her cries.

Too soon, she turned off the water. Before he could breach the silence, she picked up the receiver for the rotary phone and dialed. "Mama, Uncle Ruben's asking for you. He said he's not feeling well."

When she hung up with her mother, Artur said, "Don't worry about him. He's milking your sympathy. Ruben's engineering it so you'll entertain his guests and do all the dirty work."

He merely parroted what her own husband had said before, namely that this family leached off of her. But she gave him a sharp, disapproving look.

Too late, he realized he'd made a major misstep.

She didn't share his disdain for Ruben and Edik, and likely she didn't see them as parasites the way Mendel did. He didn't actually know how she felt, what she thought.

He couldn't afford to alienate her. More importantly, he had to win her over if he hoped to be successful in seducing her. "I only meant that they are both enjoying your company and taking full advantage of it."

"You think they're faking," she said. "And they're trying to use me."

"Who could blame them?" he asked with a winsome smile, but she turned her back on him and pulled teaspoons out of the silverware drawer.

Sofia seemed immune to the charm that had always served him so well. Worse, she seemed irritated with him. With him and not Edik or Ruben!

He didn't understand her at all, a rookie mistake.

He didn't try to talk with her again. He needed to get a better sense of her before he made another gaffe and forever spoiled his chances of seducing her.

He worked silently beside her in the kitchen, matching teacups and saucers. None of his tactics would be effective if he didn't understand what motivated his targets, if he couldn't anticipate their next moves.

The water heated quickly. Sofia poured it into the teapot and laid it on the tray, and Artur carried the tea service back into the living room.

Sofia perched beside Ruben, while he told the same story he always did about sharing a cab with the KGB agents assigned to follow him.

Unsure what to do or say, how to act so that Sofia might embrace him, Artur poured hot water into the guests' cups, drawing out the task so that he could gather his thoughts.

Right now, he was still thinking and acting too much like Artur Gregorovich, a KGB outsider, and not enough like Yosef Koslovsky, one of them. He had to overcome his own natural resistance.

He didn't want to be one of them.

But what if he were?

The thought jarred him, and he sloshed the water from the pot over the edge of the cup he was pouring. A few drops of scalding water hit his hand. He cursed.

"Are you all right?" Sofia asked. Her concern seemed to override her earlier pique with him.

"It's fine. Nothing," he said. The burn was minor, a few dots of achy pink skin and nothing more. As for the rest, he had to be fine. There was no other choice.

He sucked on his hand to soothe the burn while Sofia watched, her attention fully diverted to him, her gaze lingering on his mouth. He could still salvage the situation with her, he thought.

As Ruben elicited a laugh from the visitors, Artur found himself wondering, was the story Ruben just told true? Everything about these visits seemed artificially constructed to put the Jews in the best light and the Soviets in the worst.

But some of the stories might be true. Yosef Koslovsky's own tragic tale lent them credit.

"I used to be an astrophysicist," Sofia told the American couple as she passed around the chipped teacups. "I have my doctorate from Moscow State University, one of the best schools in the world," she boasted. "Do you know what I do now? I clean toilets at that same university. That's been my job for six years. No one would hire me for anything better once I requested to leave the Soviet Union."

Sofia hadn't struck him as a bitter person, but there was a deeply bitter undertone to her words. Artur sat on the couch beside Edik and listened, really listened, to what Sofia said, trying to get inside of her head.

"I feel trapped here. With no way out. My career is the least of it," she said. "I worry for my son who might one day have to go to the army. For my sister who's about to graduate high school. What future will they have—will any of us have—in this country that hates us?

"Stalin killed my grandparents because they were Jewish and part of the *intelligentsia*," she said. "They were upstanding members of the Communist Party when it happened. This beautiful apartment," she gestured at the walls with their ornate pre-war moldings, "was theirs. They were successful, respected people," she said. "They didn't think their own colleagues and friends would turn on them. And then they were executed."

Sofia had potent charisma and a knack for storytelling. Tying the apartment to her story made it real for her visitors, but she was capitalizing on events from a bygone era. Stalin's actions had been repudiated under Khrushchev.

She moved onto the story he'd heard her tell before about her brother-in-law, Max Abromovich and his family.

To hear her tell it, her brother-in-law had been a renowned scientist who, like Sakharov, had become uneasy about how his nuclear research was being used. Max had spoken out publicly, and the government had retaliated by arresting him.

The true story, the story Artur knew, was that Max Abromovich had been a traitor. He could have been executed for his crimes, but the court had accepted a plea bargain, a decision that Semyon rued every time his name came up in international negotiations. Increasingly, they suspected the man had not only proliferated dangerous propaganda about Soviet human rights violations, but that he had been selling nuclear secrets to the West.

"The KGB came for him in the middle of the night," Sofia said. "And then they returned a few days later and took his wife. And their daughter, Nadia. She was only fifteen."

"Fifteen?" one of the American tourists repeated, spellbound.

"Yes, fifteen, but they convicted her and sent her to the gulag, too."

Sofia smeared their country for events that Max himself had orchestrated and that had nothing to do with his Jewish nationality. It was Max's own fault. He was the one who had named his wife and young daughter as co-conspirators as part of his plea. Either she didn't know these details, or she lied to her audience by omission.

She moved onto the story of Mendel's arrest. This too she painted in the most negative possible light.

"He was tried on false charges. They said he was a drug dealer and sentenced him to five years in the gulag. Because he was teaching Hebrew."

Was that what had happened? Until yesterday, he would have dismissed the story, but Sofia had been so convincing. She hadn't wanted him engaged in visits like the one today without his understanding the dangers. She had said she'd seen the agents plant the marijuana, that it hadn't been Mendel's. Sofia presented Mendel as a tragic figure who bravely and heroically faced persecution for embracing his identity and teaching it to others.

What was true, and what wasn't?

It didn't matter, Artur decided. Mendel had been and likely still was a threat, an enemy to the state, a purveyor of Zionist propaganda about how Jews belonged in Israel, a symbol of the oppression and human rights violations the Americans used as excuses to flout the Helsinki Accords and continue their own nuclear program.

His country's future rested on silencing this criticism and holding the Americans to their promises for nuclear disarmament.

Next in her narrative of supposed Soviet atrocities and crimes, Sofia told the story of their attack near the synagogue. She painted Yosef and Edik as heroes, Davids to the Soviet Goliath that supposedly hated Jews. She conjectured what the militia would have done if they had arrived during the attack, how they wouldn't have defended her innocent party but instead would have sided with the anti-Semitic hoodlums who wanted them dead.

Artur couldn't fault her for her conclusions. But did his whole country deserve to be drawn into nuclear war because it contained a few bad people?

She magnified this example to indict the whole society to these receptive foreigners, who nodded and murmured in sympathy. "The neighbors cheered them on and told them to finish what Hitler started," she reported.

She chose the perfect detail for reeling in her American audience. The mention of Hitler seemed to resonate with their visitors. "Never again," the husband muttered under his breath, while his wife pursed her lips in a determined line.

The American Jewish community had done little to help their fellows during the Holocaust or to protect them from Stalin, and Sofia deftly played to their shame.

Sofia, he now understood, imagined she had an evil enemy to fight, an important mission on behalf of her family and her people. She sought partners in fighting what she believed a noble cause. No wonder she had endless patience for her uncle and cousin. Likely, she saw these visits and the related black market activity as a means to support the community in the face of persecution, a contribution to the larger cause.

Artur bet she didn't know how much of the money Edik and Ruben kept for their own personal use.

He now had the key to unlocking all of her secrets, to seducing her. He needed to prove himself her comrade in arms, wholeheartedly devoted to the same cause.

The American couple readily swallowed whole her woeful tale of an evil Soviet machine that manufactured horror upon horror and the threat of annihilation if it went unchecked. Of course they did. Sofia offered them more than tales of sorrow and horror. She offered them a path to redemption. In showing solidarity with Soviet Jews, they could redeem themselves for their failure to save their brethren from Hitler.

They wanted—no, they needed—her story to be true, her plea for help to be real. They would eagerly retell these stories of oppression, true or not. Meanwhile, the American government with its supposed interest in the rights of Soviet Jews would use these same tales to hold hostage all Soviet citizens by refusing to negotiate on nuclear disarmament.

"This is the life we live here as Jews," Sofia said to the visitors. "Our neighbors hate us. The government hates us. They would rather hurt us or kill us than let us leave."

"We're between a rock and a hard place. No matter what we do," Artur said. He adopted her solemn tone. "They even kill us when we serve in the military. My father and Sofia's cousin were both victims of supposed accidents in the army. Because they were Jewish."

Sofia tilted her head and studied him. While her expression gave nothing away, the directness of her gaze made him feel he had gained ground.

"I'm worried about my son's future," she said, appealing to the visitors as parents. "I want Kolya to grow up in a world where he doesn't have to be afraid." Her eyes filled with tears, and they spilled down her cheeks. She swiped away at them and fought to hold them back. One of the visitors patted her arm.

Sofia's voice cracked with emotion as she continued, "A world where he doesn't have to hide who he is or constantly look over his shoulder. Where he doesn't have to worry the KGB will come and steal away his family. Or that his life will be cut short because his fellow soldiers in the army hate him. I want him to be free."

"Amen," one of the visitors said, and then the others joined in chorus, as if concluding a prayer.

Artur reached over Edik, grabbed the box of tissues on the side table, and offered them to her. She took one with a sad smile that twisted his insides.

He steeled himself against the tender vines of sympathy reaching for him with insidious tendrils.

While she fretted over her son's future, the stories she so convincingly shared of Jewish oppression would be used to block disarmament talks and let Reagan continue with his deadly Star Wars program. Those stories threatened the futures of *every* Soviet child. They threatened the entire nation's hope for peace.

Artur had been sent to silence the human rights criticisms of the Soviet state, to stop the persecution stories leaking out of the country, to stop the traitors.

To stop criticisms like hers. Stories like hers. Traitors…like her.

Even if every word she spoke were true.

CHAPTER THIRTY-EIGHT
SOFIA

"**W**HAT'S THIS?" VERA asked when she came to pick Kolya up for school. She pointed to Sofia's kerchief and frowned with disapproval.

"Mendel wants me to wear it," Sofia said.

"Why? It's ugly," Vera said. Sofia couldn't disagree. She felt like an old *babushka.*

"I think that's the point," Sofia said. "He's worried some man will see my hair and be tempted to take me away from him."

"What next? Will he insist you wear a veil? Where will it stop?"

"I don't know." Sofia sighed heavily. "I guess I'm hoping that if I go along with him for a little bit, he'll return to himself."

"Good luck with that," Vera said dryly. "Yesterday he told me my dress was too short and also that God would punish me if I ate ham for lunch."

Sofia glanced surreptitiously toward the kitchen, where Mendel puttered with his breakfast. Asking her to wear different clothes and avoid certain foods was one thing, but he shouldn't be forcing his demands on the rest of her family.

"That's not why she's in a hurry," Kolya piped in.

He struggled over the laces on his shoes and pulled on his sweater. Sofia stuffed her hands in her pockets so that she wouldn't succumb to the intense urge to help him. Ever since Mendel's return, Kolya had developed a fierce, independent streak, as if he felt he had to prove to her that he was all grown up and that they didn't need Mendel.

"She wants to make sure we catch the same bus as Gennady."

Gennady. Kolya had mentioned him before, too. Vera hustled him out the door before Sofia could ask any questions or Kolya could incriminate her any further. Her rush was telling in itself.

This Gennady was a secret for Vera, one she clearly didn't want to share with Sofia. Her parents hadn't said anything about Vera seeing someone. Did they know?

Sofia joined Mendel in the kitchen. He had emptied one of the cabinets. Sugar, flour, her limited stock of spices, and a carton of kasha cluttered the faded and battered formica counter. Mendel scratched his head and huffed.

"Are you looking for something?" she asked.

"Sugar," he said.

"It's right there." She pointed to the canister beside him.

"Not that kind," he said.

"I don't know what you mean."

"Don't you?" he challenged.

He turned on the faucet. "It's only a matter of time before the KGB comes to search the place. I want to make sure there's nothing here for them to find."

"What makes you think they're going to come searching?" she asked cautiously. His confession echoed ominously in her head, *They sent me home so they could catch you.*

"I'm going to start teaching again."

"Hebrew classes?"

"No. Not Hebrew. A religious study group." His eyes were bright with excitement.

"What about the rabbi? Shouldn't he be the one to do this? Surely he knows more than you," she suggested.

"The rabbi isn't trustworthy. He doesn't have our best interests at heart." His voice dropped low. "As you know," he said, and she assumed he was referring to the bugs they'd found.

"You're waving a flag at them to come raid our apartment," she said.

She could easily imagine how the agents would invade their space, the way they had five years prior when they'd ripped Mendel from their bed. They had dumped every drawer and bookcase, put their hands on all of their things, and then taken him away from her and Kolya.

She shuddered at the remembered violation. Even now, she awakened with nightmares of that event, and she hadn't suffered a tenth of what Mendel had.

If the KGB swarmed in, they would go through every inch of her apartment, just as they had the night they arrested Mendel. They would find Paul's note and the cameras...

"Possibly," he agreed. "But better this apartment than another," he said nobly. "Especially when there won't be any *sugar* or anything else here for them to find."

She had to remove the incriminating items from the crawl space. She needed a new hiding place.

"Never mind the search. They arrested you for teaching before," she protested.

"Yes, because that was about solidarity with a different country," he said. "But this is different. This is about our relationship with God."

"You think the KGB cares about the distinction?" she asked with disbelief.

"Name one case of a religious Jew they have arrested and sent to the gulag," he challenged.

When had he lost his mind and become so horrifically naïve?

"Mendelevich," she said quickly. Her father kept lists of all of the Jews, like Max and Irena and Nadia, who had been sent off to prison and what was known about their whereabouts and status.

"Yes, Mendelevich was religious," Mendel conceded, "but they arrested him for trying to hijack a plane. We're not spies or hijackers.

There won't be a problem."

But she was a spy. And if the KGB found the evidence, she'd be executed.

"We have to adjust to the reality that we're not leaving this place, and we have to figure out how to survive anyway," he said. "The Jews here don't know who they are. They don't know the legacy of our traditions. The people here will attack us because we're different, and we have no knowledge of the pride we should have about these differences. They would have us feel shame and think we're dirty. That we're less than human. But you can't study our tradition without being proud. And this is a way to fight back."

"That's not fighting back," she said. "It's giving up. Covering our heads. Putting things on our doors. Retreating into religion and praying to God for the Soviets to leave us alone. You're not in prison now. You don't have to hide in a book of psalms to survive."

"I'm not hiding or giving up. Don't you see? This is my plan to protect you."

"Protect me? You said the KGB wants to flush out the activists," she said. "Your plan invites them to come here and look."

"And then they'll see there's no one to catch. Nothing to find," he said. "Whatever you're doing, it's time to stop."

Stop? Everything he'd told her about his release only made her more determined than ever to keep fighting.

Her actions, her family's action, had pushed the KGB to act, to try to shut down their activities. Their response meant their efforts were working enough to be a threat.

She couldn't stop now. Wouldn't. Even if the risk of discovery was greater than ever.

"Promise me you'll stop."

"I won't make that promise," she said.

"Why do you have to be so stubborn? I'm trying to protect you!"

"What about Irena and Max and Nadia? Who's protecting them? Fighting for them?"

"Forget about them," he said. "They've been in the gulag even longer than I was. They might as well be dead. If they aren't already."

"How can you say that? About your own sister? And what about the other people who've been arrested?"

"You've done enough," he said. "Let someone else carry the burden for a little while."

"It's not enough. I think of what happened to you—what might be happening to them—and I have to do everything in my power to spare someone else the same fate."

"No," he said. "It's too dangerous. I don't want the KGB coming for you."

"If that ever happens," she said, "then I hope there will be someone just like me fighting on my side."

Mendel turned his back on her as if the conversation between them were over. He left the faucet running and dragged a chair over to the crawl space.

"What are you doing?" she asked, suddenly nervous.

"I told you. I'm looking for *sugar*. Since you won't help me, I'll have to find it on my own."

He climbed up on the kitchen chair and reached for the handle to open the hatch. Then he levered himself up into the crawl space.

She ran through things she might say, "There's no sugar up there," or, "You won't find anything," or "What exactly are you looking for?" She realized that anything she might say would only convince him to look harder.

Her only hope was that he wouldn't find the things she'd hidden behind the clutter of boxes and old belongings.

She climbed up onto the chair, stood on tiptoe, and stuck her head into the crawl space. The cramped space couldn't accommodate both of them.

Mendel crouched on his knees under the naked lightbulb.

"It's just boxes." He sounded almost lost. He closed his eyes.

"Yes, just boxes. Max and Irena's stuff," she said.

He surveyed the area, and she held her breath.

"What's this?" Something caught his eye. She watched in horror as he crawled into the corner where the cameras were hidden. He picked up one of the Tropels. He held it to the light. "Lipstick?"

She swallowed hard. This would be the moment to tell him about Paul. About her activities. About the opportunity to be exfiltrated.

But she wasn't ready. She didn't want to stop.

"It must be Irena's. Or Nadia's." She brazened out the discovery.

He pulled the cap from the cherry red Tropel and frowned. "It's not lipstick. What is it?"

"I don't know. Let me see," she said.

"Stop lying to me," he snapped. "I know you too well."

He snatched up something else in his hand and moved back under the light. That's when she saw he had the new roll of rubles and Paul's letter. She could see the strings of numbers and her neat print underneath.

Now he would know everything.

His eyes scanned the page, moving rapidly over one line and the next. Then he crumpled the paper in his hand and roared at her. "How could you?"

The madness in his eyes made her back up. She clambered down from the chair and retreated to the sink.

He scrambled out of the crawl space and flew at her. His fists clenched the money roll, Paul's letter, and the tiny cameras, and he waved them in her face. "What the hell were you thinking?"

She reached behind her and turned the water up to full force.

"It was bad enough when I thought you were involved with whatever your father's latest scheme is," Mendel said. "But this? This is far beyond anything I could ever imagine. How could you? How could you risk yourself like this? You're a mother."

"I do it because I'm a mother," she said. "Because I want a better world for Kolya."

"You do it because you're a fool," he said. "Max's fool. Right? This is all connected to him."

He too easily put the pieces together, uncovering the secret she'd guarded so carefully.

"We're taking all of this down to the incinerator," he said. "It's over. Done. Do you hear me? It stops now. No more risks. I forbid it."

"You forbid it?" she echoed in disbelief. "Don't tell me your God demands that, too." She regretted the words as soon as they escaped her mouth.

He struck her hard across her face. The strike and the pain shocked her. She shielded her face with her hands, and for a moment she couldn't see in front of her. He had never raised a hand to her before, but she braced herself for another blow.

CHAPTER THIRTY-NINE
SOFIA

"OH, GOD. I'M so sorry," Mendel said. "I didn't mean it. I didn't mean to hurt you."

Warm liquid trickled against her fingers, and she slowly realized she was bleeding. She glared at him over her bloody hands.

She heard the scrape of a key in the lock.

"We're back," Vera called, and Sofia heard the front door open. Mendel hastily stuffed the cameras and letter into his pockets.

"Kolya forgot his lunch." Vera jogged into the kitchen, caught a glimpse of Sofia, and gasped. "*Bozhe moy!* What happened?"

"Here. Sit. Tilt your head back." Mendel pushed a chair toward her, suddenly gentle and solicitous. "I'm sorry. I'm so sorry."

He pressed her into the chair and pushed a towel against her nose.

"You hit her!" Vera accused Mendel. "What's happened to you? All this nonsense about God, and now this? You're an animal. You've gone insane."

"Never speak to me that way! You're a child. Do I need to teach you your place?"

Mendel had always been hotheaded, but now he seemed unable

to control his temper, no matter that he had been so contrite only a moment before.

Kolya elbowed past him. "Mama, are you okay?"

"I'm fine," she said for him. The physical pain had already started to recede. "Don't worry, either of you. It was an accident," she lied.

To Vera, she said, "Kolya's lunch is on the counter. Go now. I don't want you to be late."

She couldn't afford anyone else learning about her espionage. She needed Vera and Kolya out of the apartment before Mendel let something slip.

Kolya pressed himself against her leg. She would have hugged him, but her hand was wet with blood. "It's okay, Kolya. It's all going to be okay," she said, even though she didn't feel at all calm herself.

When they were finally convinced to leave for the bus, Mendel rounded on her. "Here's what we're going to do," he said. "We're going down to the incinerator, and you're going to burn the... lipstick and the letter."

"No," she said.

"I'm not giving you a choice," he told her. He hoisted her out of the chair by the arm.

Mendel grasped her arm tightly, as if she were his prisoner, and marched her to the elevator. She was ready to explode, but she bit her tongue, not wanting to fight with him in the corridor, where the neighbors might hear.

Her nose was still bleeding, and she pressed the kitchen towel to her nostrils. She'd seen another side of Mendel this morning. Her face ached with the bruising evidence of the change in him.

He had become feral, a wild, wounded, territorial animal likely to startle and attack at any moment.

The other night, she had longed for him to hold her, to kiss her. Now she couldn't stand his touch.

He repulsed her. With his long, frizzy beard and black skullcap, he appeared a throwback to the *shtetls* of the early 1900s, utterly alien. Gone was the cosmopolitan intellectual she had married. She saw no trace of that man now.

Apparently, Mendel had learned in prison to be a bully, not a defender, despite all of his talk of wanting to protect her. But she had learned important lessons of her own. Pretending to be meek and subdued would buy her time to plot and plan.

Mendel jabbed repeatedly at the button for the elevator. A tense minute passed, and he lost all patience. Rather than wait, he pulled her along swiftly down the eight flights of steps to the basement, as if they were running for their lives.

The janitor was nowhere to be seen when they reached the trash room. A high pile of trash bags sat at the bottom of the garbage shute, waiting for the janitor to dispose of them in the hot incinerator. The room smelled of oil and garbage. She could hear the roar of the hungry fire that fueled the incinerator.

Mendel retrieved Paul's letter from his pocket and threw it into the flames.

Her chest ached as she watched the paper, full of urgent questions from U.S. intelligence about how to mitigate the Soviet threat, ignite and curl in on itself.

He reached into his pocket again and produced the fat roll of rubles. "You can't burn that."

"Watch me," he said.

She wrapped her hands around his arm to keep him from hurling the money into the flames. "Do you have any idea how many people that money helps?"

"At what cost?" He tore himself out of her grasp and fed the whole roll into the fire. For a moment, she stood stunned, watching the paper money ignite and then turn to ash. She could scarcely believe what he had just done. Thousands of rubles. Gone.

Next, he pulled the cameras out of his pocket.

"Please, please don't do this," she begged.

"You know I have to," he said. He held an arm out to stave her off. "To keep you safe. This is for your own good."

"I won't forgive you for this," she said.

"I don't care if you hate me. At least you'll be safe. Not in prison. Not raped. Not beaten. Not dead!"

He hurled the cherry red camera into the flames. She watched it warp and melt in the heat, and she burned along with it, her rage white hot.

"Stop! You have no idea what you're doing," she said as he pulled the metallic blue Tropel from his pocket and prepared to throw it into the furnace.

"Do you?" he asked. "Do you have any idea how much danger you've put yourself in?" He threw the camera with such force that it pinged against the back of the furnace before bouncing into the flames.

She grabbed his arm before he could dispatch another Tropel. "Please stop. Please."

When he didn't yield, she tried to tear the camera from his grasp. He raised his arm high until she could no longer reach.

"Maybe you can pry these out of my hands, but you won't get far with them," he threatened.

She knew when she was beaten. Even if she could wrest the cameras from him, she had nowhere to run and hide where he wouldn't find her.

She crossed her arms over her chest. She hated feeling so damn powerless. Hated him.

Where was the man she had loved? He would be applauding her one-woman rebellion, not trying to quash it.

Her own rage and fury burned brightly, flaring with the flames as Mendel threw the gold camera into the furnace. He could have tossed them in all at once, but he seemed to like making her watch each one melt away, as if she might accept the finality of this act.

Her eyes burned and watered. He fed the metallic black Tropel into the greedy fire, and then his hands were empty.

He'd only burned four cameras. But Paul had given her five. Five! Mendel had missed the silver one.

Hope fluttered inside her. The silver Tropel, the one already holding photographs from the prototype report, was still hidden away in the crawl space. Along with the substantial sum of rubles Paul had given her previously.

"It's over," he said. "You're done with all of this. Now you'll be safe."

But it wasn't over, not for her. And none of them were safe. Not yet.

She turned her back on him, refusing to look at him. How could he do this to her?

All this time, she had prayed for him to return to her, to have a partner, and in this moment, she almost wished he hadn't returned.

She closed her eyes and took a long moment to steady herself. Then she prayed, not to Mendel's god but to her own, for the strength to finish what she had started and the grace to overcome the many obstacles in her path, including Mendel himself.

He clamped his hand onto her shoulders. "Promise me you'll stop."

He tried to exact the promise she had refused to make before. "Or what? You'll turn me in? Hit me again."

"God, no. Sofia, how could you even think I'd want to hurt you?"

"You hit me. You dragged me down here against my will," she reminded him.

"I'm sorry." His words surprised her. The old Mendel had never been quick to apologize. "You're right. I lost my temper. I could have handled this differently. But I saw the letter, and I got so scared."

He let go of her and came around to stand in front of her. He took her hands in his and clasped them gently.

"It would kill me if something happened to you. You're my world," he said.

"Your world?" she scoffed. He had barely touched her since he'd returned. He'd admitted to an affair with another woman. Right now, she couldn't stand the sight of him. She looked away, staring at a point on the floor.

"My world," he repeated. "I need you to be safe. It's what I prayed for every night in prison when I couldn't be here to protect you. It's what I pray for now, knowing that the KGB is watching me. Watching us.

"Please, Sofia, I know you're angry," he said. "But you need to understand." He waited for her to look at him. Stubbornly, she held her ground, held on to her anger.

He didn't force her chin up to look at him. Without letting go of her hands, he sank to his knees. He looked up into her face. "I know my return has been hard for you. I've let you down in so many ways," he said. "I know I'm different now. I've seen too much. Lost too much. I can't be the man I was before. I don't know what I can give you now," he said.

His dark eyes implored her to listen, to understand. She felt her heart breaking.

The tears she'd held back washed over her now. Her own knees buckled, and she knelt across from him on the dirty basement floor.

It was over. Her Mendel wasn't coming back. He was gone, and in his place was this strange man with his short temper and superstitious beliefs.

"I want you to know I would give my dying breath if it would keep you safe." He cupped his hands to her cheek and wiped away the streaming tears with his thumbs. "I love you."

I love you. His quiet declaration had the force of a bomb, exploding all of her doubts and fears about him.

He loved her.

He was on her side.

He wasn't an agent for the enemy.

There was still hope for them.

She leaned into him until their foreheads touched. He didn't shrink from the contact this time.

It wasn't a kiss, but it was closer, so much closer than they had come before.

"I love you, too," she said.

He exhaled and pulled her into his arms, embracing her, hugging her close. He cradled the back of her head with one hand, the way he used to. Then he slipped his fingers under her kerchief and buried them in her hair.

She reveled in that small intimacy and let herself cling to him, cling to the hope that if he could embrace her like this after everything, maybe there could still be more.

Maybe they could find their way back to each other.

He whispered, "I can't lose you. Please, Sofia. Please promise me you'll give this up. Please."

"I promise," she lied, because it was what he needed her to say and because she desperately wanted a future for them.

CHAPTER FORTY

ARTUR

THE MORNING DRAGGED, with no sign of Sofia. Even without foreign visitors, Ruben happily talked for hours. Unfortunately, Artur quickly discovered the man had little of use to say, but nonetheless repeated the ideas and small tidbits of information that happened into his possession. His stream of consciousness monologues offered up more useless musings than an interrogation goosed with truth serum.

For his part, Edik had turned even more taciturn than before the attack. Artur wasn't sure whether to blame the fact Ruben monopolized every available topic of conversation, Edik's concussion, or his concerns about his upcoming move.

When Edik finally spoke, he did offer a useful new lead. "Mendel's holding a study group."

"To teach Hebrew?" Artur asked, wondering what on earth would possess a man fresh out of prison to return to the activity he claimed had been the reason for his arrest.

"He said it's to talk about religion," Edik said.

"Are you interested in talking about religion?" Artur asked, mildly curious.

"No. But I'm going to go." It wasn't hard to guess the real reason Edik wanted to go. Sofia had yet to drop by today, and it wasn't clear that she would. "Do you want to come?"

"Sure. It's better than sitting around here doing nothing." Artur didn't need to be convinced to go. He was eager to expand his network, and he wondered who else Mendel would recruit to this new venture. He was also eager to put his new insights to the test and try to move things forward with Sofia.

They left later in the morning, leaving Ruben alone in the apartment. Today, even without the audience, Edik's father still complained of not feeling well. Artur chose to believe the man would lay abed and not engage in clandestine activities while they were away, but he was glad Ruben had his own KGB watchers to keep tabs on him.

No one seemed to follow Artur and Edik, but when they arrived at Mendel and Sofia's apartment building, they found ten KGB agents milling outside the entrance.

"There are a lot of KGB agents out here," Edik said as they approached.

Artur recognized four as Ilya's watchers and two more as Mendel's. He supposed the others were assigned to other Jews likely to cause trouble, ones he would no doubt recognize from the files. Or perhaps the KGB had caught wind of the study group and had sent extra muscle as intimidation.

"Do you think it's safe for us to go to the study group?" Artur asked. "Will we be arrested?"

"Maybe," Edik said. "Worst case? We'll get fifteen days in jail for public disruption. Mendel might get it a little worse."

"Fifteen days in prison," Artur repeated, trying to understand Edik's mindset.

"Three hundred sixty hours," Edik confirmed.

"That's a lot," Artur said. "You could miss your window to leave the country. Do you think the class will be worth it?"

"Doesn't really matter," Edik said, and Artur surmised that Sofia's presence would be enough to make the event worthwhile to Edik.

Getting arrested might even present an added bonus, a convenient excuse for Edik to stick around.

Despite his rather nonchalant attitude about arrest, Edik ducked his head as they passed the agents. Artur followed suit. He didn't know any of these men and supposed they belonged to a task force with lower security clearance.

After they passed the agents, Edik whispered, "If we get arrested, then the news will go out to our friends in Israel or America. And they'll pressure the government to let us go." Edik described perfectly the very cycle Artur had been sent to break.

"Who will send the story out?" Artur asked.

"Someone," Edik said cryptically, but Artur suspected he really had no idea.

Edik opened the door to the apartment building and held it for Artur. Sofia's father stood in the small anteroom opposite the mail slots, looking up at the numbers above the single elevator.

Ilya greeted Edik warmly, kissing him on both cheeks, and then he turned to Artur and did the same.

"Is the elevator working? Have you been waiting long?" Edik asked.

"It's working today," Ilya said. "A few of us arrived at the same time. It was crowded. So I decided to wait."

"So there's a large turnout?" Artur asked.

"No," Ilya said. "The elevator is just very small. And someone smelled like onions and stinky cheese."

"I'm surprised you're going to this class at all," Artur said. "I thought religious teachings weren't your taste. And now, with stinky cheese…" He tried to joke with Ilya.

"And onions," Ilya agreed. "You're quite right. But it's my daughter's apartment that's about to be clogged with zealotry and unpleasant smells, and she might need a little support."

Artur detected the censure in Ilya's voice. The man didn't approve of his son-in-law's new direction, and, he surmised, neither did Sofia, even if she had started covering her abundant hair.

The battle lines were being drawn, and he planned to exploit the tensions among the players, especially the rift between Mendel and Sofia.

"I understand you brought the KGB," Artur said and nodded toward the agents standing outside the door.

"Consider it a public service," Ilya said dryly. "This way we can't forget we're being watched."

Artur chuckled as if Ilya had made an excellent joke.

CHAPTER FORTY-ONE
SOFIA

W HEN SOFIA AND Mendel returned from the basement, Sofia yearned to go immediately to the crawl space .

But she didn't dare.

She went into the bathroom. She splashed cold water on her face, washing away her tears and the traces of blood still on her nose and hands.

She had promised Mendel she would stop her spying. She couldn't risk his discovering she had lied. She couldn't give him any cause to doubt her. So far as he was concerned, she had made her promise and given up espionage.

She needed him to believe her wholeheartedly if she had any hope of continuing undetected.

When she shut off the water, she heard Mendel's footsteps. Was he headed back to the crawl space? Would he find the last Tropel before she could save it?

There were other treasures there still, too. Earlier, he hadn't noticed the English book, banned in the Soviet Union, that Paul had given her for decoding his messages. And he hadn't found the substantial pile of money.

Mendel must have bypassed the kitchen. She heard the front door open. For a brief, hopeful moment she thought Mendel might leave.

She needed to retrieve those remaining items from the crawl space. Before Mendel destroyed them. Or before the KGB descended on their apartment.

Slowly, she eased open the bathroom door and watched as Mendel greeted four men.

"Welcome. Welcome," Mendel said. "I'm so glad you could come."

He had been expecting them, she realized. How long had he been planning this study group? Looking back, she suspected he had made arrangements on Saturday, when he had preached from the steps of the synagogue, perhaps issuing the invitations right after she had left.

Gracious and calm, he shepherded them into the living room and invited them all to sit and make themselves comfortable.

She came out of the bathroom, and his eyes tracked her movements. She didn't miss the nervous, almost guilty look on his face.

He obviously hadn't wanted her to know ahead of time. He had never expected her to cooperate or agree. He had known all along he would have to force her into surrender.

"I'll make tea," she offered. She noticed some of the tension leave his shoulders.

"Thank you." His voice cracked with what sounded like relief.

Let him think he had won.

She would smuggle the camera, book, and money from the crawl space with Mendel none the wiser.

He didn't need to know she planned to continue her espionage. The knowledge would only drive an impenetrable wedge between them. In the inevitable battle of wills, he would do anything to win, and so would she.

But if he didn't know? Poof! No battle. No conflict. Maybe they could finally start their lives together.

Mendel followed her to the kitchen, where she began to tidy up the mess he had made when he had emptied the cabinets earlier.

He stopped her and took her hand in his. For a moment, he looked at her the way he used to, with love shining so clearly in his eyes. It made her smile, and then he smiled, too. He squeezed her hand and then returned to the living room, a spring in his step.

She brought her hand to her heart and stood quietly for a moment, daring to hope.

He was soon caught up in his role as host and teacher. There was something comforting about seeing him resume the role he had once so loved.

She filled a kettle and set it on the stove. She glanced out at the men in her living room. From where they sat, they wouldn't be able to see her opening the hatch to the crawl space and climbing in and out. Even if one of them happened into the kitchen and caught her up there, they wouldn't think it strange. Most apartments had similar storage spaces. There was nothing inherently suspicious about retrieving objects from one.

She only had to worry about Mendel. He would suspect immediately.

He seemed engaged in conversation with his guests. She made some more noise with the teapot, and he didn't even dart a glance in her direction. Good!

This was her best chance. Maybe her only one.

The chair was still positioned beneath the crawl space door. She climbed up and lifted herself into the small, dark space. She pulled the string to turn on the overhead bulb and searched the shadowy corner behind the boxes where she had stashed the items from Paul. There! The silver of the lipstick tube caught the light.

She scrambled to reach it. She breathed a hefty sigh of relief when she clutched the cool metal in her hand. All wasn't lost. She had a few more nights of photographing ahead of her, but Paul would have the document on the prototype, all of it.

Assuming she could get back into the laboratory office and the file cabinet.

Assuming she could avoid getting caught.

She shoved the precious camera in her pocket and then swiftly grabbed the rubles. The money was still loosely wrapped in its original package from Paul, which may have been why Mendel hadn't noticed it earlier.

He had tossed tens of thousands of dollars worth of equipment into the fire. He had burned up thousands of rubles, even though people in their community depended on that money to make ends meet. She wouldn't let him find the rest and destroy it.

She had to smuggle it, along with Paul's book, out of her apartment.

She folded the paper more tightly around the remaining stack of money and refastened the twine. Even without the amount she had already smuggled to her parents, the package was still roughly the size of a book, slightly smaller than the one Paul had given her for decoding his messages.

She tucked the book and the package of rubles under her arm and shimmied out of the crawl space. She needed to keep them temporarily hidden until she could get them out of the apartment. While a KGB agent might find the book itself incriminating, there was nothing about a book or a brown paper package that would immediately raise anyone else's suspicions. No one who came upon her this moment and saw her holding the items would suspect her of spying—except for Mendel. But it would be even better if no one noticed the items at all.

When she came out of the crawl pace, she couldn't see the guests from where she stood in the back of the kitchen, which hopefully meant they couldn't see her either. She heard Mendel, talking to his guests in the living room, making introductions.

She hadn't been caught.

Where could she hide the book and the money? They were bulky and not easily disguised. She glanced wildly around the kitchen. She found and discarded several potential temporary hiding places.

Her father called. "Sofia?"

She was out of time. She tightened her arm against her side, hugging the rubles and the book close.

Ilya poked his head into the kitchen. "What are you doing in here?"

"Making tea," she said.

"What happened to you?" Ilya asked. Crossing the small kitchen in a few quick strides, he caught her by the chin and inspected her face.

"An accident. Nothing to worry about," she said.

"Are you sure?" He gave her arm a gentle shake as if to rattle the truth out of her and dislodged the items she was holding.

She managed to catch the book but fumbled the heavy brick of rubles. The paper and twine package fell to the floor with a dull thud and landed at her father's feet.

He bent to pick it up. The brown paper had torn in the fall. The corner of a stack of rubles poked through the wrapper.

Her father straightened and seemed to weigh the money in his hand. His gaze locked with hers.

He couldn't know how she had gotten the money, but he would easily grasp its significance and recognize how much more it was than the already substantial amounts she regularly delivered to his sugar bowl. He had been involved in more than his fair share of underground enterprises.

He opened his mouth, about to speak when they both realized someone else had joined them. Sofia pressed the book close against her side to hide the cover in the folds of her skirt. Then she turned to find Edik and Yosef hovering in the kitchen doorway.

Edik's gaze dipped to the package of rubles. Her father tried casually to hide it behind his back.

But it was too late. Yosef and Edik had both seen it. Worse, the congregation by the kitchen had drawn Mendel's attention. He moved quickly toward them.

As Mendel approached, she opened the door to the refrigerator, blocking his view into the kitchen. She grabbed the package from her father and stuffed it and the book into the fridge next to last night's leftovers, while Edik and Yosef looked on from the doorway.

"What happened to your face?" Edik asked, once she closed the door. She could have kissed him for the distraction.

All three men—Ilya, Edik, and Yosef—crowded into the kitchen to take a closer look. She touched her nose with her hands, as if she had nearly forgotten the trauma that had bruised her. "It's nothing. I'm sure it looks worse than it is."

"It looks pretty bad. What happened?" Ilya asked again. Her father now turned to Mendel, eyebrows raised, a hint of a challenge in his question.

"We had a fight," Mendel admitted. His shoulders stooped, and she believed he was truly ashamed for having struck her.

"It was an accident," she said.

"Did you accidentally walk into his fist?" Yosef asked. He stood tall and squared off with Mendel.

"Stop it. It wasn't like that," she said, stepping between them. She turned to Mendel, eager for him to move off before he might discover her plan. "Go get started. I'll bring out the tea when it's ready."

Mendel gave her a tentative smile. As he headed back toward the other students in the living room, Sofia whispered to her father, "I need you to keep him distracted."

More loudly, she asked her cousin, "Edik, would you mind helping me with the tea?"

As if on cue, the kettle whistled. She moved to the stove to turn it off. Yosef followed a step behind.

"If he lays a hand on you again, I'll kill him," Yosef muttered darkly so that only she could hear. She turned to him with surprise. She wasn't prepared for the intensity of his gaze, the passion in his eyes, and she stood, spellbound, wondering what it meant.

Had their trials together forged such a strong bond?

"Sofia and Edik have things well in hand." Her father tugged on Yosef's sleeve, and the spell between them was broken. "Come on. Let's go see what the charlatan has to say."

She turned her back on him and busied herself with preparing tea. She steeped tea leaves in hot water and gathered cups and saucers, buying time until Mendel was fully engaged with his class.

Then signaling Edik to join her, she opened the refrigerator. He immediately spied the package with rubles. He pulled it from the shelf and weighed it in his hands. "At least thirty thousand, but possibly more depending on the weight of the wrapper," he breathed in hushed awe.

He had a knack for money that way, intuiting amounts by feel and effortlessly summing complex calculations. "Where did the money come from?"

She pressed her finger to her lips, signaling him to hush. "It's a secret," she said. "And people might be listening."

His nod showed he understood she wouldn't or couldn't discuss the matter with him now, and she knew she could trust him to keep quiet. Like her, he had been raised with a healthy respect for surveillance.

"Can you hide all of this for me?" she whispered, indicating the money as well as the book.

She hated to ask him. In only a few days he would be on his way to America or Israel and free to let the world know of his achievements. Carting around this much money was a risky proposition. If he was caught, he would lose his opportunity to leave.

"Anything for you," he said.

Without further discussion, he untucked his shirt, loosened his belt, and inserted the package along with the book into the back of his pants.

The package stuck up just a little past his belt, and he covered it with his shirt.

"Good?" he asked her, turning his back to her for inspection.

"It will be invisible once you have your coat on," she said.

"I'll take it out to the *dacha*," he said. Their families owned a cottage seventeen kilometers outside of Moscow.

"That's perfect," she said. "Thank you."

"Is there anything else I can do?"

Spontaneously, she threw her arms around her cousin. "Just be careful, and be safe."

He murmured something at the top of her head. It sounded suspiciously like, "I love you, too."

CHAPTER FORTY-TWO
ARTUR

THE MONEY! ARTUR had seen the huge stack of money Sofia had hidden in the fridge, and he had the heady sense that his case was about to burst wide open. Soon, so soon, he'd be able to hand the traitors to Semyon and come home a hero.

Ilya plunked himself down on the threadbare velveteen sofa and patted the seat beside him. At the invitation, Artur sank deep into the misshapen cushions, although he would have preferred to sit on one of the hard chairs set up in a semicircle around the sofa, a position that might have allowed him to keep an eye on the doorway into the kitchen.

"Good," Ilya said once Artur was sitting beside him. "I didn't want to get stuck next to Misha." He gestured to a bearded man deep in conversation with Ruben and Mendel.

"Cheese and onions?" Artur ventured.

"*Tak.*" Ilya folded his hands over his mound of a belly and sat back in his seat, as if ready to nap, but Artur noted how he seemed to watch everyone through the slits of his half-closed eyes.

Artur shifted uncomfortably on the too-soft sofa. The springs were worn. Maya wouldn't have allowed such a shabby piece to remain in their apartment.

He looked forward to putting this case and Yosef Koslovsky successfully behind him and returning full-time to his life as Artur Gregorovich.

The Reitmans' apartment boasted none of the luxuries of his own—no Turkish rugs or oil paintings or fine knickknacks. Judging by what he'd seen, his conspirators had access to enough money to furnish several apartments decadently and still have money to burn. Why wouldn't they use some of it to fix up Sofia's apartment? Perhaps they were being careful not to draw suspicion. But at the very least, they could have splurged on a pile of toys for her young son.

He supposed Sofia was so dedicated to the cause that it never occurred to her use the money for her own family. She would never conscience skimming from the top like her cousin, who showed no compunction about his fast spending on food and drink.

Artur and Ilya sat side by side, their legs touching, in an uncomfortable silence, while the room filled with men. A dozen in total crammed into the living room.

From his position, he could see Sofia and Edik whispering urgently in the kitchen. Then she opened the refrigerator, and the two were shielded from view.

Sofia had her back to him. A few errant curls peeked out from the kerchief she had taken to wearing.

The curls tantalized him. Artur anticipated the moment when he would bury his fingers in her waves of hair, lock his lips to hers, and deliberately claim all of her secrets.

Sofia was keeping secrets, many, many secrets.

Normal people with secrets suffered with them. The bigger the secret, the greater the pressure, the more they yearned to relieve the tension and reveal themselves. He merely had to seem like a sympathetic ear at that perfect moment of ripeness, and all of those juicy secrets would pour right into his hands.

Ilya jabbed him in the ribs, dispelling his daydreams of making his daughter come undone.

"I see the way you look at her. Don't get any ideas," Ilya said in a low voice so that only Artur could hear. "Just because they're fighting, don't think you have a chance. She stayed faithful the whole five years he was in prison. She loves that man."

Artur was struck once again by Ilya's shrewdness. "I meant no disrespect."

"No harm done," Ilya said. "I'm just letting you know how things are."

How things were, Artur thought. She'd stayed faithful while Mendel was gone. Now that he was here making her life hell, she might very well choose to seek comfort elsewhere.

"So, Mendel, Yosef and I are curious," Ilya said, pinching Artur's arm. "If God cares so much about what we do, then why do bad things happen to good people?"

He recognized Ilya's question as an attempt to divert his too-obvious attention from Sofia and perhaps Mendel's as well.

Out of the corner of his eye, Artur observed Edik leaving the kitchen. Edik slinked into the hallway toward the door. Most people wouldn't have noticed the added bulk at Edik's lower back, but Artur did.

He heard the front door open. He had no doubt Sofia had colluded with Edik to smuggle the money out of the apartment. To what end?

Artur debated following Edik but didn't have a good way to extricate himself from the conversation Ilya had started. He decided his best course was to play along.

"Why, for example, do so many Jewish accidents happen in the army?" Artur contributed, doing his part to keep Mendel distracted, as Sofia had requested. The KGB agents gathered outside would note where Edik went, and Artur would wring the information from him later when they met back at the apartment. In the meantime, he would use the chance to prove himself a worthy ally.

"There is great evil in the world," Mendel said. "God is powerful and all-knowing, but He cannot work His will alone. We must all do our part."

"So, are you saying that the men who died weren't somehow doing their part?" Ilya challenged.

"You think I'm foolish and that my faith is stupid," Mendel snapped.

Artur noted how Mendel's temper ignited so quickly and with only the slightest provocation. He found himself worrying that Sofia's injuries might not turn out to be a onetime occurrence.

His rage over Mendel's abuse stunned him. He shouldn't care. If anything, he should be glad. Mendel's violence could only serve to drive Sofia into his arms.

"I don't think it's foolish or stupid," Ilya soothed. "I just want to understand. You've come home to us so different. With all kinds of *rules* and new ideas about religion."

Mendel visibly struggled with his temper, clenching and unclenching his fists, until the redness receded from his face. Eventually, he gained control of himself. He managed to sound civil, even reasonable, when he finally answered Ilya's question.

"Not so much has changed," Mendel said. "Like you, I believe we must all do our part to bring about a better world. You have your ways," he said cryptically, "and I used to embrace them."

Artur would have liked to know just how Mendel and Ilya had tried to change the world. Mendel had spent the past five years in prison, where he wouldn't have been capable of much contact with outsiders. For his part, Ilya had been saddled with a team of watchers, but Artur suspected he'd been actively creating trouble all along, right under their noses.

"I used to think that the way forward was to speak out, to fight." Mendel paced the room and stroked his wispy beard. Based on the introductions and what he had gleaned from the files at the Lubyanka, Artur knew the men in the parlor to be reasonably intelligent people, out-of-work engineers and scientists. They watched Mendel curiously. No one spoke or interrupted.

"I lived by those convictions. I sacrificed for them. Those convictions got me arrested. Those convictions got me a further sentence in solitary confinement." He had the appearance of a wise, old sage, and the sonorous voice and cadence of a gifted orator. "And in the years away from my family, away from my community, away from my wife"—he acknowledged Sofia, who chose that moment to enter with the tea tray—"in a cell so small I couldn't even lie flat on my back, I had a revelation."

Sofia pressed her lips together, as if she longed to comment but would not permit herself. What did she make of all of this?

"Alone in my cell, I was forced to look inward. To listen to the voice that I had not been able to hear before over the roar of my own ambition and will." Mendel took a moment, looked each of the men in the room in the eye, even Artur. "My friends, I came to understand that to change the world, to make it better, we must first change ourselves. We must first be better men."

Artur couldn't deny Mendel's gift for rhetoric. But what was his angle? Such lofty words about being a better person meant little if he beat his own wife.

"The only way to do that is to embrace God's teaching," Mendel said. He began to expound on this idea, telling them there were commandments, long lists of rules that had to be learned and followed.

"I don't know about all of this religious stuff," someone said, and he seemed to speak for the others as well. "I'm interested in learning about Jewish history. About my heritage. If the Soviets hate me for it, then at least I should understand it. But I'm not interested in becoming religious. I'm not going to grow a beard or start spouting off about God."

"Or spend long hours in the Grand Choral Synagogue with the old men," someone else added, and another man said at the same time, "We have no desire to isolate ourselves from regular society. Like in the days of the Jewish *shtetls*."

Mendel's students talked over each other, each adding another aspect of religious observance that failed to appeal. They were united in their resistance. Mendel's face grew taut. His lips formed a thin line, and he tugged at his beard. He appeared as if he were at the end of a tether stretched to its limit. He closed his eyes and mouthed a few unintelligible words, maybe a prayer, Artur thought.

When Mendel spoke, his voice was surprisingly soft and calm. "I would never ask you to."

Artur saw through Mendel's false claim. He knew the man had forced his wife to take on new customs she and her father found objectionable. Mendel would undoubtedly press his agenda here, too. What did he hope to gain?

Had Victor and the rabbi put him up to this, to make it seem as if the Jews were free to follow their traditions, as Ilya had suggested when they'd first heard Mendel preaching?

"We'll start the study group by learning more about our heritage, about the Bible and about the great legal minds of our forefathers. Give me three months, and then we'll revisit the question of God and commandments. Right now, you don't have the tools to argue with me." Despite his strangeness, Mendel managed to persuade his audience to give him months to present his case and convert them to his cause.

Artur would ensure he didn't get that chance. He planned to shut this whole operation down in a matter of weeks, if not days.

Sofia plastered on a brittle smile and wove her way between the men. "Edik remembered he had an errand to run," she told him.

"Where'd he go?" Artur asked.

"He didn't say." Whether or not she knew Edik's destination, Artur was sure she had arranged for him to leave with money. "Only that he'll meet you at home later."

When she offered him tea, he steadied her hand with his own. She didn't allow the touch to linger, but his fingers tingled from the contact with her skin.

Once more, Ilya jabbed him in the side with his elbow and made him slosh his tea on his trousers. "Stop staring. You're making a fool of yourself."

"I don't know what you're talking about," Artur said, and Ilya grunted at him.

As soon as the tea was served, Sofia gathered her coat and bag and slipped out of the apartment. Where was she going? To meet up with Edik?

Artur had a feeling of near desperation as he watched her leave. Now he would have no chance to get her alone.

The door closed behind her, and the sound galvanized him. He pretended to check his watch. "Sorry. I have to go. I have a job interview," he lied.

Ilya rewarded his subterfuge with a darkly suspicious and disapproving glare, but Artur couldn't worry about that. With Edik scheduled so soon to depart, he knew his opportunities to pursue Sofia would be greatly curtailed if he couldn't establish some relationship between them now.

He gathered his coat and hat and headed at a quick clip into the hallway. Sofia was already gone.

He didn't waste time on the slow, ancient elevator. Instead, he jogged down the seven flights of stairs to the ground level. He exited to the street and caught a glimpse of her about a block away.

Mindful of the windows from the apartment, he didn't run after her. He didn't want Ilya or the others to see him obviously pursuing her and to speculate about why, even if Ilya already harbored some suspicions.

He passed by the group of KGB agents on the corner, barely noticing them, his attention riveted on Sofia.

One of the agents called out. "Hey! You there. Jew!"

He ignored the agent and kept walking, the way he thought Ilya might. For a moment, he imagined numerous sets of eyes boring into him. He glanced up at the window of the Reitmans' apartment, and wondered who there might be watching him.

"I'm talking to you, you worthless Jew." Artur's attention shifted to the agents on the street, to their crossed arms and the menacing expressions on their faces, to the numerous sharp stares.

An agent intercepted Artur and grabbed him by the sleeve. Artur shook him off and quickened his pace. He had to catch up with Sofia.

Up ahead, he saw her turn left down the next block. He spotted a taxicab coming down the street and waved his arm to hail it. He would overtake her in the taxi and then offer her a ride, he decided.

"Hey, Sasha, help me teach this disrespectful Jew boy a lesson," the agent said as the taxi pulled up to the curb.

Sasha, who had been standing closer to the curb, jumped into Artur's path and tapped on the roof of the cab, sending it away.

"Where do you think you're going, *Zhid*?" Sasha postured in front of him, getting in his face, blocking his view of Sofia.

Artur wanted to shove him out of the way in frustration. He wanted to berate the agent for impeding his investigation, then remembered he couldn't break his cover.

Sasha shoved him hard, and he stumbled back, tripping into the agent who had first called to him. The agent laughed and shoved him harder. Artur stumbled into Sasha who caught him, snatched a fistful of his hair at the crown, and pulled his head back.

"Let go of me," Artur said.

Sasha only laughed, "Quiet, Jew."

Artur's fellow agents jeered and mocked with the same bloodthirsty glee of the neighbors who had encouraged the mob outside the synagogue.

The KGB agents had no idea who he was! They thought he was a Jew, an outsider, an enemy.

Inside, Artur burned with anger. This was all a mistake, a dangerous mistake, that put him at unnecessary risk and compromised his mission.

He vowed to get Sasha's identification and report him to his supervisor. The agents might not know who Artur was, but they should have known there was an operation going on and not stuck themselves in the middle of it without any provocation.

Sasha said, "We need to teach this Zionist proper respect."

The agents pushed him back and forth between them with enough force that his heart started to pound. The others shouted their encouragement. "Show him what we do to enemies of the state."

What should he do? He couldn't break his cover and tell them who he was. Should he meekly bow his head as they pummeled him?

Other agents converged on him, the extra men Artur himself had suggested they put on Ilya. They laughed, shouted, and took turns shoving him. Oblivious to how they threatened a top level investigation, they took obvious pleasure in bullying him. His heart raced until his chest hurt. His face felt hot. His fury threatened to boil over.

Even Edik had tried to fight back against the mob, he thought.

He regained his footing and swung a punch at Sasha. His blow connected solidly, and he heard the huff as he knocked the wind out of his tormentor.

There was a moment of stunned silence, and Artur quickly realized his mistake. Fighting the mob outside the synagogue had been one thing, but this was the KGB. And they hadn't expected him to fight back.

The agents crowded him in, and Artur knew real fear.

What if he became the victim of a "Jewish accident"?

If the agents got overzealous in their terrorizing of Yosef Koslovsky, then Artur Gregorovich would never return home to his wife and son.

"Look at the tough guy," Sasha wheezed, one hand planted in the middle of his chest where Artur had struck him. "Assaulting an officer of the law. Right? You all saw it?"

The first agent pulled his gun. The others, including Sasha, also pulled theirs.

Ten guns. More than a firing squad. Artur was surrounded.

There was no escape, no one to help him. He felt the truth of Ruben's and Sofia's rants deep in his bones. Everyone was against him because they thought he was a Jew.

The first agent yanked Artur's arm violently. "I'm the KGB. You do what I say."

Artur was KGB, too. He outranked these street agents. He could have all of them fired or reprimanded. But not now. Not today. Today he was Yosef Koslovsky, a lowly Jew. Subhuman. They could kill him with impunity.

Artur bowed his head. Meekly, he asked, "What do you want me to do?"

"Get in the cab." The agent stuck his thumb and forefinger into his mouth, making a high-pitched whistle. A moment later, a different taxi came around the block. The agent opened the door, and Artur got in. "Move over. I'm coming with you," the agent said.

Artur slid across the seat as instructed, and the agent climbed in beside him and slammed the door.

The cab started driving. "Where are we going?" Artur asked.

"You're going home," the agent said, holstering his gun. "You're taking the day off from undercover work. There's a reception tonight. Semyon wants you there. Everything's been arranged."

Artur blinked at the agent and took a slow, deep breath.

He was safe.

"Did the agents all know I was undercover?" he asked.

"Of course," the agent said.

The anger eased out of Artur's muscles as he realized the violence had all been for show, designed to keep his cover intact.

It had all felt too real. For a moment, he had felt what Ilya and Ruben and Mendel might feel every time they left their apartments and met the cadre of agents who were supposed to intimidate them to behave.

He hadn't wanted to behave. He had wanted to lash out, to exact his vengeance and make the agents pay.

"It would have been too risky if they didn't know," the agent chuckled. "Someone might have actually shot you."

Artur forced a smile and pretended he shared the man's amusement. *You can't afford to be soft-hearted. To have doubts,* Maya had told him, and he couldn't display the slightest weakness to this underling.

Artur wasn't supposed to see his targets as people. Wasn't supposed to feel any sympathy for them. Wasn't supposed to feel what they felt.

But he did.

CHAPTER FORTY-THREE
VERA

AFTER SCHOOL, VERA hurried with Kolya to the bus stop. He gripped her hand and dragged her along almost at a run. "I need to get home. I need to check on Mama."

She felt a sharp pang of guilt. Over the past week, she had resented how Kolya's complaints about Mendel had delayed their departure, the extra time she'd had to spend waiting for the next bus and coaxing him to go home to his father when she could have been with Petya, cultivating a friendship with someone her own age.

But this morning she had seen for herself the hideous kerchief Mendel suddenly insisted her older sister wear. She had seen Sofia's bloody nose.

She no longer believed Sofia's calm mantra that Mendel and Kolya merely needed time to get used to each other again. Something was very wrong.

They waited at the stop amid the crowd of students who, like them, had just finished their classes. Usually they hung back, a little apart from the crowd.

He pushed his way to the front of the line, showing an assertiveness she hadn't seen in him before. When the bus came, he was the first one on, calling impatiently, "Come on, Vera."

He barreled headfirst into Gennady, who was about to get off at their stop. "*Oomph*," Gennady groaned and backed up.

"Sorry," Kolya mumbled and climbed into the first available seat. Gennady turned sideways, out of Vera's way, gesturing for her to pass him.

Gennady was always lurking around. Too often, she caught herself falling into the old, familiar fantasies of him, only to shake herself free with the memory of how he'd turned on her. How he'd laughed at her.

She slid into the seat beside Kolya, and Gennady stood at her side, even though the bus had plenty of empty seats. She tried to ignore his intrusive presence and focus on Kolya. She'd spent most afternoons with her nephew since he was a toddler, and she couldn't stand to see him so distressed.

"I'm sure she's all right," Vera tried to soothe him.

"He made her bleed," Kolya contradicted in a whisper. Even so distraught, he kept to the lessons his grandfather had taught him. With cautious awareness of his surroundings, he did his best to keep their conversation private. "Do you really think it was an accident?"

The comforting phrase was on her tongue, but Kolya sounded so like a jurist, and she felt for a moment that she was the one on the witness stand. Sofia always said that the boy had an old soul, that he understood things far beyond his years.

"You don't think it was an accident," she said carefully. In her heart, she didn't believe it was an accident, but she avoided telling Kolya anything that might pit him against Mendel or might later be repeated to Sofia.

She never knew whether Sofia would sympathize with them or get defensive on Mendel's behalf, saying that they needed to give him some time to reclaim his life after all he had suffered.

Vera recognized a fantasy when she heard one. She spent so much of her time indulging in daydreams about her own life being different.

"He wants everything his way," Kolya complained. "He wants

us to change everything." Despite her ongoing efforts to keep her opinions to herself, Kolya gave the same indictment of Mendel that she would have.

Vera took pains to limit situations that put her in proximity with her brother-in-law. His comment the other day about the length of her skirt had sorely tested her endurance. The nerve! She would have liked to complain to Sofia, but she had kept the incident to herself, until this morning when Sofia had asked if Mendel had done anything to upset her. This time, Sofia hadn't tried to minimize the incident or explain it away. She had shown the first stirrings of real concern, the first evidence that she might be waking to her own harsh reality.

Judging by her sister's bloody nose and Kolya's unceasing complaints, Vera instinctively understood the reality to be even harsher than she had let herself imagine.

Kolya clenched his fists at his sides. "She wouldn't give him his way. And so he hit her."

Vera said the only thing she thought would make him feel better, "I'll talk to your *dedushka*."

Kolya idolized his grandfather, who she had to admit had made a better father than Mendel seemed to be. "Good. He'll know what to do," Kolya said.

Vera nodded her agreement, but she doubted her father would intervene. Like Sofia, he always sided with Mendel.

When Mendel had proposed they renounce their Soviet citizenship and request to emigrate, her father had followed his lead. Ilya had wooed the family with a tale of how wonderful it would be to live free as Jews in the Land of Israel. Now, they were all stuck with the consequences of that choice, waiting for permission that would likely never be granted, non-citizens excluded from Soviet society, eligible only for odd jobs, with no prospects for making things better, and living in constant fear of the KGB.

Together, her father and Mendel had ruined their lives.

Mendel's jail time had given them some reprieve. But now he was back, and he demanded more concessions, more changes. She feared

Ilya would go right along with him.

Deep down, she believed that only one key thing had changed about Mendel. Before he had gone to prison, her sister's husband had always had to have his way, always had to be right, and he had badgered anyone who disagreed. After prison, he had learned he could use his fists to get what he wanted. He didn't have to be right, didn't have to marshal reason and logic. Now, he only needed to be stronger than his opponent.

Gennady pressed the bell and cleared his throat. "It's your stop," he said.

Lost in thought, she would have missed her stop without his prompt, but she couldn't bring herself to thank him.

She took Kolya by the hand and exited the bus. Gennady followed and trailed a few steps behind. They walked the couple of blocks to Sofia's apartment.

Vera noticed her father's KGB agents stood outside, accompanied this time by several others, and she stopped short.

Gennady bumped into her. He caught her arms to keep her from falling and pulled her up against him. She wrenched out of his hold just as he asked the question that was on her mind, too. "Why are there so many KGB agents here?"

Kolya ran ahead into the street without looking. A line of cars sped toward him.

"Kolya!" Vera screamed.

Gennady took off and raced toward him. Fast and light on his feet, he snatched Kolya out of the way of an oncoming car and scooped him up into his arms without missing a step. The car swerved and the driver leaned on the horn, but by then, Gennady had already cleared the far curb.

Vera waited for the light to change and crossed on shaky legs. She covered her heart with her hand, feeling as if it might leap out of her chest. If not for Gennady, Kolya might have been killed.

When she reached them, she threw her arms around her nephew. All of her worry and love—for him and for her sister—poured out of her, and she clung to him. "Don't scare me like that!"

She knew she should acknowledge Gennady for his bravery, but she buried her head in Kolya's neck until she felt Gennady move on. Kolya held himself stiffly, but she remembered how not so long ago he used to snuggle against her and fall asleep. The family used to joke that Vera was his second mother. For so many years, she had chafed at the responsibility for him that they had all heaped on her, especially when he wasn't hers.

But Kolya had become hers. Hadn't he? And she didn't know how she would have survived if she had lost him.

"Ugh! Auntie Vera, you're getting me all wet," Kolya protested and pulled away. She hadn't realized she was crying.

She straightened and wiped at her eyes. She glanced self-consciously at the gauntlet of KGB agents. She recognized four of the agents. She had seen them outside her building, waiting for her father. Gennady spoke quietly with one of them, something she had been warned never to do.

Her father would condemn Gennady as one of the enemy. But who was the real enemy?

Gennady had risked himself and saved Kolya's life.

"Come on, Kolya," she sniffled. "Let's go see your mom."

Kolya darted ahead, still spurred by the urgency that had sent him shooting so incautiously across the street. Inside, he pushed repeatedly at the elevator button, but the noisy gears seemed to have gone silent.

"Do you think it's working?" he asked. The elevator needed chronic repair and often glitched out of service. He shifted impatiently where he stood and glanced at the door to the stairwell, likely weighing which option would get him home faster.

Gennady joined them. "Your mom's not here. She left for work," he said.

"She's not here," Kolya repeated as if slow to digest the information.

"See? She's fine," Vera said, as much for herself as for him. "She wouldn't have gone to work otherwise."

They should have expected Sofia wouldn't be home. She always left for work before Kolya returned. Inside, Vera shuddered at the direction their thoughts had taken, the fear that had driven them both to worry what state they would find her in, despite Sofia's assurances to them that the episode had been an accident.

She had the terrible premonition that one day she would arrive with Kolya to find her sister dead.

She shook off the dark thoughts, dismissing them as another daydream, this one dark instead of rose-colored, full of violence instead of silly romantic notions. Her gaze flitted to Gennady and then quickly away.

Either way, her daydreams were equally unlikely.

CHAPTER FORTY-FOUR
GENNADY

VERA WAS CLEARLY upset. She stood on the sidewalk a long moment after Kolya disappeared into his apartment building. Gennady could see how much she was hurting.

He fought to keep his hands at his side, when what he really wanted was to pull her into his arms and offer whatever comfort he could.

"What can I do?" he asked.

She tensed. He understood with no small hurt that she had forgotten about him. She hadn't let down her guard in front of him. He had merely caught her unguarded, and she didn't like it.

With a noisy breath, she straightened her shoulders and lifted her chin. When she looked at him, her usually expressive eyes were shuttered. She called to mind a soft, vulnerable creature retrenched in its hard shell.

"We should go. Petya's waiting," she said.

She didn't paper over the incident with a tidy white lie that she was fine. Nor did she go so far in the other direction and lash out and push him away with an insult. She merely closed in on herself, shut him out as if he didn't matter, and moved stubbornly on.

Here he fell deeper and deeper for her with each passing day, but she still wasn't comfortable with him, still only tolerated—barely—having him around.

When would she finally let him in?

She started walking in the direction of the apartment, first at a fast pace, and then eventually at a more measured one. She didn't speak, and he didn't push her.

He worried she would run, for good this time, if he pushed at the boundary she had so clearly drawn. Much as it killed him, he had to wait for her to open up.

The silence wasn't uncomfortable as they walked along, but neither was it companionable. Separate people. Separate worlds. For the next twenty minutes, she didn't so much as glance in his direction.

Her extended silence made him doubt himself. Maybe he'd read the whole thing wrong. Maybe he was imposing. Maybe he should stop pursuing her and leave her alone the way she had asked.

Maybe he couldn't win her after all, despite what Uncle Semyon had said.

When they arrived at his building, she preceded him up the stairs. He lagged a little behind to watch her long, graceful legs and torture himself with the same question that had plagued him since their first kiss.

Did she even like him?

He caught up to her before she reached his apartment. She stepped aside while he unlocked and opened the door. As soon as they crossed the threshold, multiple voices talking all at once drifted to them from the living room.

Giggling chatter. Loud jokes and guffaws. It sounded like a party. He couldn't see from the hallway into the living room, but he surmised his brother's classmates had come to visit.

He stepped ahead of Vera and stopped her in the hall. He wasn't ready to relinquish her to her classmates. She stopped and studied him in her quiet, serious way, but he had no idea what she might be thinking. He wanted to break through the wall of silence she'd thrown up between them.

"Let me take your coat," he said to buy himself time as he wracked his brain for the magic words to unlock her. He noticed the slight tremor in her hand as she undid the first button.

"That's probably Vera now," he heard his brother say to his guests in the living room as if delivering the punchline of a joke. Vera stilled.

"This should be good," someone replied, and Vera's shoulders jerked with tension.

Someone else, maybe Petya himself, made the next comment, voice too low for Gennady to hear, but the raucous, derisive laughter that followed was unmistakable.

Vera hugged her books to her chest. Gennady stepped toward her just as she whirled on her heel. She bumped into him.

"Sorry," she said. Her gaze flashed up to his then, and her lovely tilted eyes swirled with powerful emotions. Just for a moment, he read in them the longing that he had halfway convinced himself he had only imagined.

Deep, deep longing. For him? And so much hurt.

She blinked her eyes and turned her head, and he was cut off once again, but that small glimpse had been enough. She ducked her head to hide her face and squeezed past him. She yanked open the door and hurried into the hall. To leave. To run.

"Vera, wait." He pursued her out the door. The carpet in the hall swallowed the sound of her quick steps. She made it halfway down the hall before he caught up to her. He grabbed her gently by the arm and pulled her to a stop.

A small sob escaped her, and tears started to spill down her cheeks, as if the dam she had tried to construct around her heart had cracked under the strain and sprung a leak.

He walked around her so that she was forced to look at him.

"Let me go." She swatted at him. He loosened his grip. He didn't want to seem threatening. But he didn't let go.

The freshly painted white doors up and down the hallway were all shut, but he could hear the sounds of his neighbors moving about their apartments. He took a step closer to her and kept his voice low as he pleaded with her. "Wait. Please. I don't want you to go."

"Don't," she pleaded. "Don't do this. Don't pretend you care."

"I'm not pretending," he said.

"I'm not an idiot." Her shoulders were high and tight. She adjusted her grip on her books and held them in front of her like a shield. "I know how this all works. You pretend to like me and then laugh at me as soon as I start to believe it."

Her words confirmed the story he'd been telling himself about her. She'd been hurt and rejected so often that she had come to expect it.

"I would never do that." He needed her to believe he was different.

"Liar." She shoved at his chest with the books. She was too slight to budge him, but he took a step back, a small concession. "Let me go. You're not going to reel me in again."

"Again?" Her accusation surprised him. "What do you mean 'again'?"

She tried to glare at him, but her wall wouldn't hold. The tears came faster now, and he felt he could see all the way into her heart, her breaking heart.

"That first night. When you kissed me. And then you laughed," she accused.

"I didn't—"

Crying in earnest now, she continued, "You and the KGB agents. You all laughed at me."

And then he remembered. He had laughed, but not the way she thought.

"That's why you ran? Why you've been giving me the cold shoulder?" Not because she was slow to trust, but because she thought he had betrayed her.

"Am I supposed to trail after you and beg for more?" she sniffled.

"I wasn't laughing at you," he said. "I was just embarrassed."

"Embarrassed to be seen with me." She tried again to pull away.

"No," he said and stepped closer to her. "To be so caught up in you that I didn't even notice our audience."

She cut her gaze away, retreating from him in the only way she could. "You're lying."

"It's the truth, Vera." He let her go then. She started to walk past him, head held high. "Why would I lie about this? Do I look like some stupid, immature schoolboy?"

She paused, and he asked, "Do I seem like the kind of person who needs to hurt someone to feel confident? You think I have nothing better to do than kiss you so I can laugh at you? Than chase your nephew into traffic just so I can mock you? Is that the man you think I am?"

She dragged her gaze back to his. She didn't answer, but she had stopped. She was listening.

"I see you, Vera. I see who you are," he said.

He risked touching her then. He placed his hands gently on her shoulders, and she didn't reject him and jerk away. "Tell me you see me, too. Tell me you want me, too," he pleaded with her.

The longing was there in the way her body leaned toward his. But so too was the fear in the way she held herself back, poised to run.

She stared at him with those wide, exotic eyes for what seemed an eternity. He waited in unbearable suspense for her answer.

See me. Please, see me.

The books slid from her hands and hit the floor with a thunk, and then, finally, she fell into his arms. She twined her arms around his neck and kissed him as if she'd been waiting for him her whole life.

He tasted her salty tears and lost himself to the soft warmth of her mouth and the heady revelation that she wanted him, truly wanted him, as much as he wanted her.

He heard surprised gasps. They both startled and angled their heads to see the shocked faces of Petya and his classmates, all of whom had congregated in the hall, several doors down, outside their apartment.

"What are you doing?" Petya demanded.

"Isn't it obvious?" Gennady asked. He stroked his thumb over Vera's swollen lips. "I was kissing Vera."

"Vera?" one of the girls spluttered. "But don't you know who she is? Who her family is?"

"Traitors."

"Criminals."

"Zionists."

He felt Vera stiffen and tense as her classmates offered up as condemnation the things Petya had already told him about her family. They expected this information would make him repudiate her.

This time, Vera didn't run or retreat into herself. She stood by his side and trained her steady gaze on him.

She'd honored him with her trust. Her faith in him gave him a confidence he hadn't realized he'd been missing.

He treated Petya's mob to the look their father, the general, had perfected for dealing with unruly subordinates, the one that made them squirm like ants burning under a magnifying glass.

"Of course I know who she is," his voice boomed in the narrow hall. "A better question is, do you?"

To his own ear, he sounded like a military commander, a formidable man. Even Petya, always quick when they disagreed to remind him that he was a sham of a father substitute, lowered his eyes and submitted to Gennady's newfound air of authority.

Gennady looked into Vera's shining eyes, and he liked the man he saw reflected there very, very much.

CHAPTER FORTY-FIVE
ARTUR

"SO, HOW'S YOUR case coming along?" Semyon cornered Artur at the reception and handed him a glass of champagne. "There's nothing like fucking a woman for the good of your country, is there?"

"Shh!" Artur warned. He felt a little sick. "Maya will hear you."

Maya stood among a cluster of men, not far from where Artur conversed with her father. She threw back her head, laughing at something one of the men said, and touched her hand to her throat. Her choker, a luminescent strand of pearls that Artur had saved for months to acquire, emphasized the elegant curve of her neck. She was exceedingly beautiful with her refined features and statuesque figure, and he knew the other men in the room envied him. She flirted and flattered and paved the way for him to step in and claim their admiration himself.

She glanced his way and flashed him a bright, cold smile, dazzling with its warnings about how much she was doing for him, about how he had better use tonight's opportunities to his best advantage, about how he best not forget she held his future in her hands.

Artur raised his glass to his wife, and then took a long sip, trying to ease his own growing sense of agitation.

"No worries, my boy. Maya's a good KGB wife," Semyon said. "She understands the rules. You belong to us before you belong to her."

Artur drank a little more champagne. He knew for a fact that Maya had no such understanding. When he had arrived home this evening, Maya had been less than pleased to see him. Her anger over his siding with his mother about Aleksei's behavior hadn't dissipated in the day he'd been gone. If anything, it had grown, finding other sources of sustenance.

She had wanted to know every detail of his undercover assignment, claiming she could help him as she had in his problem with Victor. But Artur couldn't reveal any concrete details to her. She hadn't appreciated being reminded that she didn't have security clearance, that despite her father's high position, she wasn't actually an agent herself.

"Your mother. Your father. *My* father. I'm sure they're all quite pleased with themselves," she had said bitingly, "to imagine they come first in your esteem. Ahead of me. Your wife."

Semyon drew him back to the present, the glittering reception, saying, "This is what undercover work is all about." He gave a hearty laugh and slapped Artur on the back. "Seducing that woman is your patriotic duty, son. Ha ha."

Artur smiled uneasily at him. He sipped the last drops of his champagne and tried to read into the Spymaster's behavior. Semyon wasn't displaying his usual discretion, talking about this aspect of the case within Maya's earshot.

Semyon wasn't careless. He didn't do things without a reason. Artur tugged at his bowtie, trying to loosen the knot ever so slightly.

He felt caught in a tug-of-war between father and daughter, each of them testing him to see where his true loyalty lay.

"I apologize for pulling you from your undercover operation. Was it that hard to give her up for the evening?" Semyon asked.

Artur hadn't yet seduced Sofia, but Semyon didn't know that. Artur couldn't help but notice that Semyon hadn't led with the question of whether seducing Sofia Reitman had yielded any significant intelligence, as if the sex alone were important in itself.

Artur couldn't help thinking of Lilya, the dangle. Her duty was always seduction, nothing more. Did Semyon think him no better than Lilya, a pretty face to lure the target and then hand things over to the real agents?

"For this? Not at all." Artur mimicked Semyon's laugh, as if they were sharing an inside joke. He pretended to be delighted to be at this fancy reception, to be talking with his father-in-law about sexual conquests.

He should have been ecstatic at tonight's opportunity to rub elbows with the elite *nomenclatura*, to pursue his career ambitions. He should have cultivated the same callousness Semyon showed toward Sofia because she wasn't part of this glittering world and, therefore, didn't matter.

But he couldn't shed Yosef Koslovsky's skin so easily.

A clean shave and a crisply pressed tuxedo weren't sufficient to transform him back into his usual self. He couldn't stop thinking about Sofia's swollen face or Jewish accidents or what his life would be like if he had been Yosef Koslovsky's son.

Certainly, if he had been born Artur Koslovsky, he wouldn't be here in this world of the Communist party, of powerful men and their glamorous and decorated women, of elegant china plates with buttered crackers and beluga caviar, of glasses full of French champagne, and bellies full of rich food and ambition.

This was Artur Gregorovich's world, the world he'd aspired to, married into. For so long, even before he'd met Maya, he'd told himself he deserved to be here. All he had to do was prove it.

Yet tonight he no longer felt secure in the knowledge he belonged. What had he done to earn the good fortune, the privilege, he enjoyed and took for granted? What had any of them done?

Semyon lowered his voice and whispered, "The news isn't out, but Chernenko's dying."

Artur looked questioningly at him. Was this the moment of opportunity that had fueled so many rumors at the Lubyanka?

Chernenko's predecessor, General Secretary Andropov, had been KGB Chairman, while Chernenko had no ties to the organization. Andropov had not approved Chernenko, but speculation was that the next General Secretary would come again from among the KGB's ranks. If so, Semyon seemed a natural choice. The Spymaster looked and talked like a camera-ready politician, and Chernenko had shown a strong distaste for him. The wheelchair-bound General Secretary had specifically requested that they not be photographed together. Likely he didn't want to appear weak next to the handsome and healthy Semyon, who could only benefit from the association and any comparisons that might be made.

The agents had a pool, with bets placed on when the crusty Chernenko might kick the bucket and whether Semyon would take his place.

"This isn't my time," Semyon said, anticipating the question. "Gorbachev is in position to be the next General Secretary."

Ah, that did explain the urgency that Artur attend the reception. Gorbachev was tonight's guest of honor.

"The transition makes your case more crucial than ever," Semyon said. If his father-in-law suffered a deep disappointment over this political setback, he didn't show it. "The Jewish problem is a liability in the Cold War, and we can't afford for our next leader to start from a position of weakness."

"I understand," Artur said, intuiting that Semyon could not start with the next regime thinking he had failed.

"I might have another angle on the case. Reitman's sister-in-law. Pretty little thing. Vera," Semyon said.

"You want me to seduce her, too?" Artur asked. The collar of his shirt suddenly felt too tight. Sofia's little sister was a mere teenager, a child.

"God, no. She's too young for you," Semyon said. "I have another man on it. Teenagers are suckers for true love."

"Why her?" Artur asked. He understood why Sofia made a compelling target. Seeing her today handing off such a substantial sum of money to Edik, he expected she was a central figure in the plot he'd been sent to expose. But the little sister hadn't been mentioned during his week undercover. He hadn't even seen Vera Soifer, save for the picture in her file back at the Lubyanka.

"Let's just say there's been an unexpected opportunity to draw her in," Semyon said cryptically. "And I anticipate a payoff to the efforts, even if she yields little useful information."

He had the impression of Semyon as a Grand Master of the chessboard, moving his pieces with ruthless calculation, in a pattern only he could see. For the first time, Artur felt himself a pawn in a much larger game, one he didn't understand, one he hadn't chosen.

"In any case, I don't trust Victor to get the job done," Semyon said. "I'm glad to have you on the case. I know you'll get me what I need."

"Yes, sir," Artur said against the sudden dryness in his throat. He should have been reassured that Semyon considered him more than a mere dangle, pleased even with the level of trust the Spymaster placed in him, but instead he felt an unaccountable discomfort in his gut.

Whether or not he liked the role he'd been given, his country's fate hung in the balance. He couldn't care about Jewish accidents or Sofia and her sister.

Maya appeared at his side, her face a chilly mask. He couldn't change the facts of his job or what he was about to do, and he knew he needed to do some damage control, perhaps reassure her of his love.

"You look so beautiful tonight. We've been watching you dazzle everyone."

She brightened with his praise. Semyon excused himself to give them a few precious moments alone before he sent Artur back to the field, once again asserting his claims.

"Did you know that Grimalsky bought his wife a fur coat and diamonds?" she asked, clearly dazzled herself. "We'll have that someday. You'll be so successful, and they'll all envy us."

He easily imagined how beautiful Maya would look wrapped in fur with those luminescent pearls circling her graceful neck. She would stand beside him as he made a speech at a podium, while reporters flashed pictures and a crowd of important politicians hung on his every word.

Tonight was evidence he was well on his way. Even though he was only thirty years old, his career had already outpaced his father's. He had the right connections, along with the driving ambition that his father had rejected.

Russian royalty indeed.

But for the first time he wondered how much the dream might cost him.

"Don't you feel the men's eyes on us right now?" He asked as he led her toward the doors. He opened the patio doors and took her out into the chilly night, hoping they could reconcile before he left again. He didn't like the idea that she might stew in anger while he was away undercover. "They all envy me now. Because I have you."

"It's cold out here," she complained.

"I'll keep you warm." He took off his suit jacket and draped it over her shoulders. She pulled the sides close around her and buried her nose in the lapel, taking a long inhale. His heart constricted at this sign of her affection.

"Did you know that Grimalsky bought a new car, too?" she asked. "He paid for everything from the money he made in bribes. Just imagine what you could get. You'll climb even higher than he can."

"I'm not looking to become a bureaucrat," he said. Grimalsky was a paper pusher.

"I know," she said. "You love being an agent." Her lips pressed into a frown. "I heard what my father said. He's sent you out to have an affair."

"Maybe we shouldn't discuss this. I have to go back into the field tonight, and I don't want you distressed at such a delicate time." He alluded to her pregnancy. Stress couldn't be good for the baby or for the prospects of taking this one to term. But also, he didn't wanted to discuss this part of the job with her.

He would prefer to keep her out of it, unsullied and undisturbed by the choices he had to make to keep his country safe.

He didn't want her to be hurt.

Maya splayed one hand over her belly. With her other, she found the pearls on her necklace. She stroked one between her thumb and forefinger. "Distressed? Why would I be distressed?"

He tipped her chin so that he could look into her lovely face. He expected to see vulnerability, not the cold, hard glimmer in her eyes.

"I know what your job entails," she said. Her gaze sharpened with shrewd and cutting insight, and she said, "It's not me you're worried about."

She stood back from him as if suddenly too disappointed in him to stay close. "It's you! You're going soft," she accused. "You've let your parents fill your head with their nonsense."

Her criticism took him aback. How did this conversation have anything to do with his parents?

"I told you not to let them get into your head," she scolded. "But you did. And now you imagine you're doing something wrong." She poked a long, elegant finger at his chest. "Don't you?"

Obviously, he needn't have worried about Maya. She was every inch the good KGB wife, just as Semyon had said, and somehow that didn't make Artur happy.

"You can't afford to lose your conviction now," she said. "Forget about your parents. Do whatever you have to do to keep climbing. Seduce a hundred women. I don't care. I understand that you're doing it for us."

Her cold indifference, her single-minded ambition, disturbed him deeply. Didn't she love him?

She cupped his cheek with her hand. Her fingers were cool, like ice, against his skin. "This is the way for us to get what we want."

To get what? Fancy strings of pearls, fur coats, and cars? Press conferences and the power to treat people as pawns?

All of the things they had wanted—things he had pursued by trying to fashion himself in Semyon's image—suddenly seemed empty, meaningless.

He wasn't sure what he wanted anymore.

CHAPTER FORTY-SIX
SOFIA

SOFIA PRESSED HER ear to the bathroom door and listened for Grisha's exit. She clutched the keys she wore around her neck. The metal edge bit into her palm.

Mendel hadn't alerted the KGB, hadn't turned her in. This morning had burned away any lingering doubt. He might not want her to spy, but he wouldn't have betrayed her.

That left the question of what the KGB knew or suspected. Why had they suddenly increased security? Would the keys still work?

She heard the hallway door open and close, and she debated her next move. Grisha might still be out there, and she couldn't afford for him to start suspecting her if he didn't already.

She had already used her trick with the bleach, entering the hall with the ready excuse of retrieving it after she thought he had left a first time, but Grisha had stood there waiting.

She manufactured a new excuse to go into the hallway, took a deep breath, and pushed the door open. "Grisha?" she called, as if she expected to find him. "I need you to…"

She had been poised to pretend she'd forgotten something in the supply closet downstairs, but the hallway was empty.

She ran to the door to Max's old office and shoved his key at the lock. Her fingers trembled. She fumbled the first few attempts. Then, finally, she managed to insert the key.

She turned it to the right. She met no resistance, and the lock tumbled open. It worked!

She eased open the office door and surveyed the room. Had new surveillance been installed? Would she get into the files, only to be caught on video?

She hesitated in the doorway. She feared she was walking into a trap. Perhaps it was only a matter of time before she was discovered.

But please not tonight. Or tomorrow. Or the next day. Not until my family and my people, all of them, are free, she prayed.

She sneaked over to the file cabinet. Her second key worked there, too.

She retrieved the file on the prototype and rushed back to the bathroom.

In the bathroom stall, Sofia opened the file to where she had left off. Page 25. She had a way to go to finish the report, possibly a week left of work. She pulled the shiny silver Tropel from her pocket and removed the cap to the lipstick tube. She set the page up on the window sill and balanced on her elbows to line up the shot. Click.

She flipped the finished page over into a separate pile, took a fresh page, and set up her next shot. Her body cast a shadow over the page, and she adjusted her position, keeping her arms in place but leaning away to take the next picture. Her motions were slow and awkward.

She tried to line up every shot just so. She didn't want her effort to be wasted. She only had the one camera, and she hoped to give her allies the entirety of the report. The Tropel came loaded with only 120 frames. She couldn't afford to waste precious frames on do-over shots.

Before she knew it, she had photographed several pages. She had a sense of quiet exultation.

She heard the door to the outer office open, and she quickly restacked the pages and put them back into the folder. A moment later, the inner door opened, and she heard Grisha's heavy steps in the hallway.

She left the folder on the window sill and exited the stall, carefully closing the swinging door to hide the papers.

She grabbed the mop and sloshed soapy water over the floor near the door to the bathroom.

Giving her no warning, Grisha pushed the bathroom door open. "Careful," she said. "The floor's wet."

He hung back by the door and watched her mop for a full minute, obviously reluctant to leave. "Do you need something?" she asked him.

"I came to check on you," he said. His words were slurred. His squat nose was red, and his eyes were bright. He was so obviously drunk that she had a hard time believing he was a dangerous KGB agent sent to guard the facility.

He didn't proposition her, but he raked his eyes over her as if she were naked and offering herself to him. She feared whatever liquid courage he'd chugged down might embolden him to make a move, and she needed him to leave.

"Something's clogging the drain in the sink, and I need to clear it out," she said, thinking maybe he would have trouble seeing her as an object of lust if he pictured her elbow deep in sink sludge.

"Won't that be messy? Why are you mopping the floor first?" He was more alert than she had expected.

"Procrastination," she said with a shrug. "I know it's going to be slimy and gross."

He made a face, and she was encouraged to embellish the problem. "Probably pieces of someone's chewed up lunch. Someone in the office really likes sausage with lots of garlic. It always smells really bad when I snake the drain. I'm putting it off as long as possible, but I know I have to do it before I leave."

"I'll leave you to it." He seemed delightfully squeamish and eager to avoid bearing witness to whatever yuck might be in the drain. She tucked the knowledge away, dreaming up a new set of deflections to keep him at a distance. "Stop by the desk when you're ready to go so I can check you out," he said.

"Will do," she promised.

He left, and she slumped gratefully over the mop when she heard the outer door close behind him.

She counted slowly to one hundred and then sneaked out of the bathroom with the file and returned it to the laboratory office.

Later that night, when she was ready to leave, she found Grisha asleep at the guard desk. Grisha wasn't being especially vigilant now, when he should have been standing guard and inspecting her bag on the way out to make sure she hadn't stolen so much as a stray pencil. His head was buried in his arms. An empty bottle of vodka lay on its side at his desk. He snored loudly into his elbow.

She took in the scene and almost burst out laughing. So much for her concern about cameras, she thought, and her tension eased.

She signed her name in his ledger and tiptoed to the door.

An incredible sense of power, of invincibility almost, ran through her veins.

They didn't suspect her. Not yet. She still had time to tip the scales and repair this broken world.

CHAPTER FORTY-SEVEN
ARTUR

ARTUR LEFT THE reception determined to do his duty, however he felt about the rest. He would get between Sofia's thighs and into her head, and he would make sure he had the information the KGB needed.

A cab waited to take Artur back to the field. He recognized the two agents in the backseat, Sasha and Leonid. They had been instrumental in abducting him from outside of the Reitmans' apartment what seemed two lifetimes ago.

He flashed back to that horrible moment of helplessness, to the fear he'd had that he might actually get shot because they had mistaken him for a Jew.

"Where to?" Leonid asked.

"Any sign of Sofia?" Artur asked. He was eager to see her, to talk to her, to see if she was really all right after Mendel's harsh treatment.

"I want to catch up with her tonight. Alone," he told the agents with a wolfish smile, calculated to impress them. He dared not reveal any sign of his sympathy for her or of his failure so far to seduce her. They were likely reporting to Semyon or Victor.

But he wasn't ashamed of his softer feelings, either. Despite what

Maya had said, it wasn't wrong to feel sympathy for Sofia or for the community he had infiltrated. They were people, with their own lives and dreams and worries, with families they loved.

Still, he wouldn't let his softer emotions, his humane sensibilities, keep him from his purpose.

This was war. A war for his country's future. A war for his family's future.

Maybe the Jewish story was more compelling than he had at first credited. He couldn't ignore the feelings his own experiences had aroused. But their alleged persecution didn't warrant the standstill on nuclear disarmament, the continued brinksmanship pointing them to Armageddon.

The traitors had to be silenced.

Sasha pressed an earpiece to his ear and relayed Artur's question. "She left the university a few minutes ago. She's likely on her way to the metro station. Unless she stops by her parents' place first."

"Sooner or later she'll head for the subway. Let's head her off there," Artur decided.

Sasha spoke into his earpiece again. "We don't have eyes on her at the moment, but it doesn't seem she's passed this way yet."

"Good," Artur said.

They dropped him at the station, and he went down to the platform to wait for her.

The underground station was clean and brightly lit, but he spared no appreciation for the bright tiles or the artwork. He watched the people entering the platform and kept an eye out for Sofia. A train arrived. He didn't see her, and he stayed put, while the rest of the platform cleared of people.

Sofia Reitman held the key to this case. Tonight he would lock her in his embrace and seduce her into trusting him with her secrets—about her husband, her uncle, her father, and anyone else who threatened his country. Including herself.

He spied her coming down the stairs to the platform. She moved briskly, her nose still swollen, her unflattering kerchief slightly askew.

His heart seemed to beat in time with her rapid steps.

Her obvious misery in her marriage to Mendel made her the perfect weak link. In his head, Artur composed the story of the affair between them, the easy way he lured her into his arms and pretended to help her with her conspiracies. Once Edik left, she would turn to Artur the way she had turned to Edik.

He took a step toward Sofia and called her name. She looked in his direction. "Yosef? What are you doing here?"

"I knew you'd be getting off work about now. I came to check on you. To see if you're really okay."

"You mean because of Mendel? Don't worry about me. I'm fine," she said with a confidence that crushed his plans.

She didn't seem to welcome any concern from him. So what was his move? He couldn't think. Every cell in his body seemed to pulse with acute awareness of her. He fixated on her lips as they moved and lost himself to thoughts of how they would feel under his, how she would taste when he claimed her mouth.

Sofia's eyes rose questioningly to his. "Do I have something in my teeth?"

Artur jolted back to awareness. Caught up in his fantasies, he was botching his approach. Badly.

What should he say? He reached for words and came up blank. A slight panic built behind his breast bone. He finally had her to himself, without her family to interfere. He couldn't waste this opportunity.

He had to seduce her. He couldn't fail.

He reached for Sofia and dragged her up against his chest. He pressed his lips to hers and kissed her for all he was worth. She gasped, and he plunged deeper.

He heard a roaring in his ears. The wind in the station picked up. For a wild moment, he felt caught up in something bigger than himself, felt the relentless momentum of history.

Then the train screeched into the station. Sofia wrenched herself out of his hold.

She slapped him hard.

The crack across his jaw stunned him. He brought his hand to his face and stood dumbfounded as she turned and raced for the open doors of the train.

She was rejecting him!

Artur's cheek stung from the wallop she'd delivered, and more than that, his pride stung. He watched, frozen with humiliation, as she ran from him. The train doors slid closed, separating them.

Maybe he'd been a green fool to believe such a complicated woman would swoon in his arms, or maybe he didn't know the tricks Semyon did.

The train pulled out of the station, taking Sofia away from him. He glimpsed her sitting with her fingers pressed to her lips. She didn't look his way.

For as long as he could see her, she continued to sit with her fingers pressed to her mouth.

Maybe he had gotten through to her.

He stared after the train until he could no longer see her.

This wasn't over.

CHAPTER FORTY-EIGHT
SOFIA

YOSEF HAD KISSED her.

Perhaps Sofia had craved his kiss and unwittingly invited it, but she didn't think so. She had taken pains all week to distance herself from his attentions, even if she had secretly savored them.

She had been alone for too long, and Mendel's return hadn't yet eased her longing for intimacy.

She sat in her seat on the subway train and pressed the pads of the fingers of both her hands to her lips. To erase the kiss? Or to press it deeper?

As the train wheels clacked on the tracks, she replayed the kiss over and over in her mind.

There had been no warning. He had kissed her deeply, with so much passion, the way Mendel used to, like his next breath depended on the flow of desire between them.

The kiss was wrong of Yosef on so many levels. What kind of woman did he think she was?

She supposed the problems in her marriage were obvious to everyone, but she wasn't in the market for a lover. She had honored her vows to

Mendel, and she would see her marriage through.

Years of love, of faithfulness and partnership, didn't simply burn to ash in the heat of another man's kiss.

But, oh, that kiss. She had forgotten what passion tasted like.

She ruminated over the kiss, savoring and detesting it all at once, until the train pulled into her station.

She exited at her stop into the brisk night air and turned her thoughts resolutely to Mendel.

Her great love story with Mendel couldn't end in betrayal and bitterness. It was her deepest wish to have Mendel, her Mendel, her great love, returned to her. She yearned to resurrect what they once had. She dreamed of the day she finally would wake up to the man who'd been stolen from her.

She had waited so long for him to return to her. She would keep waiting, as long as there was hope.

There was hope. Wasn't there?

He had said he loved her.

He had said she was his world.

As she trudged the scant blocks to her apartment, doubt crept in. Was she foolish to believe the violently protective stranger in her apartment might yet transform into the man she used to adore?

The lights were off when she entered. The sound of Kolya's deep steady breath as he slept instantly calmed the turmoil inside her. She wasn't foolish to hope. Her son deserved to know his father—the real Mendel.

Careful not to disturb Kolya's slumber, she lightly kissed his forehead and brushed his unruly hair from his face.

She heard a scuffling sound in the kitchen and quietly went to investigate. Coming to stand in the doorway, she saw light spilling into the darkened kitchen from the crawl space. The hatch was slightly open. She heard the sound again, boxes being moved and pushed aside quickly. She suspected Mendel had waited for Kolya to fall asleep, and now he was now frantically searching for more evidence of her spying.

She hoped she was wrong.

She backed out of the kitchen. She moved slowly, soundlessly toward the front door, keeping her eyes on the kitchen. Mendel didn't emerge.

She opened and closed the front door, hard this time, ensuring it made a sound loud enough to carry to him in the crawl space. Immediately, she heard the creak of the hatch and the muffled thump as Mendel levered out of the crawl space and hopped down in hasty response to the sound of her return.

She opened the closet and fussed with the hangers, clinking the empty metal ones together. She picked up and dropped her shoes noisily on the closet floor.

He didn't come out of the kitchen or call out to her in greeting.

With growing dread, she returned to the kitchen. He sat at the kitchen table in the dark. The light in the crawl space was off, she noticed. He lifted a mug to his lips and went through the motions of sipping tea. There was no kettle on the stove. She was willing to bet his cup was empty.

"Why are you sitting here in the dark?" The scene was all too familiar, this time with their roles reversed. She didn't ask about the crawl space. She waited to see what he would say.

There were myriad reasons he might have been up in the crawl space. He could tell her he had been reminiscing, going through Max and Irena's things. He could say he had been searching for a specific item that he needed. Maybe he would even admit that he had doubted her.

He said none of those things. He didn't mention the crawl space. He took another imaginary sip of tea and said, "I was praying."

"Praying," she repeated. She didn't let her doubt show. Didn't he usually pray at the synagogue? With a prayer book? There was nothing on the table but the salt and pepper shakers. And the mug he plunked down beside them.

"Yes, praying," he insisted. "For your safety." Perhaps he had been praying, but he had also been searching the apartment. To thwart her.

He didn't trust her.

And she couldn't trust him.

She felt suddenly exhausted. She braced her hand against the door frame for support. Mendel got up from the table and approached her. She breathed deeply. Fighting the urge to take a step back, she dug her fingernails into her palm. He stopped just short of where she stood.

Tentatively, he lifted his hands to her face. His calloused fingers were rough against her skin. He untied the kerchief she'd worn for him, and her hair spilled free. The touch lasted only a moment, and then he dropped his hand, as if she were a flame and the contact had singed him. This time, she was glad when he pulled away.

"I can't lose you," he said. "I don't know how I would live without you."

What she heard him say beneath his words was, "I will do anything in my power to stop you." He wasn't her partner any longer. Her cause was no longer his.

"You're not going to lose me. I love you," she said, adding another lie to the mountain growing between them.

He was a traitor. But she wouldn't let him know that she knew.

***

THANKS SO MUCH for reading. Ready for more? The saga continues with *To Hunt a Spy*. Or check out the *Kings of Brighton Beach* series, which picks up the saga in present-day Brooklyn, New York. Keep reading for a preview. Or pop over to dbshuster.com to get FREE books and other offers.

KINGS OF BRIGHTON BEACH EXCERPT
VLAD

"**I** TOLD YOU, I didn't kill him," Vlad said. He tried to stay calm, but he was getting impatient with Detective Sharp's endless repetition of the same question: "Why'd you kill him?" Either this was some kind of advanced interrogation technique, akin to water boarding, or Sharp was not the sharpest knife in the drawer.

Vlad wondered what time it was. He felt as if he had been in the interrogation room for days. He couldn't waste time here. He needed to get out, regroup with Artur. Brighton Beach was on the brink of a mafia war, and Inna was in imminent danger.

"Zviad was already dead when I came in," Vlad said.

"Don't lie to me." Sharp threw his pen on the table and jumped to his feet as if ready to smash in Vlad's nose. The cop smelled like stale coffee and really needed a breath mint. His eyes were bloodshot with thick, dark bags underneath. "It'll go worse for you."

Vlad didn't expect a friendly chat over coffee and donuts tonight, not when he had been two-fisting guns in a room where a man had taken a bullet to the brain, but his handler was a little too intense, a hungry shark that had caught the scent of chum.

Vlad's nerves stretched taut. He remembered other visits to the station, other lengthy interrogations. Then he had been defiant, maybe even unrepentant. Vlad hadn't done anything arrest-worthy tonight, hadn't even fired his gun, but he still felt like a no-good kid with guilt itching to be confessed and threatening to show on his skin like an angry rash. If he wasn't careful, he would give himself away.

"I'm telling the truth." *About this, anyway.* "The door was locked. I kicked it in. She was trapped under him, and he was dead."

"You said they were having sex."

"I said he raped her," Vlad said.

His handler cast a frustrated look at the mirrored wall, where his fellow officers were likely monitoring the questioning, as if Vlad were obstructing justice. "You said you weren't in the room. How do you know what the hell happened?"

Vlad reminded himself that the cops hadn't seen what he had seen: Inna half-naked, trapped under Zviad, and screaming her lungs out.

"He was lying on top of her. His leg was over hers like he was holding her down. His pants were pulled down around his ankles, and her dress was torn," Vlad said. "What the fuck do you think happened?"

"Maybe she liked it rough. Maybe she wanted it," Sharp said.

Vlad's temper threatened to explode like a grenade, and he tightened his fists under the table to hold it in check.

"Maybe you got jealous and shot him. Did you know him? Were you friends? We can easily find that one out, so just tell us."

"I told you, I didn't kill him." He squeezed his fists tighter, but his hold was slipping. "And, no. I didn't know him personally. We've met a couple of times on business."

"What is it you do for the Koslovskys?" his handler asked in an obvious attempt to try a new tack.

"I'm in charge of surveillance and security for Koslovsky Industries," Vlad said. "And before you ask, yes, I'm licensed to carry guns in New York." There was nothing illegal in the job he did, part of the brilliance of Artur's scheme. Problem was, the scheme was almost too brilliant.

Vlad still had so much to learn from Artur about his business enterprise. The buyers and suppliers. The "products." The relationships with the other small businesses in Brighton Beach and in the New York metropolitan area, never mind the connections overseas. He still didn't know how it all worked, where all the money came from. Artur provided only crumbs of information, a faint trail that hinted at the larger enterprise. Sometimes Vlad felt certain Artur knew his angle and was baiting and teasing him: *I have everything you want. Come and get it.*

The door slammed open and Detective Saul Hersh stalked in. "I don't fucking believe it," Vlad blurted as one of the few men who could blow all of his plans to hell strutted into the room.

"Believe it," Saul said. He was short and on the slight side for a cop, but his threat wasn't in his physical strength. The man was clever, sneaky. He used to have a reputation as a hardcore interrogator, the kind who always got his answers. Sharp was only the warm up. The real deal had just arrived.

Another test, Vlad thought, as dangerous as the others. Artur had eyes and ears on the police force.

Saul placed scarred hands on his narrow hips, and the circular marks drew Vlad's eyes, just as they had the first time he had met Saul. Ivan's abuse hadn't left visible scars on Vlad, other than the cleft in his eyebrow from where his head had hit the corner of a coffee table. Saul had told him his own father used to burn cigarettes on his hands. "I had a choice," Saul had said, "to be like him, or go another way. You have that choice too. What will you choose?"

"Never thought I'd see you here again. On that side of the table," Saul said now. "Thought I'd scared some religion into you. Guess I was wrong 'cause here you are. Playing your father's favorite role—gangster with guns."

"Stuff it, Hershey. We both know you're the one who tried to play my father's role," Vlad said. "You thought if you saved Nadia from Ivan she'd shower you with … gratitude."

"Does your mother know you're here? That you're gunslinging for Koslovsky—just like your old man?"

"I don't talk to Nadia. The worthless whore," Vlad said. He made a spitting sound for extra effect.

Saul got up in his face, grabbed him by the collar. "Don't talk about your mother that way."

"You're defending her?" Vlad couldn't hold back a mirthless laugh. The poor fucking sap, sucker punched by love for a woman who would never love him back, who would never love anyone save Ivan, even her own son. Ivan had beaten Nadia so hard she couldn't stand and then turned his rage on Vlad, who had been too small to defend himself or his mother, and still she had professed her love. Sickening.

"She's practically signed your death warrant," Vlad said with a shake of his head.

"You want to talk about death warrants?" Saul tightened his grip on Vlad's collar as if to prevent any sympathy from leaking out of him. "Let's talk about what you were doing armed to the teeth at Troika."

"My job," Vlad said.

"Get a new job," Saul said.

"Did they send you in to play good cop or bad cop, Hershey?" Vlad taunted, and Saul winced at the jibe. "It's amazing they kept you on the force after what you did."

"We all make mistakes, son, and that was a long time ago," Saul said.

"I'm not your son."

"I'm willing to help you—for your mother's sake. Is there something you want to tell us?"

"Why don't you speed things up and write my statement for me?" Vlad said.

Ivan had been guilty of plenty of murders, just not the one for which Saul had arrested him. If anyone deserved a life sentence, Ivan did, but Nadia had turned on Saul the moment the truth of what he had done came to light, despite the fact that his actions may have saved her life and Vlad's. She had taken the story to the papers and spent every moment since lobbying to get Ivan's case appealed, to have him freed, even knowing that the first thing Ivan would do once he got out was kill Saul Hersh.

Saul cuffed him on the ear. "That's the way you want to play it? Fine by me." He pulled a metal chair back from the table and sat down. "Maybe your statement goes like this. You and Artur walked in on Inna doing the horizontal tango in the nightclub."

Vlad interrupted. "Say you're right. Why would I bring out the heat? Not like I give a damn who she screws."

"But Artur does. Heard he doesn't want his little princess dating a gangster."

"So Artur kills Romeo to keep him away from Juliet? In his son's nightclub. In the middle of prime time when he might get caught. When he would bring the cops breathing down his neck. Are you out of your fucking mind? Artur Koslovsky doesn't even carry a gun."

"But you do. Two of them," Saul's partner interjected. He tapped his pen against his notepad.

"Thanks, Einstein. And we've already established that neither of them fired tonight," Vlad said.

"All right," Saul agreed. "Let's say you and Artur weren't the shooters. Inna fired the gun."

"Because Zviad was raping her," Vlad said, again imposing his favored theory. Sharp raised his eyebrows at Saul, sending him some secret communication.

Saul cleared his throat. "Because of what he knew," Saul said quietly.

The statement wasn't a question, and it caught Vlad off guard. There was something else going on here, some part of the story Vlad didn't know. He was missing something. He needed to focus. He sat up a little straighter, alert now to whatever clue Saul or Sharp might cast in his direction.

"You think he was blackmailing her?" Vlad asked. The detectives exchanged another glance. They didn't like this theory any more than the one about the rape. Why didn't they want to see Inna as a victim?

"While we're playing this game of hypotheticals, tell me this," Vlad said. "Inna's in her little dress, hot and heavy with her Romeo. I didn't see a purse or a holster on her. Where exactly did she hide the gun if she was planning all along to seduce and kill him? Even strapped to her thigh, the Glock would have been conspicuous."

"Maybe the gun was his," Saul said.

"Sure. Okay. So why don't you think he might have held her at gunpoint? That there could have been a struggle, and she won?"

"We're asking the questions," Sharp said.

This time the defensiveness was unmistakable. Another shifty look from Sharp to Saul, and realization hit. The detectives couldn't stomach the idea of Inna as a victim because they didn't want Zviad to be guilty—of anything. It was as if they were protecting one of their own.

One of their own. Vlad's mind started to race with the possibility. What if Zviad was an undercover cop? He would have been investigating the Georgians. What could he have found out about Inna? Was she involved with whatever was happening at Troika—the drugs and women Dato had mentioned?

People did stupid things, sure. Supposing Zviad had something on Inna, Vlad still didn't buy that she would off him like that at the club where they were sure to be found. If silence were her game, she had nothing to gain from a messy murder that would lead to so many questions. And why at Troika?

A nasty suspicion took hold and stoked the rage inside Vlad even higher. The Georgians would surely benefit from killing the cop who was spying on them and framing someone else for the deed. Even better to have the murder at Troika, have the cops swarm the place, and shut down their supposed competition.

But why involve Inna?

Vlad silently kicked himself. He should have paid more attention to Inna these last few months. She worked closely with Artur. She pointedly avoided Vlad. Come to think of it, Artur actively kept Vlad away from her. He always sent Vlad on an errand when she was in the office. Vlad had assumed Artur had been giving him a signal, well within his rights, that his daughter—his much younger daughter—was off limits. Vlad had done his best to dampen his natural interest in her long legs and inky hair and the smoky quality of her voice that made his thoughts wander. *Not for me. Not for me.*

Now he wondered whether there was more to Artur's separation of them. Perhaps Inna was central to Artur's plots and schemes and Artur still didn't trust Vlad enough for him to know. Or perhaps Artur wanted to keep her clear of the intrigue.

She might be innocent. Or she might be another spider at the center of an elaborate web. She wouldn't escape Vlad's notice now. He would learn all of her secrets. First, he needed to stop the Georgians from killing her.

"Dato and Goga were eager to blow her brains out," Vlad said. "Said they wanted retribution. But maybe it was a smoke screen. Maybe one of their crew killed Zviad—because he had something on them. And now they want to make sure Inna stays silent about the murder."

Saul shook his head with sad wonder. "You're in the wrong profession. With a mind like yours, you should have been a detective."

"Yeah? Would that help you sleep at night? You could say it was all worth it, all the lies, as long as Ivan's son turned into one of the good guys?"

"It was worth it," Saul said solemnly. "Whatever happens—to me, to you—it was worth it." Saul's intense gaze, the fatherly worry etched in the strained lines around his eyes, unsettled Vlad. He looked away.

Saul clutched Vlad's forearm, squeezed, made him meet his eyes. "I would make the same choices all over again."

Detective Sharp coughed, and Vlad was aware once more of the awkwardness of his predicament, the need for the utmost discretion. "You're a piece of work, Hershey. You know that?" Vlad shrugged him off. "Let me tell you the real difference between us. We both tell lies when it suits us, but at least I don't lie to myself. And just for the record, I tried my hand at law enforcement. It fucking sucked."

Saul blew out a heavy breath and pushed back from the table. "You're free to go."

***

Want to keep reading? Buy Kings of Brighton Beach today or download an extended sample to enjoy for free.

ACKNOWLEDGMENTS

THIS BOOK IS the happy product of taking the long and difficult way around, getting tangled up in criss-crossing paths, losing my way, and finding it again. I am immensely grateful for the people who helped light the way and pushed me—sometimes hard—to continue when doubt and fear obscured my path.

To Catch a Traitor kicks off the family saga that runs through both the *Sins of the Spy* series, which takes place in 1980s Moscow, and the *Kings of Brighton Beach* series, which takes place in modern-day Brooklyn. However, the epic story was written and published out of order, with *Kings of Brighton Beach* appearing first as a serial comprised of three episodes and later as a novel. Despite hundreds of pages written toward the next installments, the series came to a screeching halt. I fell into a trap familiar to many writers. Pages accumulated, but I second-guessed every decision. I convinced myself nothing was good enough.

Along came my dear friend, Kristine Rosales, and the Deer Park Moms Book Club with their enthusiasm for the saga and their tough love. Thanks to Kris's suggestion, *Kings of Brighton Beach* had been a book of the month. Now, years later, the book club wanted to know, where the hell was the rest? Kris guilted, wheedled, cajoled, and encouraged me to keep writing, reminding me that I had eager readers, including first and foremost herself. She engineered yet another invitation to the book club—and a deadline—lighting a fire under me. I've dedicated this book to these lovely and wonderful women.

There are not enough thank-you's to give my writer friends, or my "wronger" friends as Gene jokingly calls them—Debora Dale, Lillian Marek, Lynne Cannon, Donna Velleman, and especially Dina Fischbein and Lisa Shiroff, who helped me navigate the way to my best version of this story. Thanks also go to the fabulous Kelly Peterson and the team at INscribe Digital for helping set this project up for success. I also thank my friends and colleagues at Queens College-CUNY, especially Anna Bounds and Holly Reed, who recognized my need to keep feeding this hungry fire and encouraged me to let it blaze.

I am grateful to my family. My mother bore witness to the highs and lows of the creative process and coaxed me back from the extremes. My father, the architect of my family's initial involvement with the Soviet Jewish cause in the 1980s, eagerly read an early draft of this book with an eye to history and lovingly provided critique. Gene, while reticent as a spy with regard to his own experiences in the Soviet Union of the 1980s, respected and supported my commitment to this project and helped me carve out the time and space I needed, even when it meant bravely guarding my door against intrusion from teenagers and small rescue animals. Said teenagers did their part, too, learning how not to starve when I didn't feed them and how to wait until it was safe to pepper me with requests. They also both willingly volunteered their skills to this project: My son provided technical support and website assistance, and my daughter lent her artist's eye and helped design the book cover.

I am thankful for these many blessings that have brought me to this moment of being able to share this story with you, my dear readers.

ABOUT THE AUTHOR

D. B. SHUSTER is married to a Russian man who regularly assures her he is not a member of the mob. By day, she is a professor of Sociology, and her research keeps her busy with facts and numbers. By night, she lets her imagination run free with dark and twisted tales of crime, espionage, and intrigue. Sometimes she sleeps. A native of Cleveland, she now lives in New York with her family.

Email: dbshuster@gmail.com

Website: dbshuster.com

CHARACTER LIST

Aleksei. Aleksei Gregorovich. Son of Artur and Maya.

Artur. Artur Gregorovich. Maya's husband. Son of Yana and Mikhail Gregorovich. KGB agent with the First Directorate, undercover as Yosef Koslovsky.

David. David Soifer. Ruben's son. Edik's brother. Sofia and Vera's cousin. Killed in the army.

Edik. Edoaurd "Edik" Soifer. Sofia's cousin. Ruben's son. Black marketeer and Sofia's partner in crime.

Gennady. Gennady "Genna" Morozov. Petya's brother. Semyon's nephew.

Grisha. Security guard at Moscow State University where Sofia works.

Ilya. Ilya Soifer. Sofia and Vera's father. Kolya's grandfather. Ruben's brother.

Irena. Irena Abromovich. Mendel's sister. Max's wife. Nadia's mother. Was sent to the gulag.

Kasporov. Igor Kasparov. Artur and Victor's supervisor in the KGB First Directorate.

Kolya. Nikolai "Kolya" Reitman. Kolya is the Russian diminutive of Nicholai and Nick's Russian nickname. Sofia and Mendel's son.

Larissa. Vera's classmate.

Leonid. KGB agent.

Lilya. KGB agent used as a "dangle" to seduce targets.

Max. Max Abromovich. Mendel's brother-in-law. Sofia's former mentor. Irena's husband. Nadia's father. Was sent to the gulag.

Maya. Maya Gregorovich. Artur's wife. Mother of Aleksei. Semyon's daughter.

Mendel. Mendel Reitman. Sofia's husband. Kolya's father. Was sent to prison for teaching Hebrew and has been released.

Mikhail. Mikhail Gregorovich. Artur's father. Yana's husband.

Nadia. Nadia Ambramovich. Max and Irena's daughter. Mendel and Sofia's niece.

Paul. Paul Salvatore. Sofia's CIA handler.

Petya. Petya Morozov. Gennady's brother. Semyon's nephew. Vera's classmate.

Renata. Renata Soifer. Sofia and Vera's mother. Kolya's grandmother. Ilya's wife.

Ruben. Ruben Soifer. Edik's father. Ilya's brother. Sofia and Vera's uncle. Frequent host to foreign visitors.

Sasha. KGB agent.

Semyon. Maya's father. Artur's father-in-law. Chief of the KGB Second Directorate, also known as the Spymaster.

Sofia. Sofia Reitman. Mendel's wife. Kolya's mother. The target Artur has been charged to seduce. A spy for the CIA.

Vera. Vera Soifer. Sofia's sister. Renata and Ilya's daughter. Kolya's aunt.

Victor. Victor Zhirov. Artur's KGB partner.

Yana. Yana Gregorovich. Artur's mother. Mikhail's wife.

Yosef. Yosef Koslovsky. Artur's undercover alias. Mikhail's Jewish friend who was killed in the army. Yana's former fiancé.

GLOSSARY

Babushka. Old woman or grandmother. Also refers to a head scarf tied under the chin. Plural is babushki.

Blyad. Swear word with multiple meanings.

Borscht. A soup made with beets.

Bozhe moy. My God.

Dedushka. Old man or grandfather.

Goluboy. Blue. Also a slang term for gay.

Konechno. Of course.

Kopek. Coin currency equivalent to one hundredth of a ruble.

Kutletka. Cutlets.

Matryoshka. Nesting dolls. Plural is matryoshki.

Mezuzah. A scroll inscribed with biblical passages from Deuteronomy 6:4–9 and 11:13–21, placed in a case, and hung on the doorposts of Jewish homes as a sign or reminder of faith.

Pilmeni. Dumplings.

Ponimayesh. You understand.

Refusenik. A person in the Soviet Union who was refused permission to emigrate, particularly Jews who were refused permission to emigrate to Israel.

Samizdat. Self-publishing house. Also refers to the copying and distribution of forbidden materials.

Shtetl. Term for a small Jewish town or village in Eastern Europe.

Sla va Bogu. Thank God.

Tak. So, thus, like.

Yarmulka. A scullcap worn by some Jewish men.

Zhid. Russian slang term for Jew.